A Troubled Heart

Kay Seeley

TO: MY FAMILY

WITH THANKS

Kay Seeley's books

Novels

The Water Gypsy
The Watercress Girls
The Guardian Angel

The Hope Series

A Girl Called Hope (Book 1)
A Girl Called Violet (Book 2)
A Girl Called Rose (Book 3)

Fitzroy Hotel Series

One Beat of a Heart
A Troubled Heart
All Kay's novels are also available in Large Print

Box Sets (ebook only)

The Victorian Novels Box Set
The Hope Series Box Set

Short Stories

The Cappuccino Collection
The Summer Stories
The Christmas Stories

Who's Who in A Troubled Heart

The Templetons
Verity Templeton
Doris Templeton (Verity's mother and Herbert Fitzroy's widowed sister)
Henrietta Williams (née Templeton. Verity's married sister)

The Fitzroy Family
Herbert Fitzroy (deceased) (father)
Elvira Fitzroy (mother)
Lawrence (eldest son)
Jeremy (second son)
Clara (only daughter)

The Carter Family
Nora Carter (mother)
Daisy (eldest daughter)
Jessie (youngest daughter)

The Hotel Staff
Carl Svenson (under-manager)
Mr Jevons (maître d')
Daisy Carter (head of housekeeping)
Mrs T (cook)
Barker (concierge)
Hollis (porter)
Bridget (waitress)
Peggy (assistant cook)
Annie (chambermaid)
Molly Brown (chambermaid)
Ruby (kitchen maid)

Significant Others

Ira Soloman (owns the bookshop where Verity works)

Charlotte Huntington-Smythe (Verity's friend)

Mr Chester and Mrs Sybil Huntington-Smythe (Charlotte's parents)

Edward and Bertie Huntington-Smythe (Charlotte's brothers)

Brandon Summerville (Lawrence's friend)

Lydia Summerville (Brandon's sister)

Matilda Perkins (married to Constable Perkins. Daisy's friend who used to work at the hotel)

Chapter One

London 1905

Verity Templeton gazed out of the window of the carriage taking her to London. Early spring sunshine bathed the countryside as they passed trees bursting into leaf. She sighed as she contemplated her lot in life. It wasn't fair. Since her mother had been laid up, struggling with ill-health, Aunt Elvira had taken on the running of her life and that of her sister, Henrietta. Henrietta was married and out of reach, so all Elvira's suffocating attention and energetic endeavours were focussed on Verity.

Her aunt meant well, but was older than God and her aspirations for her nieces were as old fashioned as hooped skirts and sending small boys up chimneys. Living in relative comfort in the country she lived in a bygone age, but what troubled Verity most was Aunt Elvira's adamant pursuit of a 'good marriage' for her. Hence the trip to town to stay with her cousin, Lawrence Fitzroy, in the family's Fitzroy Hotel during the London Season.

Marriage was the last thing on Verity's mind. At eighteen she had her whole life ahead of her. She had no intention of spending it pandering to the wants of some man, just because he could provide for her. She was intelligent, well read and not averse to working for a living, which horrified Aunt Elvira. But Verity was determined to make her mark in ways other than the proverbial 'good marriage'. She'd decided long ago to stand on her own two feet.

"I know Lawrence will baulk at the cost," Elvira, sitting opposite Verity, said, tutting and taking a long breath, "but you will need some new outfits if you are to make an impression."

Verity frowned. "Make an impression? I'm sure the clothes I have are quite serviceable. Why would Lawrence have to pay for my things, Aunt? I have a small allowance and I am quite capable of paying for my own garments."

"You have no idea of the standard expected at the events to which I hope you will be invited. And, anyway, no lady should have to pay for her own wardrobe."

"But I'm not a lady, am I? I work in a bookshop."

Elvira shuddered. "You assist a good friend with his inventory. It's not the same thing." She shook her head.

It was true, Ira Soloman was an old family friend and working for him was more of a pleasurable indulgence than an actual job. He treated her like the daughter he'd never had and encouraged her love of all things creative and artistic, even letting her put some of her watercolours on display in the shop.

"Really, Verity, I know your mother was a bit vague and not always quite the ticket, but you are a Fitzroy and you will be treated as such."

Verity pouted. She didn't want to hurt her aunt's feeling, not after she'd been so good to her, but sometimes she thought she must live on another planet. She had no idea of the actuality of life in the real world. Working in the bookshop had opened Verity's eyes to a world of possibilities, none of which included being shackled to a man for the rest of her life.

She glanced at her aunt and, seeing the haughty expression on her face, her heart softened. She smiled. "If you say so, Aunt Elvira. I'll do my best to live up to the Fitzroy name."

She sat back in the coach. The Fitzroy name, she thought. Her mother had been a Fitzroy, until she married, but it hadn't done her much good. Grandfather Fitzroy had gambled away the family fortune and if it hadn't been for her mother's brother, Herbert, Elvira's husband, they would have been bankrupt. Now they were hanging on to respectability by the skin of their teeth and thanks to the prudent management of the hotel they owned and the income from the Maldon Hall estate.

She sighed. Her own father, Douglas Templeton, had been a successful businessman until poor health had forced early retirement and premature death. Verity had little memory of him, but it was the proceeds from the sale of his business that provided her small allowance. Verity felt more pride in his achievements than she felt for someone who'd never worked a day in her life.

As the coach drew up outside the hotel her cousin Lawrence came out to greet them. He helped Elvira out. "Good morning, Mama. How was the journey?" He kissed her lightly on the cheek.

Elvira huffed. "Dreadful as always. I swear the roads get worse and more congested daily. They should do something about it."

Lawrence smiled. "Well, you're here now. And you, Verity, how are you?" He turned towards her and leaned forward to brush his lips lightly against her cheek too.

"I'm well, thank you, Lawrence. It's good to see you." Her smile was spontaneous. It really was good to see him again.

"I'm in dire need of refreshment," Elvira said. "And some of Mrs T's lemon tarts. Come along, Verity, the porters will see to the luggage."

"I can have tea sent up to your rooms if you prefer," Lawrence said.

"No. We'll take it in the tea room. Are there many guests in?"

"We have a few rooms vacant, but overall I'm satisfied with the occupancy." He escorted them to the tea room. "I'll have the porter put your luggage in your rooms," he said. "I've put you in the Admiral Nelson suite, as usual. Verity will be next door in Florence Nightingale."

"Thank you, Lawrence, you are a dear. Now, is Jeremy around? I have a task for him."

"I told him you were coming. He should be here. I'll find him and send him to you." Verity could have imagined it, but she could have sworn Lawrence's expression was one of relief.

Once Lawrence had left them settling down to wait for their tea he went in search of his younger brother. He found him in the bar chatting to a girl, the daughter of one of the guests. With his boyish good looks he'd often attract the attention of unattached young ladies, but was far too canny to get caught by any of them. "Mama wants to see you," Lawrence said. "She's in the tea room with Verity. She has a task for you."

Jeremy grimaced. "If she's with Verity I can guess what that is. She's looking for introductions to all the eligible young men in town for the season. Why she thinks I'll be of any help when, according to her, all my friends are so disreputable, I'll never know." He took a deep draw on the cigarette he was smoking before crushing it out in the ashtray on the bar. "Well, duty calls." He bid the girl he was talking to goodbye, kissed her hand and then went to find his mother.

Lawrence sighed. With his mother in town tensions would rise and there'd be stormy seas ahead.

Downstairs in the kitchen Daisy Carter, head of housekeeping, had been informed of the imminent arrival of Mrs Fitzroy with her niece. She'd had chambermaids give the allocated rooms an especially thorough clean and checked them herself. Barker, the concierge, and Hollis, the head porter, had also been inspected by Mr Lawrence.

"It's a while since she visited," he'd said that morning, as he brushed a speck of dust from Hollis's shoulder. "I don't want her to think standards have slipped. I know I can rely on you all to do your best."

"Hrumph. Who does she think she is?" Mrs T, the cook, said when she heard about the special arrangements. "I suppose our best ain't good enough for Her Highness. I've served better than 'er and never had any complaints. Mr Herbert 'specially was always very complimentary about my suet dumplings. Still – trade. What can you expect? She might have high and mighty ideas but it don't make 'er any better than us." She slammed the baking tins she was collecting onto the table and Ruby, the kitchen maid standing next to her, jumped out of her skin.

5

Mrs T had worked for the gentry and never let them forget it. Daisy sighed. "I'm sure he didn't mean anything," she said. "We all know what an asset to the hotel you are, Mrs T. Best cook in London."

Mrs T sniffed. "You better believe it," she said and carried on with her pastry making. Daisy hoped the visit would go well. She liked Mr Lawrence. If it hadn't been for him the hotel would have closed when his father died, and they'd all be out of a job.

"I'll take it up if you like," Daisy said when Bridget, the serving maid, came down with the tea and cake order. "I'm sure Mrs Fitzroy will appreciate the personal service." Not only that, Daisy wanted to see Mrs Fitzroy again and Mr Lawrence's cousin, Verity. She'd seen Verity Templeton at Maldon Hall, the Fitzroy family home, when she was helping out at a family wedding a few years ago. She'd liked her. Now she was in London Daisy wanted to offer her any assistance she could. It's never a bad idea to get into the good books of a member of the family who are responsible for paying your wages, she thought.

Chapter Two

Verity's heart fluttered a little when Jeremy joined them. It had been a while since she'd seen him but he still had the youthful good looks and twinkling blue eyes she remembered from childhood. He was her favourite cousin when she was growing up. More recently she'd heard of his reputation with the ladies and his rackety friends, but she'd also heard about his capacity for kindness and understanding so she wasn't sure what to expect.

"Mama," he said as he approached the table where they were sitting, "you look in splendid good health. The country air must agree with you." Elvira rose slightly to receive the brush of his lips on her cheek. Verity didn't miss the warmth in his voice as he spoke. "And you, Verity. What a pleasure it is to see you again." She caught the scent of citrus in his sandy hair as he kissed her in greeting. "What brings you to London? A shopping spree I'll warrant. Spring sunshine always means shopping." He grinned and Verity managed to suppress a giggle.

"Don't be facetious, Jeremy," Elvira said. "I haven't come all this way to spend my time going around the shops. I want you to escort Verity around town and see that she's invited to the most eminent social gatherings. I'm far too long in the tooth to be gadding about town, but you'll know the best place to be seen and I know I can rely on you to look after her."

"It would be a pleasure, Mama, although I'm not sure about looking after her. You've never approved of my friends."

"Nonsense, Jeremy. Your friends are all from the best families. I just feel that, at times, their behaviour hasn't always done them credit." She paused and tapped Jeremy's hand. "High spirits are all very well and I suppose young people have to enjoy themselves. Heaven knows, there's little to enjoy in old age." She looked pensive and her face softened into a smile. "I know I can trust you to do your best."

"Thank you, Mama."

"Now," Elvira said pulling herself up to sit straight in the chair. "I have to speak to Lawrence so I'll leave you two to get better acquainted." She rose to leave the table. "I'll see you upstairs, Verity. Don't be too long. I've arranged to see the dressmaker this afternoon."

Again Verity wanted to protest at the expense, but, knowing how futile that would be, she nodded. "Very well, Aunt." Her heart sank as she said it.

Left alone with Jeremy she glared at him. "I'm not a child," she said. "I don't need looking after."

Jeremy chuckled. "Don't blame Mama," he said. "She still thinks Queen Victoria's on the throne, Disraeli's Prime Minister and nothing has changed since 1880. But seriously, it's your reputation and your future she's worried about. She has your best interests at heart."

Verity bristled. "She'll dress me in gowns Lawrence will have to pay for and parade me around town on offer to the highest bidder. That's not what I call having my best interests at heart."

"Oh, I see," Jeremy said. "There's a streak of independence trying to get out." He laughed. "Or is it perhaps that you already have your future planned nearer to home? Is there someone you're keen on?"

Verity blushed as Ned Garraway's face popped into her head. His family ran one of the farms on the estate and as far as Aunt Elvira was concerned, he was quite beyond the pale, but Verity had always been close to Ned. They'd grown up together. He'd taught her all she knew about horses and how to pick the best hunters or fastest gallopers. It was because of Ned she could ride as well as any man and knew as much about horseflesh as the canniest dealer. Ned had filled the space left by her father's early death. Thoughts of him brought a flush to her cheek and a warm glow to her heart.

"No," she said. "No one."

His eyebrows rose. "No one? A pretty girl like you? I bet you have legions of admirers."

Verity shrugged. "If I do I wouldn't talk about them," she said.

Jeremy's face lit with a smile. "Modest too. How becoming."

Verity huffed. If she'd wanted to be patronised she could have stayed at home. "I have a friend in town," she said. "A girl I was at school with. Her family have a house here. I've been invited to stay if I wish. I'm sure she could show me around if you find it too onerous."

Jeremy's eyes twinkled and Verity understood how he'd got his reputation as a charmer. "You can't visit the places Mama has in mind unless you're appropriately escorted," he said. "A duty I'm more than happy to undertake if you'll allow me. It would be my pleasure. In fact why don't we start tonight? Cocktails and dinner somewhere smart but not outrageously so. Somewhere you could be seen, just as Mama wishes."

"Tonight?"

"Unless you'd prefer to dine in with Mama and Lawrence."

9

"No. Thank you. Dinner would be lovely." She finished her tea. "Now, if you'll excuse me I have to go and do battle with Aunt Elvira and the dressmaker to ensure they don't spend too much of your brother's money."

"Oh I shouldn't worry about that," Jeremy said. "Lawrence is a match for Mama in that department and anyway, I'm sure, whatever you spend, it'll be worth every penny."

When Daisy arrived back in the kitchen Mrs T was admonishing the new under-cook, Peggy. "Needs more salt," she said, adding a sprinkling of the condiment to the soup bubbling on the stove. "Never be afraid of seasoning."

Peggy tutted and glanced at the ceiling, folding her arms as she did so. Daisy felt her pain. The words 'too many cooks' sprang to her mind. Peggy was the third under-cook in six months and Daisy hoped she'd stay. She seemed like a nice girl, willing and keen to please. Of course they all started like that, but often fell short of Mrs T's demanding standards. Daisy thought Peggy had more to her than the others. She managed to stay calm and unruffled despite Mrs T's unwarranted put-downs, warding them off with a smile, or a jovial remark which made Ruby, the kitchen maid, giggle.

Daisy too had her hands full with a new chambermaid. Annie, the second maid, had been made up and a new girl, Molly, taken on when the last girl left to get married. Daisy had been reluctant to take Molly on. She was pretty, seemed bright and quite spirited although Daisy did detect some belligerence in her behaviour. Daisy thought she could do better than the work she was offering, but in the end had decided it unfair to reject her on the grounds that she was likely to be too good. She even wondered if she'd done the right thing promoting Annie. She was hard working and loyal, but not the sharpest knife in the box. Of the two of them Molly was easily the quickest worker and most conscientious, even to the point of calling the laundry boy out over a missing pillow slip. Annie would never have done that.

"Settled in 'ave they?" Mrs T said. "I 'spect they'll be wanting lunch in the private dining room. As if we 'aven't got enough to do."

"I'll help serve if Bridget's busy," Molly, who just arrived back in the kitchen, said. "I never mind serving Mr Lawrence."

"Mr Jevons will decide who's to serve," Daisy said. "I'm sure he'll let me know if he requires any assistance upstairs."

Molly pouted. "I'll get meself some tea then," she said. "I've finished the top floor."

Daisy sighed. That was another thing about Molly. She didn't understand boundaries. The maids worked in the dining areas under the supervision of Mr Jevons, the maître d', in the afternoon and evening as required. He'd mentioned to Daisy that he thought Molly had 'potential' and that customers liked her, which Daisy took to mean she flirted with them. She was also a bit too enthusiastic when it came to serving Mr Lawrence's afternoon tea, always offering before she was asked. I'll have to watch her, Daisy thought.

Molly wasn't the only new member of staff Daisy worried about. Mr Svenson, the new under-manager had been appointed shortly after Christmas and several things had changed in the few months he'd been there. "I don't know why we need another manager," Daisy said to Mrs T one evening when they were finishing up for the day. "We've always managed before."

"I like 'im," Mrs T said. "'E's got some good ideas. About time they smartened the place up a bit."

"You don't mean that," Daisy said. "There's nothing wrong with the way Mr Lawrence runs the place."

Mrs T shrugged, "No, but with Mr Jeremy not doing so much, I expect 'e appreciates the help. Maybe he's wanting to take a step back now. Spend more time with 'is family. Mrs Fitzroy's not getting any younger and there's the succession to think about."

"The succession! What on earth are you talking about?"

"We'll Mr Lawrence ain't getting any younger either is 'e? It's about time 'e settled down an' all."

Daisy huffed. Mr Lawrence was in his prime. So far Carl Svenson had only taken on the role Mr Jeremy no longer had time to undertake. She still met with Mr Lawrence every morning for a list of bookings and departures, briefing him about any problems with the rooms, any replacement items required and all other aspects of housekeeping. He relied on her and it made her feel special. Surely there couldn't be any question of his handing the reins over to someone else, someone who'd only been there months? No, he wouldn't. "You only like him because he turned on the charm and said your lemon tart was the best in London. Buttered you up, that's all."

Mrs T chuckled. "That's as maybe, but at least I know enough not to get sweet on someone you can't have, and never will be able to have."

"I don't know what you mean."

"Soft on Mr Lawrence ain't you." She shook her head. "You've got a bug in your belly, 'cos you think Mr Svenson's going to take your place."

Hot blood rose up Daisy's face. The denial she was about to make died on her lips as Barker, the concierge, came into the kitchen, rubbing his hands in anticipation of the cocoa Mrs T always made for them. "What's going on 'ere then? Bit of a do?"

"We were just talking about Mr Svenson," Daisy said. "What do you think of him?"

Barker chortled. "Young, energetic, new broom like. Still, take some of the weight off Mr Lawrence. 'E deserves a break. Any biscuits with that cocoa?"

Daisy tutted, grabbed her cup of cocoa and stalked out. Mrs T's remark still rankled. Sweet on Mr Lawrence? What nonsense. Is that what they all thought? She liked him, yes. And respected him. He was a good man to work for, but if Mrs T thought there was any more to it than that, she was off her rocker.

Chapter Three

The evening out with Jeremy was everything Verity hoped it would be. Attentive and protective he made her feel special; that was his charm.

The number of well dressed young men, out for an evening's entertainment, milling around the cocktail bar they visited impressed her too. All so young and eligible. They kissed her hand and said how glad they were to meet her and hoped to see her at many of the season's events. She thought them all sweet, if a little young and immature.

He took her to a restaurant that buzzed with life, but they seemed to know him. "Your usual table, sir," the maître d' smiled, leading them to a table in a prominent position.

As they settled into their seats, a tall, broad shouldered man with dark hair passed by. He nodded to Jeremy as he did so. She'd noticed him before, in the bar. She'd even smiled when he glanced in her direction, but he'd turned his back as though she were quite inconsequential. How rude, she thought, but a strange sensation had fluttered in her stomach. "Do you know him?" she asked.

"Brandon Summerville? I only know him through Lawrence. They served in the Guards together. He's just returned from America. Made a fortune, I understand." Jeremy glanced down at the menu. "He's also a womaniser and one of the most ruthless businessmen you'll ever meet. They say he has a soft spot, but if he has I've never seen it. On the whole I think he's best avoided."

Verity's heart dipped. She'd thought him the most intriguing thing in the place. "But if he's a friend of Lawrence?"

Jeremy glanced up. "I didn't say he was a friend. Shall we order?"

Chastened she bowed her head and read the menu. All the dishes look extremely rich and probably expensive. She chose the fig and stilton salad followed by venison in madeira sauce. Jeremy went for the oysters in champagne.

"So," Jeremy said, grinning. "Tell me about Verity Templeton. The last time I saw you was…?"

"Your father's funeral."

"Oh yes. Of course." Jeremy nodded. "You would have been…?"

"Fifteen."

Jeremy nodded again.

Verity sighed. "Your family have been very good to me and I appreciate all they've done, but I'm a big girl now. I can look after myself."

"Can you?" Jeremy looked doubtful. "My family is your family too, Verity. Don't forget that."

Verity sniffed. "That maybe true, but it doesn't stop me feeling like the poor relation, depending on your charity for everything."

Jeremy's face clouded over. "I'm sorry you feel like that, but there really is no need."

"But there is. Can't you see? We live in a house you own, you pay all our bills, now Aunt Elvira insists upon finding me a husband to take over that responsibility and relieve you of the cumbersome burden of providing for my future."

Jeremy's eyes sparkled with mirth. "My dear girl," he said. "Finding girls a suitable husband is food and drink to Mama. It's what she lives for. Please don't deprive her of her only pleasure in life. I remember the year she brought Clara to town. My goodness, we all suffered that year."

Verity laughed. She remembered the fuss there was over her cousin Clara's wedding. Then the food arrived. It was impossible to remain serious in Jeremy's company. She glanced down at her plate. It looked just as mouth-wateringly delicious as she knew it would be. Far grander than she could ever afford at home. She picked up her fork and speared a succulent, syrup-coated fig, twirling her fork around to inspect it. "If I do decide to marry he'll have to be obscenely rich," she said. "That at least would be some compensation." She bit viscously into the fig.

After the main course, they both had lemon custard soufflé and talked about the summer ahead. Verity told him of her hope to visit some of the famous galleries that housed paintings she'd only seen in books and magazines.

"I'm sure that can be arranged," Jeremy said and suggested various other outings she might enjoy.

The rest of the evening went pleasantly enough for Verity. Jeremy took her to a show at a cabaret club and introduced her to more of his friends. By the time he called for a carriage to take them home, she felt as though she'd been on a merry-go-round of people, none of whom she remembered, as their faces, apart from one, melded into a dizzying blur.

It had been a pleasant evening, and Verity had learned a lot about her cousin. He was his own man, made up his own mind about things and didn't let anyone push him around. He was also intensely loyal to the family and if she were ever in trouble she could rely on him to come to her rescue.

*

The next morning Lawrence joined his mother and Verity for breakfast. He arrived as Molly was placing dishes of scrambled egg, kedgeree, devilled kidneys, bacon and sausages on the heated plates on the sideboard. "Good morning, Mama, I hope you slept well." He kissed Elvira's cheek.

"Well enough," Elvira said helping herself to a generous portion from each of the dishes. "Is the tea fresh?"

"Yes, Mrs Fitzroy," Molly said, "but I can bring more if you wish."

"Just some hot water. I can't bear it too strong."

Molly bobbed a curtsy and backed out of the door.

"And you, Verity. How was your evening?" Lawrence said.

"It was lovely, thank you," she said, with a smile that lit her face. "Jeremy is a generous host. I enjoyed it very much." She too selected several items from the dishes on the sideboard.

Elvira sniffed as she took her place at the table. "I hope he wasn't too generous," she said, 'with our money' Lawrence heard in his head.

"He introduced me to several well connected young men, Aunt, and we were seen in what he assured me were the best places." Verity sank into a chair beside her aunt.

"And what about you, Lawrence?" Elvia continued. "It's about time you got yourself married. It's unusual for a man of your age not to have settled down."

My age, Lawrence thought. I'm only thirty-one. "I can assure you, Mama, I'm quite settled and the hotel keeps me busy." He gazed at the dishes on the sideboard and took the rest of the bacon with sausages and egg.

"Nonsense. Every successful man needs a wife and the Fitzroys need an heir. I won't be around forever. Maldon Hall will need a new mistress and a family within its walls, which it's your duty to provide." She sat back. "I remember when your father and I..." She sighed and patted Lawrence's hand. "It's what your father would have wanted – you in the Hall with a family around you." Her eyes gleamed with hope as she spoke. "You spend too much time in town. You should come home more often."

Molly arrived with the hot water which she put on the tray next to the silver teapot.

"The hotel doesn't run itself, Mama."

"No but you have other things to think about. How will you entertain when you're a successful businessman without a wife?"

"I can entertain perfectly adequately here."

"Here? In the hotel? Don't be ridiculous. No. Arrangements must be made." She glanced at Molly. "Could you pour me some tea while you're there."

Molly nodded and poured the tea, placing the cup on the table next to Elvira who carried on her conversation as though Molly were invisible. "I've received several invitations from some very old and dear friends who have daughters as well as sons, Lawrence. It wouldn't do you any harm to come with me sometimes. The girls have breeding and pedigree and will bring substantial dowries. I should have thought you might be interested in the latter at least."

"Thank you, Molly, that will be all," Lawrence said noticing the girl still hanging around.

"Who's she?" Elvia asked when she'd gone. "I haven't seen her before."

"No, Mama, she's new."

"Hmm. Pretty girl. I don't suppose she'll stay long."

Daisy was surprised to see Molly in the kitchen at that time of day when she should have been cleaning the rooms. "Have you finished already?" she asked.

Molly grinned. "No. I bin serving breakfast to his nibs. His ma's on at 'im to get married. What do you think of that?"

A cold chill washed over Daisy. What right had the girl to talk about Mr Lawrence like that and why was she serving breakfast in the first place? "I think you spend too much time listening to gossip and too little doing your work, that's what I think. Why were you serving breakfast anyway? Your job is cleaning the rooms."

"Mr Jevons asked me." Molly stared at Daisy, a look of defiance on her face.

"He never mentioned it to me," Daisy said, anger curling in her stomach. "Get back to work. I'll sort Mr Jevons out." She stomped out to find him. How dare he, she thought, make use of one of my staff without telling me.

She stormed into the restaurant where Bridget was clearing the tables after the last guest had left. "Is Mr Jevons about?"

Bridget shook her head. "I haven't seen him this morning," she said putting the last of the cutlery onto a tray to take out for washing. "And, if last night was anything to go by I doubt he's in the best of spirits."

Daisy's heart turned over. Bridget meant that he'd been at the bottle again. She didn't like to say anything but even she'd noticed the late attendance in the mornings, the slight dishevelment in his dress, the way his mind often wandered off the point when he spoke to her and his inability to recall what he'd told her the night before. It wasn't like him, not the old Mr Jevons who was the epitome of good service and moral fibre, but since his wife died...

"I see. So that was why Molly was serving in the private dining room. Mr Jevons was... unwell."

"No." Bridget's voice rose with surprise. "She offered. I was going to do it and leave Hollis to do in here, but Molly insisted and I'm not one to turn down a favour."

"So Mr Jevons didn't ask her?"

Bridget shrugged. "Not as far as I know." She chuckled. "She's a bright one, that Molly. Wants to get her feet under the table with Mr Lawrence." She grinned at Daisy. "As if."

Daisy thanked her, but her comments had done nothing to ease Daisy's mind. She's up to something, that Molly, she thought. Then her remark about Mr Lawrence's mother wanting him to get married sprang into her mind. Was that one of the reasons he'd employed Mr Svenson, the new under-manager? He was thinking of leaving the hotel? That was something else she'd need to think about.

Chapter Four

After breakfast Verity wrote to her friend Charlotte Huntington-Smythe. She'd promised to call on her while she was in town and Charlotte had said she looked forward to seeing her again. They'd been at boarding school together. Although Verity didn't consider her more than a passing friend, she remembered her as lively, outgoing and lots of fun.

"She has brothers," she told her Aunt Elvira, so the association was encouraged.

The next morning Verity received a reply to her letter with an invitation to spend the weekend with the family and to attend the Boat Race Ball. Charlotte had written: *Please come. It'll be so much fun.*

Elvira huffed when Verity told her. "Who's going to look after your wardrobe?" she said. "I knew we should have brought someone from the Hall. I'll ask Lawrence if he can spare someone."

"No don't, Aunt," Verity said. "There's no need." She showed Elvira the letter which said: *Please don't worry about bringing a maid, we have a girl here who can take care of you.*

"I don't like it," Elvira said. "They must think we can't afford a maid."

"I'm sure they don't," Verity said. "It's just a matter of convenience. It'll be quite an informal weekend."

Elvira sniffed with obvious disdain. "An informal weekend, with no maid. I'm not sure the arrangements will be suitable," she said.

"But the Huntington-Smythes move in the best circles, Aunt. There will lots of opportunities for me to meet the right sort of people at the Ball. I thought that's what you wanted for me."

"Oh. Very well. But I'm making arrangements for us to visit some well connected family friends myself," Elvira said. "I do hope you won't let me down, Verity."

"Of course I won't." Verity's heart dipped. She appreciated all Aunt Elvira was trying to do for her but her attention was suffocating. At least with Charlotte things would be different.

*

On Friday Annie the chambermaid was sent up to help Verity pack her trunk, despite her protestations that she could do it very well herself.

"Young girls shouldn't travel unaccompanied," Elvira said, on Saturday morning when Verity was ready to leave. She was somewhat mollified when Lawrence organised a carriage for the short journey to Belgravia. "Could have had better weather," Elvira said, glancing out at the dark clouds and April drizzle.

Verity buttoned up her coat and put on her hat. She'd chosen a fitted, puff sleeved, beige coat and straw, wide brimmed, cream hat decorated with pink satin flowers, feathers and lace. She kissed her aunt goodbye. "Please don't worry," she said. "I'm sure it'll be fine. It'll brighten up later." She hoped she was right, but took her pink flowered umbrella, just in case.

When Verity's carriage pulled up outside the house Charlotte Huntington-Smythe ran down the steps to greet her. She carried an umbrella against the rain. "I'm so glad you decided to come," she said. "I thought perhaps you wouldn't and I'd have to spend the entire summer with no chance of any fun at all." She kissed

Verity's cheek and guided her into the spacious hall while a footman collected her luggage.

"You'll have to excuse the rush. We're all in a tearing hurry. The Boat Race starts at 11.30 to catch the flood tide, and Daddy likes to get there early. Bertie narrowly missed getting in the boat. He's a reserve, so he's supporting the Oxford crew in the boathouse. Daddy's really proud of him." Bertie was Charlotte's younger brother, up at Oxford and a rower. Verity had met him once several years ago: a gangly youth, rather juvenile and immature.

Entering the house Verity saw what Charlotte meant. Charlotte's father, Chester Huntington-Smythe, a grey-haired, well-whiskered man in his early fifties, paced the hall like a demented pigeon with his fob-watch in his hand. The butler stood at the foot of the wide stair-case staring upwards as a housemaid took the last two steps and disappeared along the upstairs hall in obvious haste. A few seconds later she reappeared followed by Mrs Sybil Huntington-Smythe, a petite woman fussily attired, in great bustle, tutting as she pulled on a pair of long white gloves.

"At last," Mr Huntington-Smythe said, stepping towards her to hurry her out to the waiting carriage, lest she should tarry further. Charlotte grabbed Verity's arm. "Come along. We'll be late and Daddy will be cross."

Verity hurried out with her.

As Verity had predicted the day did brighten. By the time they reached Putney Bridge the rain had died out and weak sunlight lightened the sky. A brisk wind ruffled the water which looked cold, grey and uninviting. I don't envy the rowers, Verity thought and shivered. She'd heard of the Annual University Boat

Race, but never seen it before. She'd seen sailing regattas along the coast, but they generated nothing like the excitement she saw today. Crowds of people milled around on the river bank, waiting for the start of the race, looking for the best vantage point to see it. A cheerful, party atmosphere prevailed, everyone enjoying a welcome free morning's entertainment. A pie seller moved among the crowd shouting his wares. Buskers played music and the smell of candyfloss drifted across on the breeze.

Mr Huntington-Smythe led them to a moored river cruiser already heavy with onlookers. "We're going to follow the boats," Charlotte told her. "You have to shout for Oxford."

Her father insisted they all go up to the front deck for a better view. Upstairs the air was fresher and bracingly sharp. Verity feared for her hat. She noticed Charlotte wore a straw boater decorated with Oxford blue satin flowers and tied beneath her chin with a huge matching bow.

Once the race started Verity's ears filled with a loud cacophony of sound. The noise blocked everything else out, even the cold as people screamed and shouted, pushing and jostling against her, vying for the best place at the railings. For a thrilling, heart-stopping twenty minutes she jumped up down shouting with the rest of the onlookers. As the Oxford boat pulled ahead, their shouts of encouragement grew louder, willing them on to victory. A loud cheer went up as the Oxford boat crossed the line. Verity shouted and waved her arms with the rest of them. Euphoria swept through the crowd and Verity felt every inch part of it. Excitement still churned inside her as they left the boat to adjourn to the comparative warmth of a nearby tavern where drinks had already been ordered ready for celebration or commiseration.

Cries of "Well done" and "Amazing" filled the air, raising the spirits of the well-wishers. "Three lengths," one said. "Great outcome." "Great show, good effort," another said. "First win in a while," someone else commented as the drinks were handed around.

Verity, Charlotte and Mrs Huntington-Smythe waited in the snug with the other ladies while the men went to the boathouse to congratulate Bertie. Charlotte squeezed Verity's arm. "That's good," she said. "Tonight we really can celebrate."

After the race they returned to the house. A footman took their coats and hats and Charlotte led Verity into the drawing room where aperitifs were served before lunch. A fire burned in the grate. Crystal chandeliers spread light on white and gold panelled walls hung with ancient family portraits. Verity's feet sank into the blue velour carpet. Another footman offered her a glass of sherry on a silver tray. She glanced around at the opulent surroundings. She'd forgotten how grand Charlotte's family were. Suddenly she felt out of place.

The lunch gong sounded and Charlotte's father led them in to the dining room with his wife. Charlotte and Verity following behind.

A selection of cold meats, cheese, biscuits, pickles and pies were laid out with salad vegetables sent up from the Huntington-Smythes' country estate. Trifle and raspberry pie for dessert and freshly made tea and coffee in pots stood on the sideboard.

"Bertie'll make the crew next year," Chester said, helping himself to a plate of beef and cold guinea fowl. "You see if he doesn't."

Verity followed Charlotte's lead, helping herself to beef and chicken. Over lunch the talk was all about the race. Verity had little to contribute, except to say how much she'd enjoyed the experience.

"You must come to Henley," Mr Huntington-Smythe said to her, his eyes shining with pride and delight. "That's a real regatta."

After lunch Charlotte took Verity to her room so they could decide what to wear for the evening's Boat Race Ball.

"Edward and Bertie will both be there," she said, "so we will be properly chaperoned, even if Mummy and Daddy leave early. We can stay and dance the night away. It'll be such fun."

Edward was Charlotte's eldest brother and Verity gathered he was 'something in the city'. Charlotte was vague about what he did. "You'll like Edward," she said. "He's a real gentleman."

The hotel was quiet on the day of the Boat Race. Leaving guests had booked out and rooms had been cleaned by lunch-time. The tea room was quiet too, owing to the chill, drizzly weather. Molly asked if she could take the afternoon off.

"It's me ma," she said to Daisy. "She's right poorly. I said I'd look in on her if I could."

Daisy wasn't convinced that Molly was that concerned about her mother, but as Bridget said she could cope in the tea room, she agreed. "You can work Monday afternoon, instead," she said. "But don't make a habit of it. Saturday's usually our busiest day."

"Ta," Molly said before dashing off.

She's up to no good, Daisy thought, but she had a lot to do so put it out of her mind. The day went on as usual and it was only when Molly hadn't returned by the time the rest of the staff were going to bed that Daisy began to worry.

"Well, I'm blowed if I'm going to wait up for her," she said to Mrs T. "The night porter can let her in, if she deigns to return."

"She got paid yesterday," Mrs T said. "I expect she's out spending it. Doesn't seem like the sort to give her wages to her ma." She made them all cocoa and they retired to bed.

Daisy couldn't sleep. She tossed and turned. It wasn't like anyone not to return after an afternoon off. Maybe she wasn't coming back at all. Daisy couldn't decide whether or not to worry. She wasn't the girl's mother, but she did feel responsible for her. She slept fitfully, her ear cocked for any sound that might mean Molly had returned.

An hour before dawn Daisy lay awake, glancing out at the slowly brightening sky. Tasks for the day ahead tripped through her mind. She'd made a mental note of rooms that needed an extra going over. Some guests were less than fastidious when they had chambermaids to clear up after them. She often wondered what their homes were like when she saw the mess they left in the bathrooms. She rolled out of bed, poured the water she'd brought up into the cracked china bowl on the chest of drawers and washed her face. She put on the plain black dress and a clean white apron that showed her authority as Head of Housekeeping and brushed her hair, putting it up under her cap.

She started when she heard doors closing and footsteps on the stairs. Opening the door she looked out to see Molly tiptoeing towards her room.

Her heart sank. She'd be in no fit state to work if she'd been out all night partying. But part of her flushed with relief at seeing her again. "Molly. What time do you call this? Where have you been?"

Molly gasped and spun round. "Sorry, Miss Carter. I got caught up. It won't happen again. I'll just change and start work. I'll soon get going and I'll be done in no time."

"Get going? You'll be in no fit state, look at you."

Molly glanced down at her clothing in disarray. "Oh, this is nothing," she said. "I'll be right as rain when I've 'ad a wash and brushed me 'air."

Daisy sighed but there was nothing she could do about it. The rooms needed cleaning, the fires raking out and relaying and Annie had the morning off for church. "Hurry up then," was all the admonishment she could manage.

True to her word Molly did catch up. She worked quickly through the rooms and showed no sign of having been out all night.

"I don't know how she's doing it," Daisy said to Mrs T. "I'd be limp as a dishrag if it was me."

"Oh, the energy of youth," Mrs T said, "it passes all too soon." She shook her head.

Daisy chuckled. "I expect she'll be worn out by lunch."

But she wasn't. In fact she volunteered to help out in the tea room that afternoon as Annie said she was feeling poorly.

"If you're sure," Daisy said.

By six o'clock when the tea room partitions were folded back to enlarge the restaurant Molly did look a little jaded.

"How was Molly this afternoon?" Daisy asked Bridget when she saw her at tea-time. "I don't suppose she was much help, being so tired."

"She did all right," Bridget said. "Still spends too long chatting to the male customers. I wouldn't be surprised if she's arranging to meet them later. I wouldn't put it past her."

"Really," Daisy was shocked. "That would be against the hotel rules. She knows that."

Bridget raised her eyebrows and shrugged. "Not a great one for obeying rules is she?" she said.

Daisy couldn't argue with that.

Chapter Five

Getting ready for the Boat Race Ball that evening with Charlotte, Verity understood her Aunt Elvira's concerns. The pink chiffon gown Mrs Henderson, the dressmaker, has insisted she really must take was far more stylish than she would have ever have worn at home. The low cut neckline with a tulle edging topped a boned bodice embroidered in pale pink rose patterns. The narrow, high waist accentuated Verity's budding curves, the skirt falling to the floor in a waterfall of flounces. Inwardly she thanked Mrs Henderson, but her creation paled into insignificance next to Charlotte's. Charlotte had cleverly chosen Oxford Blue satin for her gown, the bodice embroidered with sequins and beads. An oakleaf pattern in forest green curved down the length of the skirt which trailed out behind her.

Charlotte's lady's maid pinned pink silk roses into Verity's dark curls swirled into a diamante band, while Charlotte chose sapphire and diamond clips to hold her spun gold hair in place.

"It'll be such fun," Charlotte said. "I'm so glad you could come."

When they were ready they swept down the stairs together to where Edward waited to accompany them.

Charlotte was right, Verity did like Edward. Tall and good looking with blonde hair like Charlotte's, Verity saw the likeness although there was a solemnity about him, unlike his sister who bounced with cheerfulness. His eyes were darker blue than hers, but glowed with the same warmth.

"Pleased to meet you," he said when Charlotte introduced him. "Charlotte's told me so much about you." Verity smiled and her heart leapt.

"Mama and Papa have gone on ahead," Edward said. "You know how impatient Papa can be. Bertie will join us later. He's meeting some friends first, but I think we'll manage."

In the coach Verity tingled with anticipation. Butterflies fluttered in her stomach as Charlotte chatted on about who might be there. When they arrived Edward waited while their coats were taken before they were announced.

Walking into the ballroom was like walking into a gilded cave filled with light. Gold and white panels lined the walls giving the impression of airy space. Tables were set around the dance floor in front of a raised platform where the musicians were seated. Verity could hardly breathe. Edward led them to a table halfway down.

"Make yourselves comfortable," he said. "I believe there's fruit punch or lemonade. What's your preference?"

They both chose the fruit punch. Edward smiled and went to get it.

Shortly after Edward had gone, the Master of Ceremonies announced the arrival of Brandon Summerville's party. Verity was intrigued to see they sported Cambridge colours. Charlotte squeezed her hand. "He'd be quite a catch," she whispered. "Loaded and highly desirable. Watch for crows."

Verity giggled as several buxom ladies pushed their protégée into his path. "They'll be lucky," Charlotte said. "He's more slippery than a bucket of eels."

The musicians struck up for the first dance and couples drifted onto the floor. Verity felt a blush rise up her cheeks as Brandon Summerville made his way over to them. She noticed his strong regular features and the arrogance in his flint grey eyes. His clothes were expertly styled to flatter and his shoes were the shiniest she ever seen.

He stood in front of Charlotte and inclined his head in the slightest of bows, there was no humility in the action. "Miss Huntington-Smythe," he said. "What a delight to see you here. May I have the pleasure?" he held out his hand. Charlotte's eyes gleamed as he led her onto the dance floor. He nodded to Verity as they left, the merest suggestion of a smile touching his lips. Her heart dropped to her rose satin dancing shoes. She felt like the last book left on the shelf when all the others have gone. Jeremy's warning rang in her ears. I hope Charlotte knows what she's doing, she thought. Then she recalled something her mother had said; 'nothing's so attractive as that which you cannot have'.

Edward returned with the drinks and, in what Verity thought an act of greatest chivalry, asked her to dance. In his arms she was swept away with the music and glamour of the occasion. Dancers whirled around them, the ladies in extravagant ball gowns, their jewellery glittering in the light from ornate chandeliers adorned with sparkling crystals. The music filled her head as Edward spun her around. He was a confident dancer and she felt herself being whisked away to the rhythm of the music. The dance was over too soon. He smiled and thanked her as he led her back to her seat. Her heart kept on dancing. She gazed around at the people stood in small groups chatting and laughing. The atmosphere in the room was one of joyful celebration.

When a breathless Charlotte joined her she brought a cluster of young men in her wake and soon

Verity was up at every dance. She couldn't help but notice that Brandon Summerville danced every dance too, every time with a different girl in his arms.

After midnight Charlotte's brother Bertie arrived. It had been a long time since Verity had seen him. The gangly youth she remembered was gone, replaced by a muscular, athletic man obviously the worse for drink. The smell of alcohol preceded him as he lurched up to them.

"I see you've already been celebrating," Charlotte said.

He nodded, looking pleased with himself. "Who's this?" He raised his eyebrows as he stared at Verity.

"You remember Verity Templeton," Charlotte said. "She came to Haddington in the summer a few years back."

"Verity, Verity," he looked blank. "Did you watch the race?"

She assured him that she had.

"Marvellous wasn't it? Come on. We have to dance the night away." He grabbed her and swung her onto the dance floor. Soon they were bumping into people as he struggled to co-ordinate his movements to the music, causing a number of huffs and sighs from the other dancers. Verity burned with embarrassment as they stumbled around the floor. She wasn't sure who was holding who up. Her only hope was to get him out of there to save them both further humiliation.

"Er. Shall we?" she said, pointing to the doors leading to a shaded terrace.

"Fresh air. Good idea." His words slurred as he spoke. Verity steered him outside. Tables and chairs were set out but stood empty.

"You're a sport," Bertie said. His breath brushed her cheek as he leaned towards her. "Lottie said you were." She tried to step aside but he pulled her into his embrace.

"And you're drunk." She tried to push him away.

"We won didn't we? That deserves a reward." He lunged closer, pushing her against the wall. "Come on. You know you want to."

"Get off me."

She turned her head as his lips grazed her cheek and his body pressed into hers. His hands roamed over her where they had no business to be. She squirmed trying to get free. He laughed. "Come on. Don't be a spoil-sport."

She felt him pulling up her skirt. "Stop it," she said. "Or I'll scream."

He chuckled. "I like a girl with a bit of fight in her." He put his hand around her neck and pushed her head back. "No too much fight though." He moved to kiss her again.

Hot blood flooded through her as anger coiled in her stomach. She took a breath, raised her leg to kick him and pushed him away with all her might. He fell backwards, smashing into a table, tipping it over as he fell to the ground with a loud crash and a string of curses. The noise brought several people rushing out from the ballroom.

Verity dashed towards the door and bumped into Edward coming out to see what all the fuss was about.

"What's going on here?" he asked.

Several people had helped Bertie up. He glared at Verity, fists curled and a look of fierce fury on his face.

"Bertie old chap," Edward said. "Have you been annoying Miss Templeton?"

"Just being friendly," he slurred.

"Well I think you've been friendly enough for one evening. Come along." He put his arm around Bertie to guide him away.

Bertie hiccupped. "She invited me," he said. "Tart wanted it."

Edward froze. He drew a breath. "Excuse my brother, Miss Templeton," he said. "I'm afraid he's the worse for drink." Verity gazed in alarm as his fist curled and a swift jab of his arm punched Bertie in the stomach making him double over. "Are you all right, Miss Templeton?" Edward asked, smiling in her direction, completely unperturbed by his brother's discomfort.

Verity's heart raced. She still shook from the experience. Bertie's accusation horrified her, but she managed to say, "I'll be fine. It was nothing. Please take him…" She waved them away. She felt sick. What had started out as a lovely evening had turned into a nightmare and the worst of it was that they were Charlotte's brothers.

"Are you all right?" Charlotte asked when she arrived back inside. "You look a little flushed."

"It's the excitement I expect," Verity said. "I am a little tired. I think I'd like to go home."

Charlotte pouted and then shrugged. "Well, I suppose it's late and the most interesting people have left already."

Verity knew she meant Brandon Summerville and his party. Edward arranged a cab for them.

"Aren't you coming?" Charlotte asked

"No. You go ahead. I'll be along later."

"It's not fair. Why do men have all the fun?" Charlotte huffed all the way home.

Chapter Six

The morning after the ball Verity hoped she wouldn't see Bertie at breakfast. She wouldn't know what to say to him. To her relief, when she arrived in the dining room Charlotte's mother was alone. "Good morning," she said. "I trust you slept well."

"Thank you, yes," Verity said.

"Meagre offerings this morning, I'm afraid," Mrs Huntington-Smythe said, indicating the dishes laid out on hot plates on the sideboard. "Will you be joining us for church?"

Verity helped herself to some bacon and scrambled eggs. Despite her hostess's comments she found the offerings more than adequate. "I'm not sure," she said.

"Don't expect to see Charlotte before midday," Mrs Huntington-Smythe said. But she was wrong. Charlotte arrived as she spoke.

"Good heavens," her mother said. "What's got you up at the crack of dawn?"

"Hardly the crack of dawn, Mama," Charlotte said, kissing her mother's cheek. "I thought Verity and I could venture over the park after church. The weather's a bit brighter than yesterday."

"Then I shall have company at the service after all. Your father and the boys are unlikely to make an appearance any time soon. They were very late coming home."

"All right for some," Charlotte muttered so quietly Verity doubted her mother heard it.

Bertie arrived just as his mother rose to leave. "Bertie," she said. "How lovely. You can keep the girls company. Well done yesterday. I'm sure you'll make the boat next time."

Bertie scowled but his mother didn't seem to notice. He kissed her cheek. "Good morning, Mama," he said. He selected something from every dish piling it onto his plate. He nodded to Charlotte and glared at Verity as he sat at the table.

"Good show yesterday," Charlotte said and he scowled again.

"I hope you're feeling better today," Verity said. "After last night's celebration." The least she'd expected was an apology for the way he'd treated her.

He stopped eating, sat back and stared at her. His eyes narrowed. "I feel perfectly fine thank you." The ice in his voice sent a chill down Verity's spine.

Verity finished her breakfast in silence but inside she seethed with rage. She picked up the coffee pot in front of her and poured herself a cup. "Coffee?" she asked.

Bertie picked up his cup and saucer, holding it out so she could pour him some, keeping his head bent so he didn't have to look at her. Verity poured the coffee until the cup was full, then she kept on pouring, lifting the jug a little higher and tilting it so the scalding liquid ran over Bertie's thumb.

He jumped up with a loud shriek, dropping the cup and saucer which fell to the table with a mighty crash.

Verity's jaw gaped. "Oh I'm so sorry," she said, eyes wide with innocence. "How clumsy of me."

Bertie glared at her, shaking his hand and then clutching it to his stomach. "You stupid bitch," he yelled. He scowled at Charlotte before crumpling his napkin, throwing it on the table and storming out, still cursing. As he went he narrowly avoided colliding with a footman, summoned by the loud crash.

"Oh dear. I'm so sorry, Charlotte," Verity said, placing the jug on the table. "I hope that isn't too bad."

Charlotte, who'd risen from the table when the cup and saucer crashed down, shrugged her shoulders. She grimaced as she mopped up the spilled coffee. "I expect he'll get over it," she said.

The footman took over the mopping up and Verity and Charlotte left him to it.

Although feeling quite smug, Verity again apologised. "I'm really sorry," she said, "but he was rude to me last night and again this morning. I know he's your brother, but even so."

"Oh," Charlotte said. "Don't mind Bertie. He's always in a grump. Second son you see. He'll never inherit. His future will be either in the military or the church, unless he relies on Edward's generosity to keep him, or finds work to support himself. He bears a grudge and we all have to suffer for it."

That doesn't excuse his behaviour, Verity thought, but didn't want to cause any ill feeling with Charlotte, so said nothing.

After the church service Charlotte arranged for the carriage to drop her mother off and take her and Verity to Hyde Park. "We can watch the Sunday parade along Rotten Row," she said. "It's where all the fashionable ladies gather. I know how you love horses and anyone who's anyone will be there."

"It's a shame we can't ride out," Verity said. "I'd love to race along there at full gallop."

"Whereas I prefer something less taxing," Charlotte said. She dismissed the carriage telling the coachman to return in an hour, and they began their walk. Verity found the parade of carriages and riders just as spectacular as Charlotte had predicted. Charlotte pointed out the most prominent citizens as they passed by. It was clear to Verity that everyone had made an effort to outdo their neighbour. Women lavishly dressed in the latest styles and colours and wearing gloriously sumptuous hats were accompanied by men in frock coats and silk toppers. Verity pictured the array of styles in Mrs Henderson's workroom. They were nothing compared to the outfits on display today.

"Now there's a magnificent specimen," Charlotte giggled.

Verity wondered if she meant the horse or the man astride it, then all became clear. Brandon Summerville, riding a striking bay, rode up to them.

He raised his hat. "Good day, ladies," he said. "What a delight seeing you. I trust you enjoyed the ball last night."

"Yes, thank you." Charlotte beamed at him. "Although it was a shame you left early."

He slid from the saddle to walk alongside them.

"You remember Miss Templeton," Charlotte said, indicating Verity.

"Of course. How do you do, Miss Templeton?"

He gave the slightest bow and Verity held out her gloved hand. He took it and raised it to his lips. A thrill ran through her. The promise in his dangerously dark eyes turned her knees to jelly. She imagined he had the same effect on all the ladies.

"How are you enjoying your visit?" he asked. "I do hope it's a protracted one so we may meet again."

"I expect to be in town for the season," Verity said. "I'm staying with my cousin."

He smiled. "Of course." He turned his attention back to Charlotte. "Please give my regards and congratulations to you brother on his team's win yesterday," he said. "We must strive to do better next time."

Charlotte linked her arm through his and walked on slightly ahead of Verity so she lost the rest of the conversation. She had a feeling that this had been Charlotte's plan and she felt like an intruder, but again Jeremy's warning ran through her mind. Still, she thought, Charlotte seemed perfectly at ease with him. And, to Verity's mind, she was a big girl and well able to take care of herself. At least she hoped that was the case.

After a short while Brandon Summerville resumed his seat on his horse and rode on.

"I hope I didn't spoil your pleasure," Verity said, slightly annoyed as she felt she'd been used so that Charlotte could accomplish something her parents would never approve of.

Charlotte laughed, a cheerful, infectious sound that made Verity feel like an aging prude. "Oh Verity," Charlotte said. "It's only a bit of fun. The gossips will have a hey-day and I don't mind a bit being talked about. You shouldn't take things so seriously."

"Well, I hope you know what you're doing. He's not a toy to be played with. Nor should you toy with anyone's affections."

"Affections?" Charlotte looked shocked. "Surely you don't think he gives a jot about us? He doesn't. It's all show. Don't be fooled by his manner. He'll take what he can and then you won't see him for dust." She patted Verity's hand. "Don't worry. I know what I'm doing."

I hope so, Verity thought, although she wasn't convinced. Judging by Charlotte's blush and the forlorn look on her face, Verity guessed Charlotte was more attracted to him than she cared to admit.

On the way back to meet the carriage they passed Speaker's Corner, where a group of suffragettes were handing out leaflets. Verity took one. She pulled Charlotte to a stop so they could listen to the speaker.

"You don't believe in all that guff," Charlotte said. "Why on earth would women want to vote?"

"It's not just about the vote," Verity said. "It's about having some control over their lives. Having a voice."

Charlotte shrugged. "I wouldn't want to be a man," she said. "Too much responsibility. I think we're better off as we are."

Verity's heart dropped and her stomach churned. She didn't want to get into an argument with Charlotte, but she couldn't agree with what she'd said. "Oh. I don't know," she said. "But I think they have a point."

Charlotte shrugged again. She smiled at Verity and took her arm. "Come along. We'll be late for lunch. Then we have the whole afternoon ahead of us to make more mischief."

Verity chuckled and went along with her. Yes, she thought. Charlotte had a very nice life. Why would she want to change a thing?

After lunch they went to Charlotte's room to plan their next adventure.

"Look at all these invitations," Charlotte said waving a bunch of gilt-edged cards in her hand. "You must come to some of them with me. It'll be so much more fun than going with just Bertie and Edward." She shuffled through them, handing Verity a couple she picked out. "This one and this one," she said. "They say *and Party*. That means I can bring a guest."

"And you're hoping to find a husband among them?" Verity asked.

Charlotte's gust of laughter rang around the room. "Mama hopes to find me a husband among them," she said. "I know most of these people and I can't say I can see husband material in any of them." She pouted. "They're all terribly arrogant, selfish and spoiled. Honestly, young men today."

Verity laughed. "You sound like my Aunt Elvira."

"I'd love to meet your aunt. She surely can't be such a dragon as you make out. Anyway, I heard you've been working for your keep. In a bookshop of all places. I can't imagine what that must be like."

"Actually, it's fine. I'm helping an old friend of my father's which brings me closer to him. Ira Soloman invested in my father's business. When Papa died his partner took over, but he lacked my father's business acumen and the firm went downhill. Helping Ira to get back on his feet is the least I can do. I enjoy it, meeting people and feeling some measure of independence." She paused. "I also work in the local school helping out with art lessons. Apparently that's more socially acceptable to my aunt. Probably because there's no pay." She laughed. "I love working with the children, they're delightful."

"I'll take your word for it. Now. Let me see if I can find you someone, even faintly suitable?" She shuffled through the cards in her hand.

"What about you, Charlotte? Is there anyone in particular you have your eye on?" Brandon Summerville's name sprang to mind. After seeing him this morning she surely couldn't deny it.

A blush rose up Charlotte's face, like a glass filling with red wine. "It's no use hoping for something that can never be," she said. She brightened. "Tell me, Verity, is there likely to be anyone among these?" She held up a bunch of invitations.

Verity sighed. "Aunt Elvira has high hopes." Her bright mood of the day dissipated at the thought. "I don't want to disappoint her. She's been so good to me since my father died, taking me in and everything."

"But there is a likelihood that you will? Tell me. Who is he?"

Verity pictured Ned Garraway in her mind. Colour rose in her cheeks. "There was someone, but it's impossible. His family have one of the farms on the estate."

"And?"

"He's good looking, kind-hearted and we share a love of horses," she said. "We've been friends since childhood. I suppose our friendship has sort of grown. I could happily spend the rest of my life with him."

"But does he make your heart race and your pulse quicken? Do you thrill at his touch and long to be in his arms?" Charlotte began dancing around the room. "Do you yearn for him when you're apart and feel you cannot live without him? Is it true love or merely infatuation?"

Verity laughed as Charlotte spun around the room. "You read too many Jane Austen books," she said.

"But does he?"

Verity declined to answer.

After tea with Charlotte's mother Verity said her goodbyes. "You must come again," Mrs Huntington-Smythe said. "Charlotte does so enjoy your company."

"Thank you," Verity said. "I hope she can come and stay with me too, sometime soon."

"That would be lovely."

Verity left determined to persuade Lawrence to invite her friend at least for some sort of dinner. After all she had to repay their kind hospitality.

Chapter Seven

Lawrence, sitting in his office going over the bookings for the next day and checking any of the guests' requests, mulled over his mother's continued comments about his duty to Maldon Hall.

It's true, he thought. I've been so immersed in keeping Papa's hotel running, with its responsibilities for staff who've given a life-time of service, I've neglected my responsibilities as far as the Hall is concerned. Perhaps she's right. I should be looking for a wife who could bear the requisite number of heirs to preserve the Fitzroy line. It's been far too long since the rooms rang with children's laughter. I suppose I've never imagined a time when Mama wouldn't be mistress of the Hall. There's always Jeremy of course, although he's shown no inclination towards tying the knot with any of his numerous paramours.

He sighed. There was no reason he couldn't spend more time on his personal life. The under-manager he'd taken on several months ago had settled in well, even winning Mrs T's approval by telling her he'd heard that her game pies were the best in London and he couldn't wait to taste one.

Carl Svenson had come highly recommended, having worked on the White Star cruise ships. They were lucky to get him. He'd happily take on more responsibility if Lawrence let him. And Jeremy could always help out.

That was his frame of mind when Verity, just back from her visit to the Huntington-Smythes, burst into his office like an unexpected ray of sunshine on a particularly grey day.

"Oh sorry, I didn't mean to disturb you," she said.

"Verity, how lovely to see you. To be honest the disturbance is most welcome." Her face was flushed and she looked a little breathless. Lawrence thought her charming.

"Paperwork getting you down is it? Perhaps I could help out. Repay some of your kindness in having me here."

He shuffled the papers together and closed the ledger he was working on. "Good of you to offer but there's no need. I'll pass these on to Mr Svenson. It's about time I delegated some of my responsibilities." He indicated for Verity to sit. "Should we have a drink? Sherry perhaps, before dinner? Then you can tell me all about your weekend."

He poured them both a sherry from a decanter kept in the cabinet and handed her a glass. She told him about the excitement of the Boat Race and the ball afterwards. She didn't mention Bertie's behaviour for fear of what Lawrence might do. He certainly wouldn't treat it with the same triviality that Edward had. He'd call him out and that would be the end of her friendship with Charlotte. She didn't have enough friends for that to be an option.

"It was glorious," she said. "All the people and the music. Charlotte looked amazing, quite the belle of the ball."

"I'm sure you looked just as spectacular," Lawrence said with a grin.

Verity sipped her sherry and Lawrence got the feeling she was holding something back, but didn't press her. Then she told him about meeting Brandon Summerville in the park.

"Jeremy said you knew him. Charlotte seemed very taken with him and I must admit he's a charmer.

46

What's your opinion of him?" She glanced at Lawrence over her glass, as if trying to gauge his response.

Lawrence pondered. He wasn't as aware of the London social scene as Jeremy and never listened to gossip. Still, he couldn't be unaware of the man's reputation. Then there was the niggly thought that perhaps Verity was asking on her own behalf, which would be a very different matter. "To be honest I haven't seen him for years," he said. "Not since we were in the Guards together. Different days, but I wouldn't believe all the stories you hear. I find people tend to exaggerate when they have little else to talk about."

"I'd like to repay Charlotte's hospitality," Verity said. "Perhaps invite her for dinner. I was wondering…"

Lawrence smiled. "I think we can do better than that. It'll be Easter in a couple of weeks. Why not invite her for the weekend at Maldon Hall? I'm sure Mama would jump at the chance to host a house party weekend there, and it'll be in time to catch the last Meet of the season."

"Really? Thank you, Lawrence. I'm sure Charlotte will be delighted."

"Good. I'll ask Mama to liaise with you about a guest list." He smiled. "It's been a while since we've entertained at Maldon Hall. It's about time we put that right."

Daisy's concern about Molly grew over time as she noticed that she rarely stayed in the hotel when she wasn't working. This wasn't unusual for staff with families living nearby, but Molly often stayed out until after midnight. When she did return she reeked of tobacco smoke and stale beer. Whenever Daisy commented on her activities she made it clear that it was none of her business.

"It's Ma," she'd say. "Proper poorly she is." Daisy could get nothing more out of her.

She did think she might follow her one evening but that felt like a betrayal of trust and there was no doubt she was a good worker. The late nights didn't affect her work, she did more than her share, so Daisy could hardly complain about what she did in her spare time.

"I wish she was more like Peggy," she said to Mrs T. "She seldom goes out and if she does she's always back at a reasonable time."

"Peggy's got her 'ead screwed on all right," Mrs T said. "She'll go far, which is more than I can say for t'other one. Always in a rush, that one, like some one's set fire to 'er bum."

Daisy smiled, but Mrs T was right. Molly never spent any longer in the kitchen than she could help, although she did seem to get on well with Peggy, both of them being new. Daisy wondered if she confided in Peggy. If she did Peggy would never say.

Things came to a head just before the Easter weekend. It had been a warm day, sunny and bright enough to entice people to spend their evenings outside walking in the park or by the river. Molly was working in the restaurant, although it was a slow night, with most of the diners finished and gone by ten. Over a late supper in the kitchen Bridget complained about Molly's absence.

"I've seen neither hide nor hair of her or Mr Jevons since early on," she said. "It's not fair leaving me and Hollis to manage on our own. I've a good mind to mention it to Mr Lawrence."

"I'll have a word with her," Daisy said. "Where is she now?"

"God knows," an irate Bridget said. "Disappeared halfway through serving dessert. An' Mr Jevons has been getting worse. I know he's not been himself recently, but it's not fair on the rest of us."

Daisy had no doubt that she would be 'mentioning' it to Mr Lawrence. "Maybe I should speak to him," she said.

She was even more furious the next morning, when Molly hadn't returned to the hotel. She'd often been out until dawn but usually arrived in time for breakfast. This is the last straw, Daisy thought. She'll have to go.

She was saying something along those lines to Mrs T after breakfast, when Molly still hadn't appeared. The conversation was halted by a loud banging on the kitchen door. "Who's that now?" Mrs T said. "Honest. There's no rest for the wicked."

When Daisy opened the door a young man pushed past her breathing heavily. Beads of sweat covered his forehead and his eyes seemed to bulge. Molly, her clothes torn, her hair in disarray and her face red and wet with tears followed him in.

"What the—"

"I want to see the manager!" the young man shouted, gesticulating wildly. "My sister's been attacked by one of the staff here. If I don't see him in the next three minutes I'm going to the police."

Shocked, Daisy stared at Molly, then at her brother. "Molly what the…?"

"Manager. Here. Now." The young man glared at her. "She doesn't have to put up with this."

Daisy drew a breath and gathered her wits. "Of course she doesn't. If anyone here has…" She couldn't imagine anyone doing anything to Molly. She just couldn't think that. "Perhaps if you tell me what has happened."

"I'll tell the manager. I ain't speaking to no underlings. Take me to 'im." The young man was getting angrier by the minute. He looked fit to explode. Molly whimpered and stared at Daisy her eyes pleading.

"Of course. He's in his office. This way." She led them upstairs and knocked on Mr Lawrence's door. "Sorry to disturb you," she said when he called for her to enter. "A gentleman here with a complaint." She gritted her teeth as she said it. She didn't think Molly's brother was any sort of gentleman.

Chapter Eight

Following his conversation with Verity, Lawrence was busy working on the arrangements for the Huntington-Smythes to spend the weekend at Maldon Hall. He could safely leave his mother and Verity to sort out the invitations, but the itinerary would be in his hands. He'd just got down to work when he was interrupted by the arrival of Daisy Carter with an unkempt young man with stubble on his chin, dragging a dishevelled, weeping Molly behind him.

"What the devil?" He rose from his chair.

"Apparently Molly's been assaulted," Daisy said, an edge of anger and incredulity in her voice. "This is her brother."

"There's no apparently about it," Molly's brother snarled. "Tell 'em, Molly."

Molly glanced fearfully at her brother and nodded, sobbing.

Thoughts jumbled through Lawrence's mind. He couldn't take in what he was seeing. At first he thought it might be some sort of joke, but the young man's demeanour told him otherwise. He could see the girl was in distress, but he wasn't sure what it had to do with him. "Please take a seat and tell me what happened." He ushered them to two chairs by the side of the fireplace. "Miss Carter, perhaps some tea?"

"Don't want tea. That's not what we're 'ere for." The young man's anger showed no sign of abating.

The thought, *well what have you come for*, passed through Lawrence's brain, but he forced a smile to his lips. "Perhaps some brandy then?"

The lad glanced at Molly and nodded.

Lawrence dismissed Daisy and went to a cabinet for the brandy and glasses. He put the glasses on a low table in front of the fire, poured the drinks and handed them each a glass. He hunkered down in front of Molly.

"What happened to you, Molly?" he asked as gently as he could manage while holding back the intense irritation rising up inside him. Whatever had happened to the girl her brother was only making it worse.

Molly sniffed, howled and then sobbed into a large white handkerchief, covering her face as she did so.

"She was attacked in this hotel by one of your staff. I've a good mind to call the police." The young man stared at Lawrence, daring him to contradict or challenge him.

Lawrence swallowed. "Attacked? Really? By whom? Who attacked you, Molly?"

Molly lifted her gaze and stared at Lawrence with watery eyes. "Mr Jevons," she said. "Mr Jevons attacked me."

Mr Jevons! Lawrence couldn't have been more surprised if the floor had opened up and swallowed him. Mr Jevons, a man in his fifties, who had worked at the hotel for the best part of his life. Mr Jevons, the man who did more to uphold the standards of morality and respectability in the hotel than anyone Lawrence could think of. Mr Jevons, who'd been the maître d' for over twenty years. He couldn't believe it. No it couldn't be true, not Mr Jevons.

"What you gonna do about it?" The lad sat back, his arms folded and a look of grim satisfaction on his face.

Lawrence rose and went and rang the bell. Daisy appeared so quickly he guessed she'd been waiting outside. "Ask Mr Jevons to step into my office," Lawrence said. Daisy hurried away. Lawrence took a breath. He walked over to the table and poured himself a brandy.

Thoughts raced through his mind. "I'm sure we can sort this out when Mr Jevons arrives," he said. "I expect you want to see him in court?"

At the mention of the word 'court' the boy's eyes became wary.

"Quite right too," Lawrence said, settling himself into the chair opposite Molly and her brother. "If he's attacked Molly he should have to pay for his crime."

The boy coughed and leaned forward. "Someone's got to pay," he said, his tone more conciliatory than before.

Lawrence sipped his brandy, watching the pair before him as they waited for Mr Jevons to arrive. The air crackled with distrust. An incongruous pair, he thought, Molly, petite and pretty and her brother, stocky but muscular, swarthy skinned, his dark eyes sharp with spite.

Ten minutes later Daisy arrived back, catching her breath. "I'm sorry, sir. Mr Jevons is not in the hotel. Bridget hasn't seen him since early last evening and he's not in his room."

Lawrence frowned. That wasn't like Jevons. He was always so reliable and since his wife had passed away he spent all his time in the hotel. He sighed. Mr Jevons hadn't been himself since he lost his wife. Taken to the drink rather heavily. Could it actually be true? Mr Jevons had attacked the girl? I should have made sure he took some time off, he thought. Damn fool.

"Well, it seems we are to be deprived of Mr Jevons's explanation," Lawrence said. "I don't think there's much I can do in the circumstances apart from reassure you that, when he returns, he will be brought to book."

"And what about Molly?" her brother said. "She's damaged goods. Can't stay 'ere now, not after... an' she won't be able to get work anywhere decent... not now."

"Perhaps, if you could tell me exactly what you're accusing him of."

Lawrence's request only brought another bout of howling, sobbing and shaking of her head from Molly and a look that would curdle milk from her brother.

"If you can't tell me more and Mr Jevons isn't here, I'm at a loss as to what to do," Lawrence said. "I'm sure there must be some misunderstanding."

"There's no misunderstanding," the lad scowled. "You can see how upset Molly is. I've a good mind to go public and let everyone know what happens in places like this."

Places like this, Lawrence thought what is he talking about, but the threat to 'go public' hit home. "What did you have in mind?" Lawrence said.

"I could go to the police," the boy said. "Or the press. Wouldn't look too good in the newspapers."

Lawrence closed his eyes and rubbed his forehead. They could tell their story to the newspapers. No doubt they could make something newsworthy of it. It wouldn't matter if it was true or not. If it was lurid enough the hotel's reputation would suffer, right or wrong, and he was sure it was wrong. He could call their bluff and send them packing, but it was a risk.

"I'm sorry this has happened to you, Molly," he said, leaning towards her. It's a terrible thing to happen to any young girl and I'm not treating it lightly. I'm unsure how to deal with it in Mr Jevons's absence. He should be given a chance to explain himself and face his accuser."

"Oh I couldn't face 'im, Mr Lawrence. Not no how." She dissolved into another bout of weeping.

Lawrence was rapidly becoming tired of this charade. "Possibly some compensation?"

She sniffed and the weeping stopped.

"How much?" Her brother sudden perked up.

Lawrence guessed she earned about ten shillings a week as she lived in plus extra for working in the restaurant and tips. Overall probably not more than thirty pounds in a year. "Would fifty pounds ease the pain?"

"Cash?" the brother said.

"Cash. To ease the pain and obliterate the memory."

"And Mr Jevons?" Molly asked. "What will happen to him?"

Maybe the girl had a conscience, Lawrence thought. "Don't worry I'll deal with him."

Molly glanced at her brother, her eyes beseeching. His lips spread into a sneer. "I suppose fifty's all right," he said. "Seventy would be better, to make sure we never come back."

Revulsion curled in Lawrence's stomach. "I have your word?"

They both nodded. Lawrence went to the safe and took out seventy pounds which he put in an envelope.

"If I do see you again I'll be the one calling the police," he said, handing them the money. "Clear?"

"Clear," they said in unison.

Once he'd ensured that Molly and her brother were escorted off the premises, taken out the way they'd come in, Lawrence sat with his head in his hands. I should have called the police, he thought. I don't believe a word of their story. Blast Jevons. If he hadn't been... but that was his fault too. He'd heard the whispers about his drinking, despite the other staff trying to cover for him. He'd hoped he'd sort himself out and get back to normal. He should have tackled him earlier. He had to protect the reputation of the hotel at all costs. He called for Hollis, the head porter, who told him that Mr Jevons hadn't returned to the hotel. No one had seen him since the previous evening.

"Thank you, Hollis. Please ensure that I'm informed as soon as he does return." Hollis nodded. "Oh and ask Miss Carter to come up. You'd better fetch Mr Svenson too."

"Sir." Hollis bowed out. Lawrence imagined the gossip that would be going on below stairs. He'd need to clear the air and make sure that nothing of the sort was ever to happen again. Irritation stirred within him. Why was the girl employed in the first place? Couldn't Daisy Carter see what a flighty piece she was? He'd heard about her late nights out and over familiarity with the guests. That should have been tackled earlier too. He sat back in his chair shaking his head. Things were changing. You couldn't rely on anyone any more. What on earth was the world coming to?

The picture of his father hanging on the wall caught his eye. He felt his disapproval. Standards were slipping. It would never have happened in his day. Lawrence sighed. There'd have to be changes.

Chapter Nine

Daisy Carter fumed. Her meeting with Mr Lawrence hadn't gone well. She felt as though she was five years old and had been sent to the headmaster. The fact that Mr Svenson had been invited in to the office to hear her admonishment made things even worse. The late nights, the over-familiarity, the wilfulness were all mentioned. Daisy burned with shame. She'd always prided herself on being firm but fair but it was true, she had allowed Molly to get away with too much. Accusing her of engendering a sense of permissiveness was, she thought, harsh and the suggestion that Mr Svenson take on the overall supervision of the staff an abomination. He was punishing her. It wasn't fair. She'd always liked and respected Mr Lawrence and her work had never before been called into question. Molly Brown had a lot to answer for.

At least she managed to assure Mr Lawrence that it wouldn't happen again and he had agreed to allow her to retain management of the chambermaids, but only because Mr Svenson would now have to take over Mr Jevons's post as maître d'. Mr Svenson's offer to help her select a new maid didn't help either.

A sombre atmosphere of resignation fell over the hotel staff. Everyone knew something was going on. There were whispers, shakes of the head, Daisy felt every gaze upon her as she walked back to the kitchen.

"Sorted it out, did 'e? Mr Lawrence?" Mrs T asked as she walked in.

Thin-lipped with fury Daisy glared at her.

"In a manner of speaking," she said.

*

Mr Jevons hadn't returned by late afternoon. Lawrence had gone over his file, reading it through several times. Jevons had been with them since his father's day. Surely he was owed some consideration for the long years of service? He knew he had a sister who lived in Clerkenwell. If he wasn't at the hotel that was the most likely place Lawrence would find him. Even if he wasn't there she might know where he was likely to be. Her address was in the file. He caught a cab halfway and walked the rest. He arrived at the house in time to see a portly woman in a beige coat and felt hat helping a dishevelled Mr Jevons in through the front door.

"Good afternoon," he said raising his hat as he walked up the path. "Mr Jevons."

"Oh. Good Lord. Oh dear. Oh my." Jevons put his hand to his head to cover his face. Lawrence heard a sob as he turned away. He'd never seen anyone look so dejected.

"You'd better come in," the woman said. "Things is bad enough without putting on an entertainment for the neighbours." He followed them in. "I'm Ada, Arthur's sister. Let me put the kettle on. I'll make us some tea."

Lawrence smiled. He'd never seen anyone look so put upon and it wasn't her fault. "That would be lovely. Thank you," he said.

Jevons led Lawrence into a small but neat front parlour that smelled of camphor and lavender. The chairs looked comfortable if a little worn, a patterned rug lay in front of the fireplace and an aspidistra in a pot stood on the well polished table. Jevons collapsed into one of the chairs holding his head in his hands. "I'm sorry," he said. "I know I've let you all down.

I've let myself down. It shouldn't have happened. I'm the one to blame. I'm sorry."

Lawrence's heart went out to him. He wasn't a young man and he'd suffered a blow when his wife died. He'd been something of a constant in Lawrence's life too. He recalled when he first visited his father's hotel Mr Jevons was there and it seemed as though he'd grown part of the place. Seeing him here felt strange. He'd never imagined him having a home life. The hotel had been his life. Now it was over and Lawrence was sorry for that.

"Mr Jevons... Arthur." Lawrence sat and stretched out his hand to place it on Jevons's shoulder. "I'm sorry too, old friend."

"I'm off it now. Sworn off it. Never going to let a drop pass my lips again. I swear." Jevons raised his head, a tear ran down his cheek. "I know I let you down. Won't happen again."

Confusion circled Lawrence's brain. Surely he didn't think... no, he couldn't... there was no way...

"The trouble is this thing with Molly, the maid," Lawrence said as kindly as he could. "I mean..."

Jevons looked baffled. "Molly? The maid? What?"

Realisation dawned. Jevons had been talking about something else. He knew nothing about Molly's accusation. Lawrence took a breath. "Molly Brown says you assaulted her when you were drunk."

An expression of sheer amazement filled Jevons's face. "Assaulted her? Who? Me? Why I never... I mean, I couldn't... wouldn't..." His voice, which had had a whiny, compliant tone, grew stronger. "I never touched the little tart, not that she didn't offer it, mind you. If she says that she's lying. ADA!" The last word was loud enough to rattle the cups on the tray of tea and scones Ada was carrying in.

"What?" she said laying the tray on the table.

Jevons seemed to have regained his composure. "That tart at the hotel says I assaulted her. Me. I never touched her. Tell 'im, Ada. I wouldn't do that. Even drunk I wouldn't do that."

Ada's face creased into a frown. "He's right, Mr Fitzroy. Arthur may be a devil with the drink in 'im, but he'd never do out to mar the memory of 'is Elsie. When did she say 'e did it? Recent was it?"

"Last night."

"Well, that settles it. Last night Arthur got drunk and fell asleep on a park bench. When the rozzers tried to move 'im on he clouted one of 'em. He spent the night in a cell and was up before the beak this morning. Paid 'is fine and an' they sent 'im 'ome. Couldn't of 'ad anything to do with any girl, maid from the 'otel or not."

Lawrence sighed. "I didn't believe her for an instant," he said. "But you must see, Arthur, dear friend, that your behaviour left you open to that sort of accusation. I have the reputation of the hotel to think about. I'm sorry."

Jevons nodded as Ada passed him a cup of tea. "You mean if I wasn't drunk?"

"That, and your absence from your post. I'm afraid I can't…" Lawrence took an envelope from his pocket and handed it to Jevons. "There's three months' wages. It's the best I can do. I'm sorry but I have…"

"The reputation of the hotel to think about," Jevons finished for him. He hung his head as he said it.

"I'm sorry it's come to this," Lawrence repeated. "If there's anything I can do, a reference or anything."

Jevons shook his head.

Ada passed Lawrence a cup of tea and offered him a buttered scone. Lawrence smiled his thanks. He felt awful but there was nothing more he could do.

"Thank you, Mr Fitzroy," Ada said. "I'm sure you've done your best. We'll get by, won't we, Arthur?"

Jevons shrugged.

"I have a little put by, and Arthur has too," Ada said. "I've always fancied a little place by the sea. Nothing grand. A few rooms, bed and board. The sea air and change of scene might suit us, don't you think, Arthur?"

Jevons looked bleakly at his sister.

"There. I knew we'd sort somat out," Ada said.

Lawrence sipped his tea, impressed by her overwhelming optimism.

Chapter Ten

Elvira sent out the invitations for the weekend, complaining loudly about the lack of notice. "Two weeks!" she said. "These things are arranged months in advance. What was Lawrence thinking? No one will come. They'll have made their plans."

But she was wrong. The Huntington-Smythes were able to come as their visit to Yorkshire had had to be postponed following Chester Huntington-Smythe's brother Jasper's fall from his horse. His injuries were not life-threatening, but bad enough for him to be laid up and unable to host the planned visit. Sybil Huntington-Smythe wrote that they'd be delighted to visit Maldon Hall for the Easter weekend. Charlotte put a note to Verity in with the acceptance saying that she was looking forward to seeing her again and, although she didn't ride to hounds, Edward and Bertie would be pleased to join the hunt.

Once the Huntington-Smythes had confirmed their attendance other invited guests found they too were inexplicably free.

Elvira and Verity went over the arrangements for the weekend. The Huntington-Smythes would arrive in time for cocktails on Good Friday. Jeremy agreed to act as host until Lawrence was able to join them on Saturday. He'd also ride out with the hunt in Lawrence's absence. They'd all go to the Hunt Ball on Saturday evening. Verity's sister Henrietta and her husband would join them after church on Sunday. Him being a vicar they would be entertaining at the vicarage until then.

"What about Mama?" Verity asked. "Do you think she will be well enough to come?"

Elvira sighed. "I'm afraid the festivities may prove too tiring for her," she said. "Why don't you pay her a visit when we arrive? Then you'll be able to see."

Verity brightened. "Yes. Thank you, I will."

"Well, I'm glad that's sorted," Elvira said.

They left a few days early to travel to Maldon Hall to prepare for the weekend. In the coach on the way Elvira carried her notebook in which she was making lists. She seemed to Verity to have endless lists. "It's a pity you're not riding out, Verity," she said. "You've such a good seat on a horse. It would be a good opportunity to impress."

"Impress?"

"Yes. I understand Edward Huntington-Smythe will inherit. I've also invited the Montagu-Brownes. Their boys hunt and they are still unattached."

Verity swallowed the sharp retort that rose to her throat. "Well I shall be spending most of my time with Charlotte," she said, vexed at Aunt Elvira's constant hints at her marriage prospects. "I'm sure she'll prove much more impressive than I ever could." Then she had another thought. "Have you invited the Garraways? They're our neighbours. They have sons too."

"The Garraways?" Elvira sniffed. "She's pleasant enough I suppose, but I don't give much for the rest of the family. I suppose they're decent enough farmers, but not the sort you'd have at your table, unless…" She smiled. "Yes. We will need extra staff. The girl could work in the kitchen I suppose, and I expect the lad could manage the horses."

Verity clenched her fists as anger boiled up inside her. The memory of growing up with Ned and how he'd always been by her side filled her mind. If it wasn't for him she wouldn't be the rider she was today. Why did their position as farmers have to make any difference now they were adults? She'd always thought of Ned as a friend, and hoped that one day he might be more than that.

Any further discussion was curtailed by their arrival at Maldon Hall.

The midday sun bathed the front of the house in a golden glow. Birds that had been lazily pecking on the drive fluttered away over the manicured lawns as the carriage scrunched over the gravel, the horses' breath sending clouds of vapour into the air. Verity's heart warmed at the familiar sight. This was home. She'd been six when her father died and her Uncle Herbert, Elvira's husband, had taken them in, providing the Dower House on the estate as a home for them. Her mother still lived there and she was looking forward to seeing her again, especially since she'd been so ill of late.

"I'd like to go and see Mama," she said as they dismounted the coach.

"Of course," Elvira said. "Meadows will see to the luggage, but do come in first and have tea. I'm sure Mrs Wilkins will find some cakes or some-such that you can take to her. I do hope she is recovering well, it's such a worry."

Verity thought her mother's health was the last thing on Elvira's mind, but the cake would be a nice idea. With only a part-time house maid and a woman from the village who cooked for her she doubted her mother's fare would stretch to cake too often.

Verity called on her mother that afternoon, taking with her some cake and some fruit from the Maldon Hall kitchen. She arrived just as Mrs Bradley, the woman from the village who called in twice a day to assist, was leaving.

"How is my mother?" Verity asked, her voice heavy with concern.

"She's lost in a world of her own, if you ask me," Mrs Bradley said. "I've given her lunch and there's a pie in the oven. I'll pop back later to see to it, if that's all right."

"That's very good of you, Mrs Bradley. I know Mama appreciates everything you do for her."

Inside Verity found her mother sitting in her chair by the fire, her face pale and drawn. She wore a heavy shawl around her shoulders, despite the warmth from the fire crackling in the grate. Verity knew to expect some forgetfulness and that her mother was often distracted, but she'd never seen her looking so vulnerable and bewildered.

Glancing around the neat little room Verity noticed the pile of photo albums on the side table. The photograph in a silver frame in pride of place on the mantelpiece was of her father. Her mother held a similar, but smaller, photograph in her lap. Verity put her parcels on the sideboard and went over to kiss her mother's cheek. She took the photograph from her hands. "I always liked this one of him," she said. "It's just how I remember him."

Doris looked up, gazing at Verity for several minutes before she spoke. "Verity," she said. "How good of you to call." She lifted her hand to brush a stray lock of hair from Verity's forehead. "You're just like him. You have his eyes." A smile twitched her lips.

"Mrs Bradley said you've had lunch, but I'll make us some tea. Mrs Wilkins sent some cake and fruit to go with it."

Doris nodded and Verity went into the kitchen to make the tea. When she returned she saw her mother lost in thought, one of the photo albums open on her lap.

She set the tea tray down and took the album from her mother. "What's this," she said glancing through the pictures. They were all family photographs taken at happier times. Aunt Elvira had said Doris was living in the past. From what Verity could see she couldn't blame her.

Over tea and cake Verity sat with her mother going through the albums, sharing lost memories from long ago. She hardly remembered her father and knew little about his passing. No one ever spoke about it but she did recall a tall dark-haired man in a good suit who smelled of lavender and cedar wood and who was sometimes serious and withdrawn. Mostly she remembered high days and holiday, the family all together. It was only going through the album she realised how seldom her father was with them.

As she put the book to one side a photograph fell out. She picked it up. She recognised her father standing next to three other men carrying guns. It looked like a shooting party. "Oh look," she said. "Here's one of Papa. Who are these other men?"

Doris took the photograph and her face crumpled. Deep sadness filled her eyes. "He didn't mean to do it," she said.

"Didn't mean to do what?"

"It wasn't his fault. These men…" Doris started poking the photograph in an agitated state. A tear rolled down her cheek.

"What's the matter? What is it?"

"He never meant to hurt anyone." Her voice became a plaintive cry and Verity worried for her. She quickly took the picture away, pushing it back into the album. She couldn't bear to see her mother looking so perturbed. "It doesn't matter," she said. "It's all in the past. Please don't let it upset you."

Doris shook her head. "Why did he do it? He didn't have to." She grabbed Verity's wrist her grip far stronger than Verity thought possible, given her frailty. "He wouldn't have done it you know. Not on his own. Not unless someone made him."

The look on her mother's face broke Verity's heart. She'd obviously brought back some terrible memory from the past and in doing so had upset the one person in the world she loved more than any other. "Oh please don't fret, Mama. It's not worth it. It's all gone now. All put away. Let's have some more tea and we could sit in the garden for a while, now the sun's come round, if you're up to it."

Her mother lapsed into silence for several minutes. She glanced at Verity, her face calm as a mill pond, her anxiety forgotten. "Tea? Yes, that would be nice. There may be some cake left from yesterday. You know how your father likes cake."

Verity sighed. Her sudden loss of memory was a blessing, but Verity determined to find out what it was that had distressed her so.

Chapter Eleven

The cocktail party on Friday evening went well, Jeremy, the consummate host, making everyone feel at ease. The Huntington-Smythes admired the house and gardens and chatted with the other guests, Edward and Bertie interested themselves in the possibilities of the Saturday morning hunt while Charlotte flirted outrageously with all the men.

"I like your cousin," she said. "Charm on legs. Who could resist?"

Verity chuckled. Cousin Jeremy was well able to look after himself and well versed in the ways of young ladies like Charlotte. He always managed to extricate himself without giving offence, a skill in itself, Verity thought, but she was glad the evening went well for Elvira, who'd worried herself into a stew about the shortness of time to prepare and the lack of staff to serve.

After breakfast the next morning Verity and Charlotte accompanied the men to the meet for a stirrup cup at a local hostelry before the hunt. Jeremy rode out on a spirited hunter while Chester, Edward and Bertie had been accommodated from the neighbouring Garraway stables; the Fitzroy stable having been reduced over the years to a mere four carriage horses and a hunter.

They sat in the gig in the spring sunshine, watching the milling crowd of hounds, horses and men, the atmosphere highly charged with eager anticipation. Around them huntsmen in red or dark blue jackets, raised glasses to their lips, hounds bayed at wheeling horses and onlookers, radiant with the thrill of the morning, chattered and whooped with delight.

Verity saw Ned Garraway adjusting the bridle of a horse across the pack from her. Her heart jumped. She raised her hand to wave, but he turned away just as she did so. For a moment she envied him the ride. She recalled the thrill of the chase, the exhilaration, the wind in her face and the intense feeling of unfettered freedom as they galloped across fields and over hedges.

"Do you wish you were going with them?" Charlotte asked.

Verity sighed. "No. Not really," she said, although part of her did.

They sat enjoying the clamorous spectacle until the Master called the hounds to order and the hunt set off. Charlotte, her face bright with excitement, called, "Good luck," to her father and brothers, and waved as they headed out. "I do hope they find good sport," she said. "They'll be in a foul mood otherwise."

"It'll be a great ride out at any event," Verity assured her. "Ned's horses are the best in the county."

Once the hunt had got underway Verity and Charlotte drove into the nearby town to sample the shops. Charlotte bought her mother a decorated Easter basket filled with marzipan fruits and jellies. She found some decorated Easter Eggs with small trinkets inside for her father and two brothers. Verity bought a chocolate Easter Egg she said she'd take to her mother that evening.

Lawrence arrived at Maldon Hall in time for afternoon tea. As the cab from the station drove up to the house nestling quietly in the afternoon sun he felt a pang of regret. Mama was right. He should come home more often. His last visit had been at Christmas and that was only a couple of days as the hotel had been a priority. It was true, he had been shirking his responsibilities. He sighed. Perhaps now was the time to put that right.

Meadows greeted him as he stepped out of the cab. "Good afternoon, Mr Fitzroy," he said. "Good to see you home."

Lawrence nodded and felt guilty all over again. The butler took care of his luggage while Lawrence paid the cab driver. Inside the house familiarity and a sense of home filled him. "Mrs Fitzroy is in the drawing room with the Huntington-Smythes," Meadows said. "They're having tea."

"Thank you." Lawrence took a breath. Best get it over with, he thought.

"Ah. You're just in time for tea," Elvira said as he walked into the room. A look of the greatest pleasure filled her face.

"Mama," he said, bending over to kiss her cheek. "And you must be Mr and Mrs Huntington-Smythe." He shook their hands.

"This is my eldest son, Lawrence," Elvira said. "He's been in town on business. Always so busy."

A maid appeared with a fresh pot of tea and a cup and saucer. Lawrence smiled his thanks. "Where is everyone?" he asked.

"The boys are playing billiards," Elvira said. "Verity and Charlotte are upstairs planning what to wear for tonight's ball. Jeremy's gone. He said he had business in town." Elvira huffed. "I hope you'll be staying the whole weekend, Lawrence."

"I will, Mama." He took the tea she offered and sank into a chair next to hers. "I'm looking forward to meeting everyone, but I will have to freshen up and change before dinner."

After tea with his mother and the Huntington-Smythes, Lawrence took the opportunity to walk around the garden before going up to change. He saw the spring flowers coming into bud, the neatly trimmed hedges and lawns, and trees coming into leaf. The rose beds near the house were well kept but as he wandered further from the house he noticed some corners had become overgrown, the beds needed weeding and the paths hadn't been swept for some time. It wasn't exactly unkempt, just not as pristine as it would have been had there been a younger family in residence, or the garden visited more often. Of course, he thought, old Ted the gardener would be getting on now and, even if he had a boy to help, it wasn't the same as it would be with two full time gardeners. He doubted his mother ever ventured far from the house or it would have been seen to. Something else that needed his attention.

Once he'd dressed for dinner he made his way down to the lounge where he found his mother with her guests. Verity arrived with Charlotte as he poured himself a glass of sherry from the decanter on the sideboard.

"Lawrence, how lovely to see you," Verity said. "I'm glad you made it in time for the ball tonight. I was worried you wouldn't."

"Good to see you too," he said bending to kiss her cheek. He stood back and looked her up and down. "You look amazing." Verity blushed with pleasure.

"You haven't met my friend Charlotte," she said, turning to introduce the most stunning girl Lawrence had ever seen. Tendrils of golden hair framed the face of an angel. Cornflower blue eyes gazed up at him. A thrill of delight ran through Lawrence. He was lost for words.

"Good evening," Charlotte said, extending a slender hand. "I'm delighted to meet you. Verity has told me so much about you."

Lawrence swallowed. Her eyes sparkled as she smiled at him. His heart melted. "Then you have me at a disadvantage," he managed to say. "Verity has told me very little about you."

Charlotte laughed, a warm enticing sound that fell on Lawrence's ears like blossom in springtime. "Good," she said. "Then I shall have the greatest of pleasure telling you myself."

They were interrupted by the arrival of Edward and Bertie. Verity introduced them just as the dinner gong sounded. "Ah dinner," Lawrence said, offering Charlotte his arm. "Shall we?"

Throughout the meal Lawrence found his gaze wandering towards Charlotte. He did his best to make conversation with her brothers, finding Edward easy to talk to but Bertie a bit of a trial. He seemed to sulk and disagree with most of what Lawrence said. Mrs Huntington-Smythe did her best to smooth over his most objectionable comments, but Lawrence felt a sense of disquiet about him. He hoped Verity wasn't keen on him. If she showed any sign of finding favour in him, Lawrence thought, he'd have to have words with her. Something he didn't relish.

*

Daisy's mood didn't improve when Mr Lawrence left for Maldon Hall and Mr Svenson called her into the office.

"'E didn't waste any time getting 'is feet under table," Mrs T said.

"No. He wants to show us who's boss," Daisy said, still smarting from the dressing down she got from Mr Lawrence the previous day. Her heart thudded as she approached the door. She hadn't realised how much she looked forward to seeing Mr Lawrence each morning and going over the expected arrivals and departures. It had come to be the best part of her day. She gritted her teeth as she knocked on the door and entered.

"Ah, Miss Carter," Mr Svenson said, sitting at Mr Lawrence's desk looking more than a little pleased with himself. "What's the position on the new chambermaid?"

None of you business Daisy thought, but said, "I have several girls to see."

"Good. Then I can expect someone to start soon?" He smiled and Daisy saw the sparkle in his ocean blue eyes beneath a thatch of Nordic blond hair.

A cold chill ran over her. *I can expect*, she thought. Like Admiral Nelson? "As soon as I find someone suitable," she replied.

"Perhaps I should see the applicants," he said. "After all we want someone reliable this time."

This time. Daisy cringed. He wasn't going to let her forget her past mistake. "I'll ensure they have good references," she said. "There's no need for you to... I mean I'm sure you have better things... more important things..."

"There's nothing more important than the reputation of this hotel, Miss Carter. I'm sure I don't have to remind you of that."

Daisy's blood began to boil. Her face burned with fury, more so because he was right. The fiasco with Molly could have done immeasurable damage had Mr

Lawrence not paid her off. "I don't need to be told of the value of the hotel's reputation," she said anger clear in her voice. "I am more aware of it than you will ever be. I suggest that you do your job and I'll do mine. Good day."

With that she stormed out. Who the hell did he think he was, speaking to her like that? Still, he had a point. The girl who replaced Molly would have to be above suspicion and that wasn't easy to achieve. She looked through the few letters she'd had from girls applying for the post and her heart sank. The person she took on would have to come with good references, be trustworthy, honest and willing to work long hours for low pay. The working environment would be better than factory work, but no less arduous. She sighed and bent her head to go through the letters again, deep despair circled her heart.

Mr Svenson wasn't the only one worried about Molly's replacement. Annie too kept asking about it. "I can't do it all by meself," she said. "At least Molly did her share. I'm going to miss her. I liked Molly."

Of course you did, Daisy thought. She did most of the work. "Don't worry I'll come and give you a hand," she said and immediately regretted it. Cleaning the rooms wasn't her job and it wouldn't take Mr Svenson long to remind her of it.

Chapter Twelve

The evening of the Hunt Ball Verity would have cried off if it hadn't been for Lawrence being there and Charlotte's enthusiasm for the event.

"All those handsome huntsmen," she said. "I can't wait."

That was just like Charlotte, full of life and eager for adventure. Verity on the other hand dreaded it. The thought of having to dance with Bertie again and the discomfort that would bring made her insides writhe with anger.

She worried about her mother too, haunted by her face, drawn and pale and her words. Every day she'd visited and watched her mother's growing confusion. There was no repeat of the distress she'd shown on her first visit, but it wasn't something Verity could easily forget.

She asked Elvira what she may have meant – what had her father done that had caused so much distress? Elvira had put it down to her mother's confused state of mind. "Lost in a world of her own," she said. "I wouldn't put too much store by it." Then she'd suggested Verity busy herself sorting out the flowers for the weekend. "I'm not sure we'll have enough from the garden. You may have to go into town."

The only positive Verity could come away with was that Ned Garraway would be at the ball. His parents' farm provided some of the horses so he was bound to be there.

Her fears faded as she dressed and the maid helped Charlotte with her gown, an amazing creation of frills and flounces in deep burgundy, embroidered with white roses. Silk flowers around the neckline and a white lace shoulder cape completed the outfit.

"You'll be the belle of the ball," Verity assured her.

"I do hope so," Charlotte said, as she gathered up her voluminous skirt. "No point going otherwise."

Verity laughed. Charlotte didn't lack confidence, that was certain.

Charlotte's parents stood in the hall with Elvira to see them off. Lawrence offered Charlotte his arm. Edward did the same for Verity and Bertie followed behind, scowling. Verity wondered why he had to be so disagreeable all the time.

When they arrived they left their coats in the cloakroom and waited in the lobby to be announced. Verity drew a breath. Well, she thought, crossing her fingers, let's hope everyone behaves and we have a good time.

The next few hours passed in a whirl of dancing, music, laughter and muted conversations. Waiters circled the room with trays of glasses filled with champagne. Verity danced with Lawrence, Edward and several of the men she knew from the hunt. To her great relief Bertie spent more time in the bar than he did on the dance floor. She looked for Ned, hoping to dance with him, but each time she caught a glance of him he was spinning around the floor with a different girl from the village. Doing his duty, I suppose, she thought, but still wished it was her in his arms.

When the music stopped for the band to take a break there was no sign of Edward or Bertie. Thankfully Lawrence appeared at Verity's elbow. "Shall we?" He accompanied Verity and Charlotte into the supper room. Inside a long white-clothed table groaned under the weight of the dishes set out for the dancers. They joined the queue making its way to the table.

"Oh look," Charlotte gasped, her voice filled with delight. "The Summervilles have arrived."

Verity glanced over at the crowd coming through the door. She saw Brandon Summerville with a young lady on his arm.

"That's his sister," Charlotte said. "Excuse me. I must go and have a word." She skipped away like a child promised an ice cream.

"I didn't know the Summervilles were coming," Lawrence said with obvious displeasure. "I wasn't aware they rode to hounds."

Verity was surprised to see them too. "Someone must have invited them," she said. "They're not part of the hunting crowd." She watched Charlotte simper in front of Brandon. "I believe they're old friends of the Huntington-Smythes. Wasn't he in the Guards with you?"

"Yes," Lawrence said, but didn't elucidate any further.

After supper the Master of the Hunt called for silence and the speeches began. First he thanked the Master of Hounds, then the local landowners. There was a presentation to the huntsman who'd collected the most brushes and, as far as Verity could see, everyone congratulating themselves and everyone else. Applause, compliments and warm felicitations brought an end of season feel to the proceedings. An atmosphere of good cheer filled the room.

As the speeches were coming to an end the Master of the Hunt said he wanted to make a special announcement. "Ladies and gentlemen, charge your glasses and raise them to two young people who have today become engaged to be married."

A murmur of approval went through the crowd as people filled their glasses.

"To Ned Garraway, who we all know is the best horse-breeder this side of the river, and his lovely lady, Miss Georgina Swanley." The Master of the Hunt raised his glass and everyone cheered.

Verity's face flamed. She felt the blood rising like boats on a spring tide. She couldn't take it in. Ned engaged? Why hadn't he said anything? Why hadn't anyone told her? She watched with burning embarrassment as he led Georgina Swanley up to the stage, beaming like a Cheshire cat. When she looked down her hand was shaking. "Excuse me," she said to Lawrence and hurried away.

In the ladies room she took a breath. Of course, it all made sense. The Swanleys had the farm next to the Garraways. They were neighbours. They had no sons, only daughters. When Ned and Georgina married the two farms would, in time, be combined. Ned could breed his horses, while Georgina managed the rest of the farm. She felt sick to her stomach. What a stupid fool she'd been thinking there could ever be anything between her and Ned. Stupid, stupid, stupid. But knowing it didn't ease the pain.

After the speeches the band struck up and the dancing began again. Lawrence was going to ask Charlotte for a dance but Brandon Summerville beat him to it. He watched as they circled the room, happiness shining from her angel face. Something knotted in his stomach. If only she'd looked at me like that when we were dancing, he thought. He recalled Verity saying that

Charlotte was keen on him, but seeing it didn't make it any easier to accept.

He glanced around but couldn't see Verity. He saw Edward talking to the Master of the Hunt. There was no sign of Bertie so he went to the bar to look for him. He was their host after all and perhaps should see he was all right. He saw him in the corner playing cards with three other men. Duty done, he went to the bar and bought himself a stiff brandy.

He was still in the bar when Brandon came in. He nodded a greeting. Brandon bought a drink, offering Lawrence another. Not wanting to offend he accepted. After exchanging pleasantries about the evening, the families who were there, the music and the elegance of the ladies, Brandon said, "I'm surprised you have the Huntington-Smythes as guests. Wouldn't have thought they were your kind of people."

Puzzled Lawrence said, "I hardly know them. My cousin Verity was at school with the daughter. They're her guests, not mine." Then he recalled the look on Charlotte's face when Brandon asked her to dance. "You seem quite fond of Charlotte yourself."

A broad smile filled Brandon's face. "Ah yes, Charlotte." A mischievous glint warmed his eyes. "Terrible flirt, but I like her. She's the best of the bunch. The others aren't quite what they seem. I'd be very careful if I were you."

"Really?"

Brandon laughed. "Take care, my son," he said, tapping Lawrence on the arm in a friendly gesture as he walked away.

He hadn't said much, but what he had said was enough to give Lawrence pause. Brandon himself was no stranger to dirty dealings and if he thought something was wrong about the Huntington-Smythes, it couldn't be ignored. He'd hardly exchanged words with the parents and he hadn't taken to the brothers himself, but Charlotte… that was different. If there was something not right about them Verity's future wasn't the only one he'd be worrying about.

He sighed and swigged back the rest of his drink. It had been a long day and he had plenty to think about.

A full moon and a thousand stars lit the sky as they left the ball. Verity's heart filled with the warmth of having spent a pleasurable evening. She'd worried that Bertie might spoil the party with his boorish behaviour. He'd spent most of the evening at the bar and she feared he might make a scene when she saw him coming towards her, his gait uncertain and a leering grin on his face. Her heart crunched and her stomach churned. She froze, her only thought to get away from him, but her feet refused to move. Then, a voice at her side said, "Miss Templeton, may I have the pleasure."

She turned as a swell of relief flooded over her. Brandon Summerville stood next to her, a disarming smile on his face and his arm held out in invitation. The next minute she was swept into the swirl of dancers in his arms. She'd never been so grateful to anyone in her life. Not only that, he was the handsomest man in the room.

The memory of that moment lingered as she got into the carriage for the drive home. Thankfully Edward had escorted Bertie out earlier, leaving Lawrence to accompany her and Charlotte.

When they got back to Maldon Hall Verity was surprised to see the lights blazing and several carriages in the drive. One she recognised as her sister's, and another as belonging to the local doctor. As soon as the carriage stopped she leapt out to see what was going on.

Elvira met her in the spacious hall. "My dear, I'm so sorry," she said, taking Verity in her arms.

"What's happened? Why is everybody here?"

Elvira led her into the morning room where guests were usually asked to wait. Lawrence, who'd followed her in, went with her.

"It's your mother, dear. I'm so sorry."

Chapter Thirteen

Deep sadness filled Elvira's eyes. "An accident we think."

"An accident? What sort of accident? You don't mean...? No I saw her earlier today, she was fine... she can't..."

Elvira embraced her again. "Mrs Bradley found her earlier tonight. She was passing the cottage and saw the lights still burning, so she went in. She found your mother on the floor in the kitchen."

Bewilderment and frustration washed over Verity. She curled her fists. No. It couldn't be true. Elvira was saying something about the doctor and sending for Hettie... It didn't make sense. "You mean she's... she's..." Tears stung her eyes, but she fought them back.

"The doctor did all he could but it was too late. He thinks it was her heart." Elvira's voice trembled with emotion. "I'm so, so sorry."

Verity turned and stared at Lawrence, who looked as shocked and bewildered as she felt. "Where have they taken her?" he asked. "Can we see her?"

"They took her to the cottage hospital, but I've asked that she be brought back here. It's what she would have wanted. To be at home." Elvira's eyes misted over. She gripped Lawrence's arm. "You'll take care of everything, won't you, Lawrence?"

Lawrence put his hand over his mother's. "Of course, Mama," he said. "Of course I will."

"Good. I'll give you a few minutes." Elvira hugged Verity again before she left the room.

The happiness of the evening ebbed away as deep sadness filled Verity's heart. Elvira's words finally sunk in. Her mother was gone. She still couldn't believe it. Haphazard thoughts scrambled through her brain. How could this have happened? How could she have not known? Why wasn't she there? Suddenly it became all too real and a strangled cry escaped her throat. She turned to Lawrence, tears running unchecked over her cheeks. He took her in his arms and held her close while great sobs wracked her body.

It was several minutes before she could collect herself enough to let him go. "I'm sorry," she sniffed, wiping her eyes on the handkerchief he offered. "Whatever must you think of me?"

He smiled. "I think you are a most amazing girl. Your mother would be proud of you."

That made her well up again. She took a breath and squared her shoulders. "Come on, let's go and join the others. I want to know exactly what happened." Tears glistened in her eyes as she strode out of the room.

She found Charlotte waiting in the hall. "I'm so sorry," she said rushing up to her to give Verity a hug. "I've just heard. Mummy and Daddy have packed everything up and we're going home." She hugged Verity again. "I'll miss you. If there's anything I can do... anything at all... you must let me know."

Verity forced a smile. "Thank you. I will," she said, and reluctantly let her go. As she watched Charlotte walk away it felt as though all the fun had gone with her. From now on there would only be grief and sorrow.

After that Verity joined her sister, Henrietta and her husband, the Reverend Owen Williams in the drawing room, where they were having drinks with the doctor. She wanted to hear every detail of mother's demise. It didn't feel real. She'd been dancing the night away with her friends while her mother lay dying.

Lawrence, shocked as he was and tired from the night's activities, felt a great weight of responsibility fall upon him. The first thing to do was to see to their guests.

He was still in the hall with his mother when the Huntington-Smythes came down the stairs ready to depart.

"Tell Verity how sorry we are," Mr Huntington-Smythe said, speaking on behalf of his whole family. There were murmurs of agreement. They all shook hands and said their goodbyes each adding how sorry they were. Charlotte kissed Lawrence on the cheek as she prepared to leave. "I'm sorrier than I can say," she whispered in his ear, gazing at him with limpid blue eyes.

"Me too," he muttered and found he really meant it.

By the time the guests had left the sun had risen on another day. Lawrence arranged for telegrams to be sent to Jeremy and their sister Clara, both of whom were close to Aunt Doris. No doubt his mother would already have a list of those needed to be informed and invited to the funeral.

"She'll be buried here," Elvira said. "With Herbert. She was a Fitzroy before she married. That's what he would have wanted."

Elvira arranged for breakfast to be served in the dining room where they could all get together. The atmosphere around the table was subdued as he'd expected. The conversation, softly spoken and reverential, was, for the most part, one of fond anecdotes and remembrances of a life well lived. He hadn't realised how fond everyone was of Aunt Doris and what a special place she held in all their hearts.

"She should have stayed here with me," Elvira said her tone one of deep regret. "I asked her often enough, but she wanted to be on her own. I think the older she got the more she found the formality of life at the Hall stifling. Herbert always said she was like a butterfly – needing her own space."

"Brings home to us all how fleeting life can be," Owen Williams said. "Like the flowers of the field."

"She was a lot more substantial than a flower," Henrietta said, sharply. "And so much more consequential." Tears shone in her eyes.

"I didn't mean… I just meant…" Owen struggled against his wife's admonishment. "Flesh is weak," he said eventually.

"Speak for yourself," Lawrence muttered under his breath. Henrietta's husband would conduct the service, so he didn't want him upset, no matter how insensitive his comments. He supposed he was used to dealing with death, and thought more lightly of it than the rest of the company.

He noticed Verity sat in silence, hardly eating. She looked so young and vulnerable his heart went out to her. She was closest to his Aunt Doris and now she had no one other than a married sister and the Fitzroys. He vowed then that he would take care of her.

Chapter Fourteen

Carl Svenson imparted the news of Mrs Doris Templeton's death and Mr Fitzroy's continued absence from the hotel at a hastily arranged meeting in the dining room. Daisy stood with Mrs T and the kitchen staff. There had been whispers that something was amiss.

"There's always whispers," Hollis said, "but this time I think there's somat in it."

"'E just wants to show us who's boss," Barker said. "'E's setting out 'is stall to take over when Mr Lawrence goes."

"No." Daisy's heart missed a beat. "I don't believe Mr Lawrence intends to leave the hotel. It's always been run by a Fitzroy. He wouldn't."

"Well, it's not 'is home is it? Not now. Maldon Hall. That's where 'e is and I reckon that's where 'e means to stay."

"What do you think, Mrs T?" Daisy asked. "You know the Fitzroys best."

Mrs T put the last of the sausages and bacon in the oven to keep warm, wiped her hands on her apron and shrugged. "Best go and see what 'e 'as to say, I 'spose," she said. "Pure speculation otherwise."

So they all went up to the dining room to hear what Mr Svenson had to say.

Once he had their attention he began. "Mr Fitzroy has informed me that he'll be extending his absence due to a family bereavement."

"A bereavement?" Annie said glancing at Daisy in puzzlement.

"Someone's died," Barker said. "Can we know who?"

"Er." Mr Svenson looked at his notes. "Mr Fitzroy's aunt I believe. Mrs Doris Templeton."

An intake of breath and a soft gasp spread through the gathered staff.

"I'm sorry to 'ear that," Barker said. "She was well known 'ere and often came to stay. Will we be expected to attend the funeral? She was one of the family."

"That will be up to Mr Fitzroy," Mr Svenson said. "I'll let you know the arrangements as far as they are applicable to you as soon as I hear anything."

Daisy had fond memories of Mrs Templeton. Memories Mr Svenson would know nothing about. A well of sadness opened up inside her. She felt for the family. "What about flowers?" she heard herself say.

"Flowers?" Mr Svenson looked bewildered. "Oh yes. I suppose. Perhaps you would arrange for something to be sent on behalf of the hotel staff, Miss Carter. I'm sure we'd all appreciate it."

Daisy nodded although her heart chilled. It felt cold and impersonal, especially since Miss Templeton has been a recent guest. She decided that she'd send a personal note to Mr Fitzroy and the family and another to Miss Verity. It was the least she could do.

Mr Svenson continued, "In Mr Fitzroy's absence it falls to me to take his place. You will all report to me as you did to him. His absence is no excuse for standards to be allowed to slip. Rest assured I will be just as diligent as Mr Fitzroy in ensuring that visitors and guests of this hotel have nothing to complain about. All guests will leave after their stay with nothing but praise for our service and compliments to the staff. Is that understood?"

A murmur went through the small group who all looked at each other, apprehension clear in their faces.

"Did Mr Fitzroy say how long he'd be away?" Bridget asked. "Only with no Mr Jevons either…"

"I shall be appointing a temporary maître d' until Mr Fitzroy returns," Mr Svenson said.

"Oh so he is returning?"

"I have no information to the contrary." Mr Svenson clapped his hands as if to dismiss them. "That is all I know. When I know more, you will know more. Now, hurry along. We have a hotel to run."

"Well, what do you think of that?" Daisy said when they'd all returned to the kitchen. "Now hurry along." She clapped her hands in imitation, her heart heavy with dread.

"I think he's enjoying his five minutes of power," Barker said. "It won't last. I don't believe Mr Lawrence would leave without telling us first. No. It'll be as the bloke said. He's staying to arrange the funeral. Then he'll be back."

Daisy hoped with all her heart that Barker was right. The thought of a future working for that over inflated stuffed shirt made Daisy sick to her stomach.

I won't do it, she thought. I'll find another job. I'll go somewhere else, but thinking about that that made her feel sick too.

*

Over the next days the absence of a second chambermaid became more of a problem for Daisy. Try as she might she couldn't help Annie and keep up with her own work. She only had a couple of girls come for the job too.

"Any joy?" Mrs T asked as each of the girls left.

"No," Daisy said. "As soon as I mention the hours they lose interest. You'd think they'd jump at the chance to live-in in a smart place like this."

"Well, any girl with owt to 'er will be after one of them new-fangled office jobs. Better pay, better hours and you can wear better clothes an' all."

"Maybe we're expecting too much," Daisy said, thoroughly disheartened.

She mentioned her difficulty when she went to visit her mother, Nora Carter. "Honestly, Ma, I don't know what they expect these days. All I want is someone capable of doing some cleaning. I'm not asking for the world."

"Reliable and respectable is hard to find," Nora said lifting the hot iron she was holding off the shirt she was ironing. "Most just want a job 'til they get wed. Factory work's hard and relentless, but at least there's a social life and chance of a way out. Domestic service is a drudge. Not many girls want that these days." She put the iron on the hob and hung up the shirt.

"It's not such a bad life," Daisy said. "I've done alright."

Her mother looked at her. "Twenty-five and still not wed." She shook head. "That's no recommendation." She moved to put the kettle on.

Daisy huffed. "Better single than shackled to a…"

Nora spun round. "What? Better than shackled to a piece of shite like your sister?"

"I'm sorry. I didn't mean…"

Nora shook her head, her face granite. "You know what your sister's been through. It wasn't her fault."

Jessie had been fifteen when she got pregnant and married Charlie Benton. That hadn't worked out well either.

"How is Jessie?" Daisy said as a swell of guilt washed over her.

"She's between jobs at the moment." The kettle came to the boil and Nora made the tea.

Daisy's heart sank. If Jessie wasn't working Ma would be missing the money she brought in. "Between jobs? Why? What happened? I thought she was settled at the factory."

"Aye. So did I. But the girls there hated her and, according to Jess, the boss was more hands-on than 'e should 'ave bin. She clocked 'im one with a sack of sugar." Nora set out cups and saucers for the tea. "You could do worse than offer her the job."

"Like I did before you mean?" Daisy immediately regretted her words. She'd asked Jessie to take on something because she didn't want to do it, not realising how fragile Jessie was. They'd all had to pay for her mistake. Jessie paid the most of all.

Just then the door opened and Jessie walked in. "Hello, Dais. What you doing 'ere?"

"She's come to offer you a job," Nora said.

Jessie froze. "What? Like last time?" It was several years ago, but Daisy saw the pain on Jessie's face at the memory.

"No," Daisy said, "Ma's got it all twisted. I'm just looking for a maid at the hotel, that's all."

"A maid? Cleaning and such like? I can do cleaning, can't I, Ma?"

"Aye, you can. An' it's live-in so that'll be somat."

Daisy died inside. Jessie was a troubled soul and a lot of the fault for that could be laid at her door. She knew that. She'd caused more harm than she liked to think about. Jessie had been frail and vulnerable and Daisy had put her in an impossible position. It was no wonder she did what she did. Despite the passing years the pain and misery still affected them all. Then there was Mr Lawrence to think about. What would he say, seeing Jessie again?

"I don't know, Jessie…"

Jessie's face said more than words could. "So, I'm not good enough? Is that it? Not good enough to be a cleaner?"

The unspoken, *I was good enough last time,* hung in the air between them.

"No. I'm not saying that. It's just…"

"What?" Hurt and anger filled Jessie's eyes.

Daisy's resolve melted in the heat of the accusation. She owed Jessie a chance and she'd have Ma to answer to if she didn't give it. The decision had been taken out of her hands. "All right. But you'll be on a month's trial to see how it goes," she said in an effort to dissuade her. "And Mr Svenson, the under-manager, has to agree."

"Fine. When can I start?"

Daisy sighed. "Give me a couple of days to sort something out," she said, hoping to think of an excuse to change her mind.

"What's to sort out?" Nora said. "You want a maid. Jessie's available. She could come with you now, why wait?"

They both glared at Daisy. She gave in. "Oh, all right – but Jessie…"

"Yes."

"It's my job on the line as well as yours if this doesn't work out."

"You worry too much. I know what's what."

Daisy sighed. Jessie was right. She'd been as good as gold last time – until… But that wasn't likely to happen again was it?

Chapter Fifteen

Verity found the days prior to the funeral went in a blur. Villagers and farmers called to express heartfelt condolences. "She was well thought of around here," they all said. The farmers' wives brought cake and stayed for tea.

"It's good of them to call," Elvira said. "When they're so busy."

When Jeremy arrived Verity was glad of his company. He managed to calm his mother down and temper her more outrageous suggestions for the funeral cortege. He insisted on taking Henrietta and Verity to lunch in town on the day the undertakers called to do their business at the house. He accompanied them when they went to choose flowers. He lightened the sombre mood around the dinner table with warm memories and perceptive comments. He even managed to charm Henrietta's husband, the vicar, with his knowledge of the scriptures and suggestions for readings.

Verity's cousin Clara, Elvira's daughter, arrived at the end of the week, wafting in like a summer breeze. Verity's heart lifted as it always did when she saw her. Growing up Verity had always been in awe of Clara. Bold and often reckless nothing fazed her. She always seemed to manage to turn things to her advantage, whatever the problem. Verity admired that.

"I was so sorry to hear the news," Clara said as she hugged Henrietta and Verity in turn. "You must be devastated."

Verity nodded. "We are," she said. "It's difficult to get our heads around what happened, it happened so quickly."

"I can imagine. Now you must tell me all about it." She ushered them indoors where Elvira was serving tea. The rest of the afternoon was spent with Clara listening to the details of Doris's passing and then reliving affectionate anecdotes about the time she spent in London with her.

"She was wiser than you might believe," she said. "She didn't miss much of what went on but never made a fuss of it. She made you feel safe somehow and she was a great friend to me."

At least with the family there, Verity felt more settled and she couldn't complain about the lengths the Fitzroys went to to ensure that her mother's funeral was everything it could possibly be. Lawrence pulled out all the stops. A Notice of Death appeared in *The Times* and Elvira sent cards to everyone in the county. Few attended.

"I won't have people saying we didn't give her a good send off," Aunt Elvira said.

The family all wore black, curtains were drawn, mirrors covered. The house was in mourning.

"I'm not sure what Mama would have thought of it all," Verity said to Henrietta. "She was a simple soul. Never wanted to cause anyone any trouble."

Doris Templeton (née Fitzroy) was laid to rest on a bright morning in May when trees were coming into leaf, bluebells carpeted shady woods, filling them with their fragrance, cows grazed contentedly in fields and birds chirped their merry songs. Verity sniffed in the air as she walked with Lawrence, slowly, slowly into church, her mind still reeling from the suddenness and senselessness of it all. Would it have been any different if she'd been there? Probably not, but she couldn't help feeling as though she'd let her mother down. I should have been here to take care of her, she thought.

The sparse congregation in the church consisted of the few villagers who could spare the time and several of Elvira's friends. Mrs Bradley, who'd cooked and cared for Doris, was visibly moved and spent the whole time, her cheeks damp with tears, sniffing into her handkerchief. Verity thanked her for coming and assured her that she'd call on her later that week.

"She was a dear soul," Mrs Bradley said. "I'll miss her."

Verity didn't doubt it.

A buffet lunch was served at Maldon Hall after the service, but Verity couldn't face it. Couldn't face the utterances of condolence from people who hardly knew her mother and cared even less about her. Couldn't face the pity in their eyes and the hypocrisy in their hearts. "I'm going to lie down," she said as soon as they arrived back at the house. "I have a terrible headache."

"Can I get you anything?" Lawrence, who'd been at her side throughout, asked.

"No. Thank you, I'll be fine." At least he cared, she thought. She couldn't even face Henrietta. They'd been so close when they were growing up but now Verity felt very alone.

Upstairs she took off her hat, gloves and black mourning coat and sat on the bed. It had been a lovely service, the words, probably written by Henrietta and the hymns they'd chosen together. Even Owen had produced the right air of solemnity mixed with compassion and solicitude. "I hope it was what you wanted, Ma," she whispered as her mother's face appeared in her mind. "We all loved you." She imagined her mother chuckling and telling her not to be so daft. *I'm still with you, always,* she thought she'd say. *I never really left.*

On a whim she got up and left the room that had never felt like home. She slipped unseen down the back stairs and out through the back door. The noise and chatter of the mourners gathered in the drawing room faded as she tripped through the kitchen garden out to the lane that led to the Dower House.

When she arrived she found the key under the stone in its usual place and let herself in. She wanted to be there one more time, to feel close to her mother. In the sitting room she sat in her mother's chair and glanced around, taking it all in: the picture of her father over the mantel, the decanter and glasses on the sideboard, the china horse ornaments on the window sill, the pile of photo albums stacked neatly on a side table within easy reach. It all felt so familiar and yet strangely different. The room stood still and empty, everything in order as though waiting for its owner to return.

The well of sorrow she'd held back for so long erupted in great sobs, wracking her body. Tears wetted her cheeks as she held her head in her hands and wept. When she was all cried out she sat back in the chair and glanced around again. She picked up the album on the top of the pile and opened it. Memories flooded her brain. They were all there, pictures of happier days. Pictures of her and Hettie growing up. Pictures of her and the horses she rode, even a picture of her and Ned, winners at the local gymkhana. That brought another stab of grief. Why hadn't Ned told her about the engagement?

She went through another album, some of the photographs going back years, pictures, yellowed with age, of her mother and father in younger days; stiff formal portraits that gave nothing of the spirit or personality of the people in them. She ran her finger over her father's face trying to bring it to mind and another wave of grief and sorrow engulfed her. Other pictures of carefree days when she was young made her smile. For more than an hour she sat lost in the past as memories washed over her.

Much later, as dusk descended and the sky darkened, she went to put the albums back in the sideboard where they belonged. As she did so she noticed an envelope pushed to the back of the cupboard. Crumpled, it looked as though it had been roughly pushed aside. Puzzled she took it out and opened it. Inside she found a collection of newspaper cuttings. Intrigued she tipped them out and began to look through them. A black banner headline hit her eye: *Disgraced Businessman found Hanged.* Next to it was a picture of her father.

Chapter Sixteen

On the bus back to the hotel Jessie appeared distracted. "What's the matter?" Daisy asked. "Regretting it already?"

"No. 'Course not." She sat chewing her bottom lip. "Miss Clara's not there now is she? Nor Mrs Fitzroy?"

Daisy smiled. So that's what's worrying her, she thought. Of course they'd immediately recognise her and the trouble she'd caused would re-surface. They'd never agree to the appointment. Oh, they'd try to be kind, but she'd still be sent packing. Then Jessie had used a different name and given a fictional account of her husband's whereabouts for a very good reason. Perhaps it would be as well to keep up the pretence.

"No. Only Mr Lawrence, but still, perhaps we should stick to the name you used before, Mrs Ferguson. It'll save confusion."

Relief filled Jessie's face. "Right. Mrs Ferguson it is then. And my husband? Still working up North?"

Daisy pondered. "No," she said. "Maybe he's on a ship. Let's say he joined the Merchant Marine. That will explain a long absence."

Jessie nodded. "Do you think Mr Lawrence will be all right with me... you know... after..."

"He's away at his aunt's funeral at the moment. I think Mr Lawrence will be the least of our worries."

Jessie relaxed and looked out of the window for the rest of the journey. Daisy wished she could feel as good about the appointment as Jessie did.

When they arrived they went round the back of the hotel, across the old stable yard and in through the kitchen. Mrs T and the rest of the staff were sitting at the long table, having just finished lunch. Ruby was starting to clear the plates.

"Good afternoon," Mrs T said. "Who do we have here?"

Daisy took a breath. "This is Jessie. She's the new chambermaid."

"Ah! So you found someone." Mrs T rose from the table. "Hello, Jessie, and welcome. I hope you'll be happy here." She smiled, a smile so rare that Daisy almost fell through the floor. A quizzical look crossed Mrs T's face. "I feel as though I know you," she said. "Have you been here before? Visiting a friend perhaps?"

Thoughts ran like wild hares through Daisy's head. Had Mrs T seen Jessie before? She couldn't remember. It was possible. "Jessie's my sister," she said, her heart hammering. "I expect it's the likeness that's thrown you."

Mrs T stared from one to the other. "Yes. I see it now. Well, welcome anyway. Now I must get on." She glared at Daisy with a look Daisy interpreted to mean: *I know there's more and I can't wait to hear it.*

"Annie," Daisy said. "Jessie will share with you and you'll need to show her the ropes. Take her up now so she can settle in. Then you can both sort the laundry this afternoon. I'll see Mr Svenson about the arrangements."

"Yes, Miss Carter," Annie said her face beaming. "Come on, Jessie."

At least she'll be happy, Daisy thought.

She didn't relish seeing Mr Svenson, but in Mr Lawrence's absence he'd have to make up Jessie's pay packet and add her to the staff. Butterflies ricocheted in her stomach. She wasn't sure whether to mention the family connection as she didn't know how he'd feel about it. If she mentioned it she didn't want him to think there'd be any favouritism, or that she'd treat Jessie any differently from the other staff. If she didn't mention it and he found out later he'd think she had purposely kept him in the dark, and that wouldn't go down well either. It wouldn't have been a problem if Mr Lawrence had been there.

She knocked on the office door and went in. Every time she saw him sitting at Mr Lawrence's desk a shudder of annoyance went through her. He'd rearranged the things on the desk and moved the chairs around. Making himself at home, she thought, and she didn't like the thought of that either.

"I have a new chambermaid starting this afternoon," she said. "Jessie Ferguson. I've written the details down for you." She passed him a paper with Jessie's terms of employment on it. "These are the usual arrangements."

He took the offered paper. "Good," he said, his face lightening. "I'm glad you found someone. I hope she's reliable."

Unlike the last one, Daisy thought. "I've told her there's a trial period. Mr Lawrence will have the final say when he returns."

Mr Svenson looked amused. "I'm sure Mr Lawrence will be guided by my advice on the matter," he said.

I wouldn't be so sure, Daisy thought. Wait until he sees her. She stood for a while not sure whether to explain further.

"Is there anything else?"

Daisy wondered if she looked as uncomfortable as she felt. "Er. It's irrelevant, but I should mention that she's my sister."

"Your sister?" He looked surprised and a grin spread across his face. "Well, then I'm sure she'll be eminently suitable."

His eyes sparkled with mirth, making Daisy feel even more uncomfortable. Heat rose up from her neck to her cheeks. "Well, I'd best get on then."

"Right."

She stood dithering. She seemed to have lost the use of her legs.

"There's nothing else then?"

"No, thank you." She backed out of the office feeling as though she'd been caught with her hand in the till. Outside she breathed a sigh of relief. Why did he have to be so patronisingly condescending, she thought, especially when he doesn't know the half of it?

When she made her way back in the kitchen Mrs T was waiting for her, as she knew she would be. She pulled her into the empty staff sitting room. "So, what's with your sister then? What is it you're not telling us?"

Daisy shrugged, but she couldn't lie to Mrs T. Not easily anyway. "She's delicate and I worry, that's all."

"Delicate?" Mrs T glowered. "She looks healthy enough to me. Quite robust in fact."

"Physically, yes, but…"

"But?"

"Well, she's troubled… I mean, she's been through a lot. Married too young and when that didn't work out… well… she went off the rails a bit." No need to give her the whole story Daisy thought.

"You mean off her trolley? Some sort of hysterical doings?"

"A nervous condition the doctors called it. She was confused, became delusional and… well…"

Aghast, Mrs T's eyes spread wide. "You mean she's deranged?"

Daisy shuddered at the word and a swirl of foreboding spiralled through her. She could hardly deny it. "She was but she got over it… unfortunately she was working for Miss Clara at the time and the family… well… it was my fault. She was doing me a favour."

"So what's she doing here now?" The anxiety on Mrs T's face turned to sharp anger.

"It was years ago. She's better now. The doctors said…" What had they said? Daisy didn't know. All she knew was that Jessie had been discharged from the institution where they'd kept her. They wouldn't have done that if she was still unwell. She felt a sudden need to protect Jessie. After all it was her fault she'd lost her mind in the first place. "I'll vouch for her. She's my responsibility and I'll answer for any problems she causes. She's fine now. I told you."

"What about the other staff. It's hardly fair on them is it?"

Daisy gasped. "I'd appreciate it if you didn't mention it to the others. Jessie's had a bad enough time as it is without anyone making more of it than it was." As if that could be possible, Daisy thought.

Mrs T shrugged. "All right, but on your head be it," she said.

The enormity of what she'd taken on hit Daisy like a rock. "She'll be fine," she said. "She's a good worker. You'll see."

Chapter Seventeen

Verity stared at the paper, numb with shock. She couldn't make sense of it.

Her father? In the paper? Hanged?

She sank on to a chair in disbelief. It couldn't be true. She scanned the page in bewilderment and confusion. The words *allegations, intent to defraud, bankruptcy, suicide,* danced before her eyes. No, it couldn't be right, not her dear papa. He was a respectable businessman. Honest as the day is long. There must be some mistake.

She looked through the other cuttings, they all said something similar. The more she read the worse it got. Words like *swindle, fraud, deception, cheat, sham, rogue* appeared in most of them.

A cold chill ran through her. Nausea rose up in her throat. She swallowed it back. Her first thought was for her mother, "Mama," she breathed glancing round. The realisation that she was gone broke over her like a huge wave pulling her under. Pain, like a punch to the stomach gripped her. Her mind spun. She shook her head trying to dislodge the thoughts racing through her brain. Her mother had kept the cuttings and never said a word about her father's death. The betrayal felt like a stab to her heart.

She cast her mind back, trying to remember the last time she saw him. She couldn't and no one spoke of it. All she could recall was being sent to stay with Uncle Herbert and Aunt Elvira at Maldon Hall. Then, a little while later, her mother came and they moved into the Dower House. "He died of a broken heart," was all her mother would say when she asked. "Far, far away," she said when Verity asked about his grave. That's why they never visited and that's why her mother was buried with her brother. I should have known, Verity thought. Why wasn't I told?

She put the cuttings back in the envelope and placed it between the pages of one of the albums. She sat for a while thinking. What should she do next? It wasn't something she could forget, put aside, never mention again as her mother had done. She didn't believe it. It couldn't be true. She got up, picked up the pile of albums and took them with her pulling the cottage door closed behind her. Perhaps now wasn't the right time, but Aunt Elvira had some explaining to do.

When she got back to the house people were leaving. Elvira and Lawrence stood outside seeing them off. "Thank you so much for coming," she heard Elvira say. "My sister-in-law would have appreciated it."

As Elvira turned to go back in she spotted Verity. "Ah Verity, there you are. What's that you've got? Something nice?" She ushered her into the hall.

"Oh, just mother's photograph albums," she said. "I thought I'd remove them from the house. They're very personal and I didn't want people going through them."

"Quite right," Elvira said. She sighed. "I suppose we'll have to have the Dower House cleared. It's where I'll live when Lawrence gets married. A house can't have two mistresses." She led them towards the drawing room.

"Are you getting married?" Clara, who'd just joined them, asked Lawrence, surprise lifting her voice. "It's the first I've heard of it."

Lawrence shook his head. "You know Mama. Ever the optimist." He glanced around the hall as though seeing it for the first time. "Although, I suppose I will have to one day."

"I'll just take these upstairs then," Verity said hoping to escape.

"Oh, old photographs. I expect there's a lot of memories hidden in those," Clara said seeing them in Verity's arms. "We could go through them if you wish."

Verity's heart sank. "Oh no. Not today. It's been very trying and I don't think I can stand any more nostalgia."

Clara chuckled. "Whatever you say. Perhaps a walk around the garden then, when you're ready. I want to hear all about your life in London."

Verity nodded and rushed upstairs. In her room she put the albums in the dressing-table drawer and locked it, putting the key in her jewellery box. She vowed to get to the bottom of her father's death but today was for sharing happy memories of her mother and she didn't want to cast a dark cloud over them.

*

As time went on Daisy realised she didn't need to worry about Jessie doing her share. She turned out to be diligent and conscientious, pleasant to everyone and quicker than Annie at cleaning a room and making up beds. Annie, who had a smile on her face for the first time since Molly left, had nothing but good to say about her.

"She's a good worker," Annie said. "Of course I have to show her how we do things, but she's a quick learner. I think we'll get on."

Daisy was hardly satisfied with that as a recommendation. Annie would appreciate any help and the fact she could tell Jessie what to do would please her.

But Jessie was making an effort too, Daisy could see that. She'd never known her so compliant. How long would that last once she got her feet under the table? Jessie wasn't above causing a row for the sake of it. She wasn't sure she wanted her to stay and already regretted her impulse to offer her the job.

Despite her resolution not to Daisy found herself watching Jessie closer than she did any of the other maids, checking her more often and, she had to admit to herself, hoping to find some fault that would allow her to let Jessie go. After all she was on trial and she had told her the job was temporary.

Jessie even managed to charm Mr Svenson when she took his tea up one afternoon. "I see your sister's fitting in nicely," he said to Daisy when she went in for the bookings the next morning. "Pretty girl too, just like her sister." Daisy had squirmed with embarrassment.

"How are you finding the work?" she asked her on the third day.

"Oh I like it well enough. It's out of Silvertown, that's the main thing." She glared at Daisy. "Don't worry I'm not thinking I'll stay here forever. I know you've done me a favour and I appreciate it. Ma does too. But I want to get on, make somat of meself. Not spend the rest of me days making other people's beds and clearing up after their mess."

Daisy breathed a sigh of relief.

"No," Jessie continued. "I see it at a stepping stone. After working here I'll get a good reference so I can better meself. I might even work in a shop. Anything'll be an improvement on that stinking factory."

So that was why Jessie was behaving herself. In the hope of a good reference and a more favourable position. Ma always said she could've made something of herself if it hadn't been for Charlie Benton. Daisy hoped she was right.

Chapter Eighteen

During the weeks after the funeral the house was in mourning, but the memory of the headlines festered in Verity's brain. Henrietta called every day and they sat and talked. Henrietta agreed to go through their mother's things with Verity. "It'll only be her clothes and personal effects," she said. "The furnishings and everything else belong to the Estate."

It was a week before Verity got up the courage to ask about her father's death. "Do you remember much about Papa and how he died?" she asked.

"Papa? Gosh that was a while ago. Let me think. I remember getting a new pony. Alicante, you remember, just after we came here. I must have been about twelve – oh yes. I won the gymkhana. The locals got a bit het up about that." She chuckled as she sipped her tea.

"No. I mean how he died?"

Henrietta pouted. "His heart wasn't it? Stress of work Mama said. I do recall seeing very little of him, he was very stern and always busy."

Strange, Verity thought. That's not how I remember him at all. "So you didn't know about this?" She showed her the newspaper cuttings. "You didn't know our father killed himself?"

"Killed himself?" Henrietta put her tea down and stared at the cuttings. She shook head, looking stunned. "All I know is that there was a great furore about some business. People calling, shouting, angry words, Mama crying, everyone upset. That's why we were sent away." She picked through the cuttings. "Where did you find these?"

"Among Mama's photograph albums."

Henrietta put her hand to her mouth, looking troubled. "This must have been devastating for poor Mama. What a terrible thing to happen. No wonder she kept it from us. She always had our best interest at heart."

"It says Papa was a crook and a charlatan. Do you believe that?"

"No of course not. But it was a long time ago. We have different lives now. It's pointless dragging up the past. It doesn't change anything. No point muddying up the waters of our lives now. It could do untold damage and no good at all."

"Don't you want to know the truth?"

"The truth? The truth is what you believe. I believe Papa was a good and honest man. No amount of newspaper coverage, rumours or gossip will change that. I believe the past should stay in the past. If I were you I'd get rid of these." She handed Verity the cuttings.

Verity gazed at the cuttings in her hand. How she longed to screw them up, shred them to pieces and the lies that went with them, but in her heart she knew she'd have to find out for sure. It was her Papa they were talking about.

The next morning at breakfast the subject of the Dower House came up again. "I've arranged to go through Mama's things with Henrietta," Verity said. "It'll only be her clothes and personal belongings. Hettie said the parish would be glad of them."

Elvira huffed. "I don't know why you don't let Simpkins deal with it. After all he is the Estate Manager. He has people who can do that."

"Because it's family." Verity's tone sounded sharper than she intended. Elvira's attitude was beginning to grate. Did the woman have no feelings? "She was our mother."

"It's such a shame," Elvira said. "You should be thinking about later on. When you can go out and about, dancing and going to balls to meet the right people. Not sorting through hand-outs to the parish."

Verity's fury boiled over. "The right people," she blurted out. "You mean like my father?" She tipped the newspaper cuttings out onto the table in front of her aunt. Elvira stared at them, her face hardening. "Is it true? Did my father kill himself? Why did nobody tell us?" Tears stung her eyes.

Elvira's face was granite. "Where did you get these?"

"Mama kept them. Is it true? Did you know?"

Elvira sighed, pushing the bits of paper away as though disgusted by them. "It was a long time ago. There were rumours. I never heard the whole story. It's in the past, my dear." She patted Verity's hand. "No sense in dragging it all up again."

"Did you know?" Verity's voice rose to a crescendo as she threw the accusation at Lawrence. He picked up the papers, a deep frown on his face.

"Me? I knew nothing."

"It was years ago," Elvira said. "Best forgotten."

"Best forgotten! He was my father. I have a right to know." All the pain and emotion of the last week, losing her mother and the discovery of the manner of her father's death rose up in a swirling mass of misery and rage that threatened to overwhelm her. "He wasn't a crook or a charlatan. I knew him. He wasn't what they said. Why would he kill himself? I don't understand."

Deep concern creased Lawrence's face. "Just because it's in the newspaper doesn't mean it's true," he said disbelief clear in his voice. "I never knew your father but I'm sure I'd have heard something if this had been the case. How much did you know, Mama?"

Elvira shrivelled under her son's glare. She took a breath to compose herself. "Not much. Your father dealt with business. I was more concerned with the living than the dead. The girls came to stay with us. We gave them a good home." She turned to Verity. "When your mother came to join you we didn't ask questions. She was upset enough as it was, losing her man. I've always thought of you as my family, you know that. I treat you as one of my own."

Verity crumbled. Elvira was right it was no good blaming her. "I'm sorry, Aunt. I know you've always done your best for Hettie and me and I'm grateful. But he was my father. I need to know the truth."

Elvira rose, crumpling her napkin and dropping it on top of the cuttings. "The best thing you can do, my dear, is to forget all about it. Find yourself a good husband. Live a good life." With that she strode out of the room.

Verity sighed, blinking away her tears. She looked at Lawrence. "He was my father. I need to know," she said.

After the conversation with Verity, Lawrence began to wonder about his uncle's death. True, he wasn't a blood relative, having married his father's sister, but seeing Verity so upset disturbed him. He'd seen his own father when he passed away and that had brought some comfort. He could only imagine the shock and distress for Verity finding those cuttings and how stupid it was of Doris to keep them. But then he relented, perhaps it was all she had of the man she'd married – his obituary.

He felt sure his mother knew more than she was saying and decided to approach her again. He found her in the drawing room where a maid was bringing her morning coffee.

"Lawrence, do come and join me." She nodded to the maid to bring another cup. "I have some letters to post. People have been so kind sending their condolences."

Lawrence took a seat beside his mother.

"I wanted to ask about Verity's father. What do you know about him?"

"Oh not that again!" Colour rose in Elvira's cheeks as she became quite agitated. "How stupid of Doris to keep those newspaper cuttings. She really is the end – I mean was the end." Her voice dropped as she spoke. She shook her head. "I'm sorry, Lawrence, but as you can see I'm quite put out about it."

The girl arrived with the extra cup and Elvira set about pouring the coffee.

"I suppose it's only natural that Verity would want to know about her father." Lawrence took the cup Elvira offered him.

Elvira sighed with resignation. "If you really must know I only met him a couple of times. Surly I thought. A Yorkshire man and proud. He adored Doris." She sipped her coffee, pausing in thought. "She was a looker in her day. Flighty though and not a thought in her head that hadn't been put there by someone else." She sat back, lost in memory. "One of life's butterflies, Herbert called her. They were close, he'd have done anything for her." Her voice hardened as she said, "What he did. That was unforgivable. Leaving those poor children."

"What about his business? Was he as corrupt as they said in the papers?"

Elvira shrugged. "Hearsay and gossip most of it I suspect. He didn't strike me as a man who'd take advantage of others, but you never know do you? Your father knew more about the business side of it. You know I don't have a head for that sort of thing."

Lawrence felt the dismissal. "I'd like to know more about it if possible, especially as I'm Executor of Aunt Doris's estate."

"Her estate!" Elvira's eyes widened. "Doris didn't have a penny to her name, I can assure you of that."

"All the same I will have to look into it."

"Oh Lawrence, I wish you wouldn't. And I do hope you'll discourage Verity from any further enquiries. It can only do harm to our reputation and she'll be tainted by it too. No man will look at her if it comes out that she's the daughter of a swindler, a fly-by-night twister and a conman."

"Tainted by it? Surely not, Mama? This is the twentieth century. We're not living in the dark ages."

"And you think that changes anything? Let me tell you that society today is just as rapacious, malicious, vindictive, poisonous and invidious as it's always been." Elvia poured herself another cup of coffee, stirring the spoon with some vigour. "A good marriage is the only path Verity has for any sort of future. At least the scandal never reached the London papers and no one will connect her to a little-known, ages-old transgression. As long as she keeps quiet she can find a husband and settle down."

"I'm not sure Verity sees it that way."

"Well, you must make her, Lawrence." Elvira's voice rose with her passion. "Without a man to keep her she'll be destined to find work in some shop or factory, or, heaven forbid, as a governess, taking care of children who will never be hers. No. You must tell her to forget this futile quest of hers and find a husband."

Lawrence finished his coffee. There was nothing to be gained by upsetting his mother further so the conversation turned to pleasanter things. When he left the drawing room he found Verity in the hall, waiting for him.

"So what did Aunt Elvira say?" Verity asked. "If it's not too personal."

Lawrence chuckled. "She wants me to persuade you to drop the matter of your father's death. She thinks it will taint you and damage any prospect you may have of making a good marriage."

"Taint me? How ridiculous. It's my father's behaviour I'm questioning, not my own."

"I know. You have to forgive Mama. She lives in a bygone age."

Verity stood, twisting her hands. She turned to him. "Will you help me? Please, Lawrence. You must know people who would have been around then and will be able to remember any circumstances they may have considered disreputable or suspicious. Even if he was what the papers say, I'd rather know."

Lawrence frowned, seeing the beseeching look on her face and the tears trembling in her eyes. "Are you sure? Do you really want to stir it all up again? You may not like what I find out."

"Whatever you find couldn't be worse than not knowing, living the rest of my life pretending to be something I'm not. If I am the daughter of a criminal don't you think it's better to know than have people sniggering behind their hands because my life was built on a lie?"

Lawrence sighed. He remembered how shocked and horrified he'd been when they discovered that his grandfather had gambled away the Fitzroy family fortune, leaving nothing but a mountain of debts. He recalled how his father worked night and day to put it all right. How the family pulled together, all working to pay off the loans, because that's what families do. They stand up for each other. Verity was very much on her own.

"Please say you'll help me find the truth. I won't give up. If you won't help me I'll find someone who will." Determination gritted her jaw and a ring of defiance hardened her voice.

Lawrence's resistance and good intentions ebbed away. "I can look into his financial affairs if you wish. It wouldn't be unexpected given that I'm executing your mother's Will. Any wrong-doings on his part may come to light. From what I read in the newspaper cuttings his actions were precipitated by some sort of financial catastrophe. Something may come of it, but I can't promise it'll be anything you want to hear."

Verity threw her arms around him in a hug. "Thank you, I knew I could depend on you," she said, immediately cheered.

It was the nicest thing that had happened to him all week. Still, he didn't relish the task he'd agreed to undertake.

Chapter Nineteen

A few days later Lawrence was ready to return to London. Verity wanted to go with him. "Honestly, Lawrence. I know I'm in mourning but I can mourn just as well in town. Much as I love your mother and appreciate all she's done for me, she's beginning to drive me quite mad."

Lawrence chuckled. "She clings to etiquette as though it's written in stone," he said. "I'm afraid it's all she has to measure her life by. I'll speak to her."

To his surprise Elvira agreed that Verity should return to London. "She's still in mourning, but a few discreet dinners with friends are permissible," she said, "and the poor girl's fretting here. A change of scenery will do her good."

They departed after lunch. Elvira insisted they take the carriage. "Always arrive in style," she said. "It's what people will remember about you."

"Thank you for everything," Verity said, kissing her aunt goodbye before Thomas, the head groom, helped her into the carriage.

"Don't forget what I said, Lawrence," Elvira said as he kissed her cheek. "Find her a good husband. It's the best thing you can do for her."

On the drive back to London Lawrence gazed out of the window at the passing scenery. The last few weeks had brought home to him how much Maldon Hall needed him and how much he needed it. The hotel was his business, but there's more to life than business, he thought. There's family and it was about time he started thinking of having one of his own. Charlotte's face came to mind. Her smile and the sparkle in her blue as the ocean eyes were mixed up with visions of

Maldon Hall in summer, children laughing and running about the place.

"Why don't you ask the Huntington-Smythes to dinner by way of an apology for their hasty departure," he said to Verity. "Nothing too grand, just dinner at the hotel. I think we owe them that at least."

"Really?" Verity looked surprised. "You wouldn't mind? With me being in mourning and everything?"

"You'll be out of mourning in a couple of weeks. I was thinking middle of June. They're your friends. I'm sure Mrs T could provide an excellent feast and Jeremy could rustle up some sort of entertainment for the evening. It'll be a pleasure to be entertaining again."

Verity smiled, the sparkle back in her eyes. "I'll write to Charlotte immediately." She turned away but Lawrence caught the laughter in her voice. "I'm guessing it's Charlotte you're most keen to invite, not her brothers."

He had the grace to blush. "Unless she's already spoken for."

"Not as far as I'm aware," Verity said. "But you never know with Charlotte."

By the time Mr Lawrence and Miss Verity returned Jessie had fallen into the routine of cleaning the rooms, sorting the laundry and helping out with serving when and if required. That didn't stop Daisy worrying about what Mr Lawrence would say when he saw her. In order to avoid any bad feeling or surprises she decided to take Jessie to see him and get his approval as soon as he arrived.

She waited until she knew Mr Svenson would be in the cellar checking the inventory against receipts and took Jessie with her to the manager's office.

"It's up to Mr Lawrence whether you stay or go," she told Jessie as they stood outside his door. "Wait here."

She knocked and went straight in. "Good morning, Mr Lawrence. I hope I'm not disturbing you." She paused as he looked up from the papers spread out on the desk. "I was sorry to hear about Mrs Templeton. I hope the funeral went well."

"Miss Carter. It's fine. It went as well as one can expect. What can I do for you?"

"I thought it best to see you about the new chambermaid."

"The chambermaid?" he chuckled. "That's your department. I'm sure…"

He didn't get any further. Daisy opened the door and Jessie came in. "You remember my sister, Jessie Ferguson," Daisy said.

He looked as though he was about to fall off his chair. "Good heavens. Er. Yes." He stared at Jessie. "Mrs Ferguson." Daisy tried to imagine what thoughts might be racing through his mind. She couldn't. "Er. How are you?" he asked at last. "Are you fully recovered?"

"Yes, sir. Thank you, sir." Jessie dropped a curtsy. "And can I say how much I appreciate your giving me a job here and a second chance, Mr Lawrence. Not everyone would be as forgiving. Your open-minded, unbiased attitude does you credit. I promise I won't let you down."

Mr Lawrence looked as stunned as Dairy felt. "Well," he said.

"I've told Jessie she's on a month's trial," Daisy said, "and that you will then decide if she's to stay. I hope that's acceptable."

Mr Lawrence stroked his chin, looking from one girl to the other. "I suppose there's no harm in it. What does Mr Svenson say?"

"I believe he's quite satisfied with the arrangement, sir," Daisy said.

"In that case…" He turned back to his paperwork. "The chambermaids are your responsibility, Miss Carter. As long as Mr Svenson's happy."

"Yes, sir. Thank you, sir." Daisy curtsied and backed out, pushing Jessie out of the door before she could say any more.

"Phew," she said when they got outside the office. "That went better than I expected."

Jessie grinned. "You worry too much, Dais. I told you he'd be all right."

For now, Daisy thought. Until something goes wrong, then there'll be hell to pay and it'll all be down to me.

*

Lawrence spent the next few days wrestling with the mountain of paperwork he'd brought back from Maldon Hall. It seemed his Aunt Doris had kept every letter, invoice and bill going back to the first years of her marriage. There were school reports for the children, notes on their attendance at church, certificates charting their achievements. Much of it, although deeply enlightening, was immediately discarded. Her daughters may find her past associations a source of pleasant memories, but they didn't serve his purpose. He was more interested in her financial statements and her husband's correspondence. It took several hours before he found anything worthy of note.

It was clear that his Aunt Doris was as penniless as his mother had said. She had never had a bank account in her name. All her bills were sent to Maldon Hall for payment, and had been since the day his father took them in. There were some bank statements in her husband's name from the early days of their marriage, notes and bills appertaining to a property they previously owned in Yorkshire. He found a letter from a solicitor relating to the transfer of the property. Nothing recent.

Douglas Templeton's certificate of death confirmed 'Death by asphyxiation'. He put it to one side. He could find no Will. He'd been in India when his uncle died so knew very little about him or his business, but, no Will? Surely a man contemplating suicide would have left something to comfort his family? If, as the papers suggested, he was a villain, where were his ill-gotten gains? There were no signs of extravagance, high-living, or anything other than normal family expenditure.

A single sheet of paper, which had obviously become detached from other correspondence, referred to a portfolio of shares and gave the name of a stockbroker in Leeds. Despite a lengthy search he could find nothing else referring to shares, investments or stock market dealings. From the scarcity of other paperwork it became clear that all evidence of Douglas Templeton's financial dealings had been destroyed, either by him before his death, or by someone else afterwards.

Lawrence sighed, folded the single sheet of paper and put it in his pocket. He made a pile of all the paperwork relating to financial transactions, slipped it into a drawer in his desk, locked it and placed the key in his pocket.

Although the stockbrokers were in Leeds, if they were reputable they would be known in London and there were several places where he could make discreet enquiries. There were also people he knew who might be more forthcoming. If he could find nothing here he'd go to Leeds. He'd promised Verity he'd look into her father's death and the more he went through his papers the more intrigued and suspicious he became, not by what he saw, but by what was missing. A large part of Douglas Templeton's life had been wiped out.

Despite good reports from Annie and seeing Jessie getting on well with the other staff, Daisy still worried. Jessie was fragile, she knew that. It wouldn't take much to set her off either. She felt uncomfortable whenever she saw her talking to anyone in the kitchen lest she let something slip about her past. Then there was Mr Svenson, always asking how she was getting on and saying how nice it must be to have her family so close. Daisy didn't think it was nice at all.

"I'm going to see Ma," she said one day when they both had the afternoon off. "Are you coming with me? Ma'll be pleased to hear how well you're settling in."

Jessie shook her head. "No. You go. I said I'd go to the market with Peggy. She wants some material for a blouse and I wouldn't mind somat new meself."

So Daisy went on her own. When she arrived her mother was in the kitchen preparing the evening meal. "Jessie not with you?" she said.

"No, she's gone to the market. She said to give you this." She handed her an envelope containing several coins. "She said to take your usual and keep the rest for her."

Nora grinned and took the offered money. "She's a good girl our Jessie." She put the envelope in her pocket. "Cup of tea?"

Over tea and biscuits Daisy told Nora about Jessie and how well she'd settled in. "She seems to get on with the others and doesn't mind pulling her weight. I still worry about her state of mind though."

"Do you think she'll stay?" Nora asked.

Daisy sighed. "I don't know, Ma. According to Jessie it's a stepping stone to better things. I hope it works out for her." She dunked her biscuit in her tea and took a bite.

"Always did have a good 'ead on her shoulders," Nora said, a look of satisfaction on her face. "Except when it came to that Charlie Benton. Talking of which…"

"What?"

"He's back. And from what I hear 'e's been asking about Jessie. Just as well she's gone."

"You mean he's been here?"

"Here? No. He knows better than to come 'ere. If your dad ever set eyes on 'im he'd be wheeled around for the rest of 'is life. Bin asking round the shops and down the market."

A shudder ran through Daisy. "You don't think he'd come to the hotel?"

Nora shrugged. "I ain't told no one where she is, but I don't s'pse it'll take 'im long to find out."

"Great," Daisy said as a stone of dread hardened in her stomach.

For the rest of the afternoon Nora chatted on about the latest gossip and snippets of local news, but all Daisy could think about was the return of Charlie Benton.

She left her mother's with her mind in turmoil. Charlie Benton was back. A maelstrom of memories swirled through her brain, not one of them pleasant. She couldn't go back to the hotel, not now, not yet. She couldn't face Jessie, knowing he was back and having to say nothing to her. Nausea rose to her throat, sickness churning her stomach, as other memories surfaced – heart-stopping memories long buried but still pricking like a thorn you can never quite remove.

Her steps turned towards the river path. The warmth of the day still lingered, the sound of boats making their way to the docks filled the air. If Charlie was back it was for no good reason. The Bentons had never been any good. They'd been trouble for as long as she could remember. Charlie was no different, as Jessie found out to her cost.

She walked for an hour, unaware of her direction, her breathing heavy as her heart. If Charlie came for Jessie there was nothing anyone could do about it. He was her husband, he had rights. He could beat her half-to-death and there was nothing they could do to stop him.

She strode on until she saw a bench where she sat, head in hands and sobbed for Jessie and all she'd been through. When she'd cried herself out she took a breath. She stared out over the undulating water, the boats bobbing on the tide and the sun slowly sinking over the warehouses lining the banks. Damn you Charlie Benton, she thought. I'll swing for you if you hurt Jessie again.

Chapter Twenty

Verity arranged to meet Charlotte at a tea room near the corner of Hyde Park to arrange a convenient date for the dinner party. She looked forward to seeing her again. Life always seemed so much brighter when Charlotte was around. The biggest problems and deepest regrets melted away beneath her sunny, optimistic disposition. Nothing was too much trouble for her and the fact that Lawrence had taken a shine to her was a bonus. The tea room was tucked away just off the High Street between a greengrocer and a hardware shop. Very discreet.

Verity arrived first and took a table where she could see the entrance. She wasn't quite sure what to expect today. It was the first time she'd been out since returning to London. The memory of her mother and the secret she'd kept most of her life still played on her mind.

Charlotte arrived a few minutes later, breezing in like a ray of sunshine on a cloudy day. "I was so sorry about your mother," she said, bending to kiss Verity on the cheek in greeting. "It must have been a devastating blow."

"It was," Verity said as a stab of grief twisted like a knife inside her. "I wish I'd spent more time with her and got to know her better. I'm afraid I wasn't much of a comfort to her at the end." Tears pricked her eyes at the memory.

Charlotte smiled. "I'm sure you're wrong. She would have appreciated everything you did for her." She sighed. "I think sometimes we take people we love for granted and only appreciate them when they're gone." A look of the greatest sadness crossed her face.

She patted Verity's hand. "She wouldn't want you to be sad. She'd want you to go on living the life you've always dreamed of." She picked up the menu, quickly reverting to her usual cheerful self. "Now, are we having cake?"

Verity couldn't help but smile. That was the thing about Charlotte. She could turn your emotions on a pin-head. You could never be downhearted for long.

They ordered tea and cakes and Charlotte chatted about the various events she'd attended and who was there. "Honestly, you haven't missed anything. Just the same people doing the same things under the guise of the latest fad." The way she said it made Verity think that Brandon Summerville must have been conspicuous by his absence.

She hesitated to mention the dinner party. Although the hotel catered for discerning, affluent guests, it wouldn't be in the same league as the hospitality Charlotte's family could provide. She took a breath. "Lawrence suggested that I invite your family for dinner at the hotel," she said as nonchalantly as she could, given that her heart was pounding. "It would go some way to make up for having to leave Maldon Hall so abruptly. What do you think?"

A mischievous glint lit Charlotte's eyes. "Will your cousin Jeremy be there? He was so much fun."

Verity smiled. "Yes. Both Jeremy and Lawrence." She didn't mention Lawrence's interest in Charlotte. She would have been flattered but not surprised. Charlotte expected every man she met to be interested in her and her expectations were generally met. "It wouldn't be a grand affair, given we're still in mourning, but I could invite a few friends. It could be a pleasant evening."

"It sounds quite intriguing," Charlotte said a note of mirth in her voice. "I imagine your hotel would be the perfect setting for intimate dinners and discreet liaisons."

"It's not that sort of hotel," Verity said laughing. "You seem to have a very warped idea of us."

Charlotte giggled as the girl arrived with the tea and cake, setting it down on the pristine white cloth. "I was only teasing. I'd love to come. Of course it would be up to Mummy and Daddy. With two eligible sons and a marriageable daughter they get hundreds of invitations throughout the season. They're hoping to marry me off to a title."

"Is that what you're hoping for?" Verity asked, thoughts of Lawrence's inevitable disappointment running through her head.

"Me? No. but it would bring some respectability to the family. We made our money through trade, just like you. I think sometimes they forget that." She picked up a cake and bit into it. "Who else will be there?" she asked, when she'd swallowed her mouthful.

Protocol decreed that the whole family be invited, but Verity dreaded spending another evening with Bertie. "As well as your family, Jeremy and Lawrence I'll ask a couple of girls from school to even up the numbers. I'm still in touch with them. Several families are in London for the season," she said. "When would be most convenient?"

"Sometime between Epsom Races, Royal Ascot and Henley Regatta," Charlotte suggested. "Bertie's back at Oxford, so he won't be able to come. I could invite someone in his place." That mischievous glint was back in her eye and Verity didn't exactly trust her, but she didn't have much option. She'd promised

Lawrence she'd invite them. She couldn't go back on her word.

"That's settled then," she said. "I'll send out the invitations tonight."

They spent the rest of the afternoon chatting about their immediate plans. "A Gala Dinner at the Savoy this evening," Charlotte said. "Something to do with Daddy's racing friends. Lots of 'the right sort' there of course."

As she was speaking a couple of women dressed in white with purple and green sashes came into the tea room. Every head turned in their direction. "Suffragettes," Verity said. "I've seen some of them at the hotel."

"Votes for Women," one of them said handing Verity a leaflet as she passed the table. "Meeting tonight. Come if you can, ladies. It's to benefit us all."

Verity glanced at the leaflet. Details of a meeting that evening at Caxton Hall in Westminster were set out together with a list of speakers, what the Movement stood for and what they hoped to change.

"Not me." Charlotte waved the leaflet away. The woman shrugged and moved on. "It's not that I don't admire them," she said, "standing up for what they believe in. I think some women do get a raw deal, but I'm not sure Daddy would approve."

Verity stared at the leaflet, Charlotte's words ringing in her ears. Her own father's approval was the last thing she needed to worry about. He hadn't given a jot about her, her mother or Henrietta when he did what he did. A surge of anger rose up inside her. Damn all men, she thought. Maybe the suffragettes were right. It was time women stood up for themselves.

After they left the tea room, Charlotte saw a young lady she knew walking along by the park. She waved to her. "Lydia," she called, pulling Verity across the road, dodging horses, wagons and various carriages. "How lovely to see you," she said, when they arrived, breathless, in front of a well dressed girl about their age. "It's been too long." She kissed her cheek.

"Yes," Lydia replied. "We've been out of town. A trip to Paris actually. How are you?"

Charlotte grinned. "I'm well, thank you." She turned to introduce Verity. "You remember Miss Templeton. From the Hunt Ball at Easter?"

"Yes. How do you do, Miss Templeton. I was sorry to hear of your bereavement."

Verity smiled as she recognised Lydia Summerville, Brandon's sister. "Thank you," she said. "People have been so very kind."

Charlotte prattled on, "Verity was just telling me about a dinner party she's arranging at her cousin's hotel. It would be perfect if you and Brandon could come. Don't you think, Verity?" Her eyes gleamed with glee.

Verity didn't know what to say. She could hardly refuse. "It's nothing grand I'm afraid, in the circumstances, but…"

"Good. That's settled then." Charlotte beamed. Verity's heart sank. Brandon Summerville was the last person Lawrence would want invited to this particular party.

Lydia noticed the leaflet still in Verity's hand. "Oh," she said. "Have you got one too? They've been handing them out all along the street. Have you heard Mrs Pankhurst speak? I hear she's quite inspirational."

Verity cheered up. "No, I haven't but I can't disagree with what she stands for."

Charlotte huffed. "They'll never get anywhere. Men have all the power. They're not likely to relinquish it are they?"

"But it's so unfair," Lydia said. "I've had a first class education, read the papers and keep abreast of the news. Yet the local pig man, who inherited his farm and has no interest in anything other than his pigs, has more right to make decisions about his future than I do about mine. It's not just about getting the Vote, it's about the subordination of women for no reason other than their gender."

"I didn't know you felt so strongly about it, Lydia," Charlotte said.

Lydia laughed. "Neither did I until today. But since reading about it I do feel one should take an interest. After all we are the fairer sex."

"Well, not me," Charlotte said. "I have a Gala Dinner to attend."

"Where you'll be put on show for any man wealthy enough to make an offer," Lydia said. She turned to Verity. "What about you? Are you game enough to at least go and listen to what they have to say?"

Verity decided she liked Lydia Summerville. She wasn't afraid to speak her mind, which was unusual. Most girls brought up in society were schooled to repeat only what ideas have been put in their heads by governesses and to please men with their unquestioning acceptance of any opinion they care to express. "Why not?" she said. "I think we owe ourselves that."

"Good. Then we shall go together," Lydia said.

As they said goodbye to Charlotte Verity couldn't help but feel that, once again, Charlotte Huntington-Smythe had got exactly what she wanted. You had to admire her for her ability to do that.

Chapter Twenty One

Lawrence, sitting in his office that afternoon with Inspector Rolleston of the Metropolitan Police, couldn't believe what he was hearing; something about Mr Jevons and the girl, Molly Brown. The memory of Molly blubbering in his office and the man she was with came vividly to mind. He hadn't believed her then and he certainly didn't believe what he was hearing now.

"You've arrested Mr Jevons?"

"Yes."

"Can I see him? I'm sure we can sort this out quite quickly. It'll be a mistake."

"No mistake, sir. We have a witness."

"A witness? Who? Not that poor excuse of a brother of hers? I wouldn't give credence to anything that comes out of his mouth. A villainous liar if ever I saw one."

Inspector Rolleston looked uncomfortable. "Well, sir, that's as maybe, but there's been a death and these things have to be investigated. I understand allegations were made. I'd like you to come to station and make a statement."

Lawrence's mounting anger subsided. The inconvenience he felt was a small matter next to the death of a girl who'd worked there. "Of course."

"We'll need to speak to the rest of the staff too, anyone who knew her. The constable here could do that if they could be made available."

The constable who'd arrived with the inspector stepped forward. "If you don't mind, sir."

Lawrence nodded. "Mr Svenson, the under manager, will be able to make suitable arrangements."

He rang the bell and asked the girl who responded to fetch Mr Svenson. Once he'd arranged for him to take over he went with the inspector.

When they arrived at the station, Inspector Rolleston picked up a file of papers from the desk sergeant and led Lawrence to a small room along a corridor. A shaft of afternoon sunlight, coming in through a window high up in the wall, lit the room, but did nothing to warm it. A table stood in the centre with four chairs arranged around it. A shiver ran through Lawrence. If he'd been guilty of anything he would have found the room intimidating.

The inspector asked his opinion of Miss Brown, which he thought quite irrelevant. He told him he knew little of the girl apart from the fact that she was a chambermaid who helped out in the restaurant. He knew nothing of any relationship with Mr Jevons and he went to great pains to let Rolleston know that, although he'd paid them off, he hadn't believed a word Molly or her brother said at the time and her allegation later proved to be totally unfounded.

"She was clearly petrified of the boy," he said. "I wouldn't be surprised if he's done it himself."

"He's not her brother," Rolleston said. "The way we understand it, sir, he's her pimp. Were you aware that she was working as a prostitute?"

The word hung in the air like a bad smell no one wants to acknowledge. Dismay and disgust coiled in Lawrence's stomach. Shocked he blurted, "Of course not. If we'd known that we would never have taken her on." The words 'reputable hotel' came to mind but he couldn't utter them. Why did Daisy Carter not guess her occupation? Was she so naive, or just stupid? His heart hardened towards her as his anger mounted.

"We did look into him," the inspector said, "but apparently she was one of his best girls. Very popular among the toffs, sir, if you know what I mean."

Lawrence cringed under Rolleston's glare. "You don't think I...? I can assure you..."

The inspector chuckled. "No need, sir. I believe you had every good intention when you took her on. I gather she was very plausible. Anyone would have been fooled."

The suggestion that he'd been made a fool of rankled. It was Miss Carter who'd been fooled, but he was too much of a gentleman to point that out.

"Mr Jevons no longer works for you, does he?" Rolleston smiled like a tiger awaiting his prey. "Despite your vehemently expressed confidence in his innocence?"

Lawrence ran his finger around his collar, which had become suddenly tight. "No. Unfortunately we had to let him go. He'd become unreliable." Even as he said it he knew how damning it would be.

"Well, thank you, sir." The inspector tidied his papers and Lawrence was allowed to go. "May I see Mr Jevons? Is there anything I can do for him?"

Inspector Rolleston shook his head. "I'm afraid not, sir. Maybe get him a solicitor. He has a sister I believe, she may need some help."

Outside the station Lawrence was at a loss. He felt helpless. There must be something he could do to stop this travesty of justice. He'd go and see Ada Jevons. Perhaps he could at least do something for her.

Verity and Lydia had a while to wait before they made their way to Caxton Hall for the meeting, so they walked in the park. Verity hoped to find out more about Lydia's brother, Brandon. She recalled how overawed she felt when she first met him, such an interesting and powerful man who drew attention wherever he went, the sort of man who needed no one else's approval. It was clear Charlotte was smitten. She had to admit that she'd been intrigued too and Jeremy's warning about his reputation only made her more so. Even the thought of him made her heart quicken.

She found Lydia easy to talk to. She was very different from her brother: friendly whereas he'd been quite stand-offish, warm where he'd been cool towards her to say the least.

"You mustn't mind Brandon," Lydia said when Verity asked about him. "He's been through a lot. He's not as fierce as he makes out. Underneath he's a real sweetie."

Verity couldn't imagine that.

Caxton Hall, when they arrived, was gradually filling with people, many of them clearly supporters of the cause. Women sporting purple, green and white, pushed forward for a place near the front. They were soon being jostled by the crowd. Verity was surprised to see men in the audience, shouldering their way forward.

"It looks as though there are a few male supporters," she said to the woman standing next to her.

"I wouldn't count on it, luv," the woman responded, scowling. "They're probably here to cause trouble."

By the time the first speaker took to the stage the hall was full of people pushing, shoving and elbowing their way in until Verity felt herself being pressed closer than was comfortable to her neighbour, a large woman who smelt strongly of sweat.

"It's a bit crowded," she said to Lydia standing next to her.

"Just goes to show doesn't it? Women want a voice. They want to be heard." She smiled at Verity.

It didn't take long before the men in the audience started to heckle the speaker. "I don't know what women are coming to," one of them shouted.

"Their senses," a woman in the audience shouted back. That brought a cheer from the women and jeering from the men.

"Does your husband know you're out?" another called. That was greeted by loud booing.

The atmosphere was one of good-natured wrangling. The women on the stage gave as good as they got, obviously used to the gibes and taunting. As the evening went on Verity found herself being pushed nearer and nearer to the front. Between the men jeering and the women shouting it was difficult to hear the speakers. A group of women at the back started chanting 'Votes for Women' which brought a chorus of shouting, shrieking and whistling from the crowd.

Suddenly the jostling and shoving became more boisterous and frenzied. A swell like a tidal wave sent the crowd surging forward. Verity, wedged between two buxom women both shouting in a ferment of excitement, got carried forward with it. Much as she tried to extricate herself she couldn't. A tingle of anxiety rose inside her as she glanced around trying to see Lydia. She caught a momentary glimpse of her hat before it disappeared into an undulating sea of heads.

She tried calling out, but her voice was lost in the chaotic melee around her. Only the sound of police whistles penetrated the noisy confusion. Two uniformed officers ran on to the stage and removed the speaker, carrying her off amid loud protests. On the floor of the hall the gathering had turned into a terrifying mass of people brawling, bickering, squabbling and fighting.

Horrified, Verity realised too late that they had been caught in a trap. She glanced around, trying to catch her breath. Her stomach knotted in fear. The men in the audience were now helping the police coral women into a corner. A policeman grabbed Verity's arm squeezing and bruising it. "Get off," she yelled trying to pull her arm away. Tears of frustration welled up in her eyes and sudden feelings of panic and powerlessness gripped her. "This isn't right. It's not fair." She tried again to pull her arm away but the policeman's hold was too strong

"Best come quietly," he said. "We've got orders. It'll go easier if you co-operate."

Fierce fury coursed through her veins when she saw a woman being pushed to the ground and another beaten with a truncheon.

Frightened for her life, she went quietly.

Together with twenty other women she was taken to the police station and charged with Causing an Affray and Disturbing the Peace.

"We weren't doing anything," she cried out when they took her in. She tried to explain that the men there were the ones who caused the trouble. Her protests fell on deaf ears. All her denials were to no avail. She was taken with the others and thrown into a cell, several of the officers taking pleasure in handling them as roughly as possible.

"At least we'll get our names in the paper," one of the women said. "All good for the cause."

Verity didn't think it good at all. She was horrified. Her arms ached where they'd been bruised and the sleeve of her coat had been ripped half off at the shoulder. All she could think about was what Lawrence would say. She'd let him down and Aunt Elvira would disown her. She'd be thrown out on her ear, like a load of old rubbish. All they'd wanted was a chance to speak up for themselves and not be ruled by men. What was so terrible about that?

She glanced around at the other women. All were older than her and most sported white, purple and green ribbons showing their support for the suffragettes. "What will they do to us?" she asked a dark-haired woman in a brown coat.

The woman looked her up and down noticing her clothes and mourning arm band. "I haven't seen you before. You're not one of us are you?" she said.

Verity shook he head. "I got caught up in the crush." As her anger at their treatment abated the reality of her situation started to sink in. "I came to hear the speakers and got separated from my friend."

The woman's face softened. "You'll be all right. It'll just be a fine. If you don't pay the fine you'll be given time." She glanced around. "See that woman over there?" She pointed out a tall lady in a white hat with purple and green feathers. "She broke a window last year and got six months hard labour. I was with her but didn't break anything so I only got two weeks. That's how it works."

Verity swallowed. "But I didn't do anything."

"No. Like I said. It'll be a fine. Pay that and they'll let you go. It's not so bad. At least we're showing we're prepared to suffer for our freedom and not be held prisoners in a world dominated by men. There are some who've done a great deal more than me, or anyone here. You have to admire them."

"Oh I do," Verity breathed. Part of her agreed with everything they stood for and wanted desperately to show support, but another part of her just wanted to go home.

By the time Daisy returned to the hotel after visiting her mother, the hour was late. Mrs T was making cocoa for herself and Peggy. "Has Jessie gone to bed?" Daisy asked, surprised not to see her sister.

"Jessie? No. She's not back yet," Peggy said, looking uncomfortable as she stirred her cocoa. "I don't suppose she'll be long."

"I thought you were together," Daisy said, sudden fear twisting to a knot in her stomach.

"We were, at the market. But she saw someone she knew. A chap. She told me to go on without her. I didn't want to go but she insisted."

"A chap? What sort of chap?" Sudden fear circled Daisy's heart.

"You know, someone she'd worked with before. She knew him anyway. She said it'd be all right."

"All right? To leave her with a man you didn't know?" Daisy's eyes blazed. "It most certainly wasn't all right. What did Jessie say, exactly?"

Peggy shrugged, a pink flush creeping up her face. "I don't know. But I thought, as she's married it would be all right. I mean she's not…"

Daisy tried to calm down. It wasn't Peggy's fault. Jessie had a mind of her own and she remembered how stubborn she could be when she wanted something.

"I'm sorry. Of course it's not your fault. What did this man say to Jessie?"

"Something about a night out. For old time's sake. That's why I thought he was a friend. I'm sure it's all right. She'll be back in a tick."

The fear turned to frenzy. "I don't suppose you know his name?"

Peggy pouted. "I think she called him Charlie," she said.

Daisy's heart crunched.

"Mr Svenson wants to see you," Mrs T said, turning back from the stove to interrupt their conversation. "Urgent, he said. You're to go to the office soon as you get back, he said." Mrs T glared at Daisy as though she'd committed some terrible sin.

"Mr Svenson? Did he say what it's about?"

"No. Just it's urgent. In a right state 'e was an' all. Looked like he was ready to do serious damage to somat."

Daisy sighed. "The laundry's probably put too much starch in his shirts," she said. "I'd better go and see him." Cold fury curled inside her. First Charlie's back and now Mr High-an-Mighty wants to make something out of nothing. If anything's happened to Jessie, I'll swing for that scrote Charlie Benton, she thought.

Upstairs she knocked on the office door and went straight in. She wasn't in the mood for Mr Svenson's smarmy greasing up or throwing his weight about. What she and Jessie did was none of his damn business. "You wanted to see me?" she said.

"Ah, Miss Carter. Please do come in." He indicated the chair in front of the desk.

"I'd rather stand," she said. "I hope this won't take long. It's late and I still have things to do."

"Er. Yes. Well. The thing is…" He looked as discomforted as she'd ever seen him. "The police have been here."

"The police?" The bottom fell out of her world. "It's not Jessie is it? Please tell me…"

He frowned. "Jessie? No. Why should it be Jessie?"

Relief washed over her. "Sorry. It's just that she's not back yet. I thought… well… that something might have happened…"

"No. It's Mr Jevons. He's been arrested. The police want you to go to the station and make a statement."

"A statement? About Mr Jevons?"

"He's being charged with the murder of Molly Brown."

Daisy heard the words but they didn't sink in. It took a while for the jumble in her head to make any sense. "Molly Brown is dead and the police think Mr Jevons killed her?"

"That's about the size of it," Mr Svenson said. "I don't need to tell you how upset Mr Lawrence is about the whole affair. It will bring shame on the hotel and ruin its reputation."

"Mr Lawrence, is he… can I speak to him?"

"No. He's out. He's gone to see what he can do. We must do whatever we can to assist the police no matter the personal cost. Is that clear?"

Daisy stood stunned. It didn't add up. Mr Jevons and Molly? No. It was ridiculous. Mr Jevons wasn't a killer. It couldn't be true. One thing she did know was that, whatever had happened, she'd get the blame. It was all her fault.

Chapter Twenty Two

It was late, so Daisy took a cab to the police station. "'E's told you then?" Barker said when he hailed one for her. "That Molly was a bit of a minx but she didn't deserve what 'appened to her."

"No, she didn't," Daisy said her heart heavy with dread. Vision of the smiling girl ran through her head, her copper curls dancing as she went about her work. She'd always been cheerful and optimistic. What on earth could have happened to her? Whatever it was Mr Jevons wasn't responsible, Daisy was sure of that.

She recalled Molly's brother, if he was her brother. Uncouth, rude and a nasty piece of work. She wouldn't put it past him to have done it.

Then she thought of Mr Lawrence, he didn't deserve any of this either. Jessie played on her mind too. No good could come of her seeing Charlie. If she went off the rails again it would be something else she'd have to account for. Making a mistake employing one chambermaid could be forgiven. She wasn't sure Mr Lawrence would put up with another.

She didn't know what she feared most, losing her job or losing his good opinion of her. She'd never do anything to hurt the reputation of the hotel, but with all that had happened, and what might happen with Jessie, she wasn't sure he'd believe that any more. She couldn't bear his disdain. She swallowed the lump rising in her throat.

The police station appeared busy, a hubbub of noise came up from where Daisy supposed the cells were housed. "Sorry, miss," the harassed desk sergeant said when Daisy told him what she was there for. "We're extra busy tonight. You'll have to wait."

She took a seat and waited. While she waited she stewed inside. She couldn't get the image of Molly's face out of her mind. The police would want to know about her relationship with Mr Jevons and the accusation she had made. It was too horrible to contemplate.

While she waited people came in and some went out again, some didn't. A woman, gaudily dressed and smelling of cheap perfume, swore like a trouper as two constables hauled her in between them. "You again, Mary," the sergeant said.

"Took a man's wallet," one of the constables said.

"Take her down."

Mary swore at him again.

The sergeant tutted and shook his head. "They never learn," he said.

A man came in. Daisy was quite taken with him. She noticed his good boots and smart attire. Tall, with broad shoulders and an easy manner, he looked out of place there. The desk sergeant seemed to know him and smiled in greeting. Daisy couldn't hear what they said, but the man's business was quickly dealt with and he left, nodding politely to Daisy as he passed. The sergeant went out the back but returned again a few moments later.

A drunk was brought in and taken to the cell, then another working girl, caught soliciting. Daisy was about to ask how much longer they expected her to wait when a constable came out and spoke to her. "Miss Carter?" he said. "I'm sorry to have kept you waiting. Follow me please."

She followed him through the door behind the desk and along a corridor, passing several rooms. He stopped at one and opened the door. "In here, please."

Daisy smiled and went to go in. As she did so she turned her head and thought she caught a glimpse of Miss Verity Templeton coming along the corridor in the other direction. But it couldn't be, could it?

The first thing Verity did when she got back to her room in the hotel was to strip off her clothes and wash the stench of prison from her person. She'd been anxious being singled out, thoughts racing through her brain like swarming bees. There was uproar in the cell when the constable who'd arrested them came to get her. "Miss Templeton, please come with me," he said. The women jeered and cheered, some cat calling others booing. Verity's heart was in her throat as she followed the constable out.

"You're in luck," he said as he led her along the corridor and up the stairs. "Or know the right people. The charges against you have been dropped."

"Dropped? But..." She must have looked surprised.

He turned and put his finger to his lips then tapped the side of his nose. His face told her not to ask, just be thankful. "I'm to see you get home safely." He accompanied her out of the station, into a cab and back to the hotel. "Goodnight, Miss Templeton," he said when they arrived. "I trust we won't be seeing you again."

The night porter nodded to her as she passed. She couldn't get to her room quickly enough. Maybe her fine had been paid, or more likely the officer in charge had been paid off. It was wrong that she should be treated any differently than the other women, but all the same she was glad to be home. She wouldn't be suffering the same indignities they were going through.

Seeing how they were treated at first hand had brought the stories in the paper to horrifying life. She wondered how they could bear it.

Exhausted from the evening's ordeal she lay on the bed thoughts whirring through her brain. She owed Lawrence a debt of thanks, who else would have bailed her out? As sleep overtook her she decided her gratitude could wait until morning.

When she left the police station Daisy walked for half-an-hour before she managed to find a cab to take her home. Another hour and the early morning sun would break across the sky bringing a new day. Her footsteps dragged. She'd made her statement and answered all their questions with a sense of deep betrayal. She told them again and again that she didn't believe Mr Jevons capable of such a thing, but they weren't interested in her opinion, only the facts. Molly Brown had been the victim of a brutal attack. They asked about her relationships with the other staff, Mr Svenson and Mr Lawrence.

"She was a chambermaid," Daisy said. "That's all. Just a chambermaid."

"She served in the restaurant. The private restaurant. Did Mr Jevons ask for her?"

"No. Well, occasionally but…"

And so it went on. They asked about Mr Jevons's drinking, his wife's death, his unreliability, his state of mind… all questions Daisy was loath to answer but had no choice. Inwardly she cursed Molly Brown, but then hadn't the girl been cursed enough? Yes, she wanted justice for Molly, but prosecuting Mr Jevons wasn't going to get it.

"Thank you, Miss Carter," the constable said when they'd finished. "I expect you'll be called to give evidence in due course." Sickness rose up from her stomach together with an abiding fear of what Mr Lawrence would think. Would she still have a job by then?

The night porter let her in and she asked him if Jessie was back.

"Aye. Hours ago," he said with a grin.

Thank God for that, she thought and she went to her room, thankful that it was over. She could probably manage a couple of hours' sleep before she'd have to be up again in the morning.

Chapter Twenty Three

Verity awoke the next morning with a well of shame and dread swirling in her stomach. How could she face Lawrence? What must he think of her, with all the trouble she'd caused? She owed him far more than she could repay. She'd sullied the family name and its reputation. He must hate her for that.

When she arrived downstairs she found him having breakfast with the newspaper spread out in front on him. The anxious look on his face didn't surprise her. Would he find her name there in a piece about the disruption and unruly disorder of the suffragettes?

"I'm sorry," she said, distress clear in her voice. "And thank you. I don't know what to say, except that I'm truly grateful." She poured herself a cup of coffee from the tray on the side. "The thought of spending another minute in that place…"

Lawrence stared at her. "Good morning, Verity. What place is that? And what have I done to deserve your gratitude?"

She took a breath. "You know. Bailing me out, paying the fine or whatever. I wasn't one of them. Well, not really. I got caught up." She sat at the table facing him. "I'm sorry."

"My dear girl," he said. "I have no idea what you're talking about."

Verity couldn't decide whether he was serious or making light of it for her benefit; denying it to save her embarrassment. "I saw Miss Carter at the police station, so I guessed it was you. Who else could it have been?"

"The police station? What on earth were you doing there? Don't tell me the police dragged you in too? It really is too bad." He folded the paper and slammed it on the table. "As if I don't have enough…"

He didn't get any further. Verity dissolved in tears, fumbling in her bag for a handkerchief. "I'm so sorry," she sobbed the shock of the night's events overwhelming her.

"My dear." Lawrence moved beside her, put a comforting arm around her and handed her his own clean white handkerchief. "I just can't see what you have to do with the Molly Brown business. It's not as though you knew her at all."

Verity sniffed. "Molly Brown? No. I don't know her. Why? Who is she?"

Lawrence sighed. "She's a person of no consequence, well, not someone you need to worry about anyway. I think you'd better tell me what you're talking about."

She nodded and swallowed before speaking. She wanted to get it clear in her head. "I met Charlotte in town to set a date for the dinner party, then, as we were leaving we ran into Lydia Summerville." As she said it the memory of the invitation sprang to mind. "Oh." She clapped her hand to her mouth.

"You ran into Lydia and…?"

"And, er…" She swallowed again; decided one confession at a time was enough and went on to tell him about the suffragette meeting, the uproar that it turned into, being arrested, the women in the cell and being released. The words tumbled out, falling over each other in the telling. "As I was leaving I saw Miss Carter going into a room with a constable, so I thought…"

"You thought I'd bailed you out. Well, it wasn't me, but I'd like to thank whoever it was. Miss Carter was there on another matter."

"Thank you for being so understanding," she said. "My name may appear in the newspaper."

"Really? Well, right now I have a great deal more to worry about. Please don't give it another thought." He picked up his paper and stood to leave.

Verity sighed with relief. It was good to get it all out. Now all she had to do was tell him about inviting the Summervilles to dine. "Can I see you later," she asked. "About the dinner?"

He smiled but in his eyes she saw the anxious look of earlier. "Of course." He bent and kissed her cheek.

As he was leaving one of the maids came in carrying a riot of daisies and peonies in a huge bouquet. "These are for Miss Templeton," the girl said. "Should I take them to your room, miss?"

"No. I'll take them." Verity rose and took them from her. Lawrence waited while she read the card it said: *I'm so sorry. I hope you got home unscathed. Thanks for your support –Lydia.*

"Lydia," Verity said. "Just sending best wishes."

Lawrence huffed and walked away. Oh dear, Verity thought. What do I do now?

Lawrence returned to his room and dropped the paper on his desk. He'd done all he could for Mr Jevons having spoken to his sister and offered to pay for a solicitor to represent him. Thankfully he'd found nothing in the newspaper so far. Given her occupation Molly Brown's death would hardly be of note. Personally he wanted to wash his hands of the whole sordid affair, but part of him recognised that, as the girl had worked there with Jevons, they would bear some responsibility. He sighed with resignation. If Jevons hadn't killed her, and he was sure he hadn't, someone else had. But who? Inspector Rolleston's words 'she was popular with the toffs' came to mind. That was an avenue that needed to be explored, but surely that could be left to the police? The last thing he needed was to get involved in a police investigation.

Daisy Carter knew the girl best. She'd be familiar with her background and where she came from. She'd be better placed than he to enquire about possible assailants among her peers. He made a mental note to speak to Daisy Carter. The thought that she might mention seeing Miss Templeton at the station, crossed his mind too. Perhaps she could enlighten him as to who may have paid for her release.

Sighing, he turned his mind to Verity's father's papers. He'd made discreet enquiries around town but no one had heard of the brokerage in Leeds. There was nothing to be gained by going through it all again.

That was his frame of mind when Verity knocked on his door a little later. He welcomed her in. She took a seat opposite his desk.

"I was going through your mother's papers," he said. "I'm afraid there nothing of any great help. Do you remember much about the house in Codlington?"

Verity shrugged. "Not much. Mama had some old photographs. They're yellowed with age and it's difficult to make out who they're of, but I've brought them with me. They may be of some help."

"There's a letter from a solicitor about the transfer of the property, but no evidence of any proceeds of sale. I find that strange. In fact the whole thing's a bit odd. There's nothing of note anywhere."

Verity pouted. "Is there nothing you can do?"

"I plan to visit the solicitor, and the offices of the newspaper that reported his death might have some further information, but other than that…" He held up his hands in a gesture of helplessness.

"When will you go? I'd like to come with you."

"I'm not sure that's a good idea. You never know what I might turn up. It could be quite unpleasant."

Verity glared at him. "He was my father. Whatever it is, I have a right to know."

Lawrence wilted under her gaze. He couldn't say no. She was so earnest, so vulnerable. How could he refuse?

"Good," she said. "Now about the dinner."

Despite the late night Daisy woke early. She wanted to speak to Jessie before she started work. She found her with Annie already started on one of the upstairs rooms. "Jessie, can I have a word?" The look on Jessie's face told her she knew what it was about.

"I'll start next door," Annie said, tactfully withdrawing.

Daisy struggled to remain calm. "What happened to you last night? I thought you were with Peggy," she said, casually as she was able.

Jessie pouted. "Not that it's any of your business but you know who I was with. Didn't Peggy tell you?"

"So it was Charlie and as long as you're working here it is my business. What did he want?"

"He said he loves me and he's sorry for what happened. He wants to make it up to me."

Daisy gasped. "You surely can't be so naive as to believe him?"

Jessie's face reddened. "Of course I believe him. He's my husband." Sparks flew from her eyes. "Is it so unbelievable that he should love me? Am I so unlovable?"

Daisy felt immediately sorry. "No. Of course not, It's just that… well… it's Charlie Benton."

"Humph. You're just jealous. He said he loves me. I believe him. We're still married. He wants us to try again."

Daisy's jaw hardened. "Did you tell Peggy anything about him being your husband?"

"'Course not. My old man's supposed to be away at sea isn't he?"

"I wish he was," Daisy muttered.

"You never liked 'im. You were always jealous of me."

Daisy took a breath. "Oh Jessie. Don't you remember how he was when you were together? What he did?"

"I know, but it's different now."

"Different? How?"

Jessie shrugged. "It just is. He's sorry, he said so and he wants us to be together again. He wants to take care of me." Jessie's eyes lit up and a broad smile filled her face. "He loves me."

Daisy's heart sank. Jessie would never see Charlie for what he was. "Got it all worked out has he? Going to take you away from all this?" She waved at the bed waiting to be made up. "You'll be putting your notice in then?"

"No. Not straight away. He wants me to carry on working until he finds a place for us."

I bet he does, Daisy thought. "So he knows you work here? Walked you home did he?"

"Not quite. He wanted to but… he made sure I'd be all right. Asked if I'd get in okay, after everything was locked up."

"What did you tell him?"

"That the night porter would let me in. You see, he really cares." She smirked. "You don't know what it's like to be loved. You've never been married." With that she picked up her basket of dusters and brushes and swept out with a huge grin on her face.

Daisy sighed. She couldn't see Charlie Benton as part of Jessie's love's young dream. He was bad news, always had been. What did he want with Jessie now?

Over the next few days, whenever Daisy got a chance to speak to Jessie alone she probed further. "When are you seeing him again?"

Jessie shrugged. "He'll let me know when he can."

"Where's he been all this time?"

"I don't know, he didn't say."

"Did he ask about anyone else at the hotel? The other staff? The guests?"

"He didn't ask about you, if that's what you mean, and no, he didn't ask for money if that's your next question." Jessie's tone was one of intense irritation.

Every day Daisy felt the bond between them lessen. Jessie became more stubborn and less forthcoming. "I thought you'd be pleased for me," she said one day. "I at least thought you might want me to be happy."

Daisy hated being at odds with her sister, especially after all her trouble, but she could see no good coming out of the situation if Charlie Benton was involved.

Chapter Twenty Four

As Lawrence dressed for dinner he wondered why he'd ever suggested it. Events had overtaken him and he now regretted his impulse. It was to see Charlotte again. That's what had driven him to such rash impetuosity. He hadn't bargained for Brandon and his sister being invited. The way Verity told it Charlotte had manoeuvred her into inviting them. Now he had to play nice and watch her making eyes at a man who had a reputation as a notorious womaniser. At Maldon Hall she'd given him reason to hope. At least he'd have a chance to get to know her a little better, even if it wasn't the opportunity he'd been looking for. His only hope was that she would see him in a charitable light.

He glanced in the mirror as he tied his white bow tie. He took a breath, ran his fingers through his dark waves and squared his broad shoulders. I'll be damned if I'm going to fail at the first hurdle, he thought. Brandon wasn't interested in anything more than a mild flirtation with Charlotte. Surely she'd see that?

Verity too was having misgivings. She'd spent most of the afternoon with Mr Svenson making sure the arrangements were just right, but even so her nerves jangled. She'd never played hostess before, always being the daughter, niece or younger sister. This dinner would show Charlotte that the Fitzroys could do as well as the Huntington-Smythes when it came to putting on a memorable event. They may not have access to the same resources, but they had Mrs T, the finest cook in London. The reputation of The Fitzroy Hotel lay in her hands. She prayed tonight would be a success.

In her mind she ran though the evening ahead, inwardly preparing for every eventuality. She'd always enjoyed Charlotte's company, seeing her as outgoing and brave. Now she wondered if she wasn't a bit shallow, added to which she'd managed to manipulate her to her own bidding. First seeing Brandon Summerville in the park, then engineering an invitation to the dinner. That hadn't gone down well when she told Lawrence, although he was too much of a gentleman to make much of it. She hoped she'd behave at dinner and not make her obsession with Brandon obvious. Lawrence would be mortified and she'd feel bad all over again.

She dressed in the midnight blue taffeta gown Mrs Henderson had included in her new wardrobe. The boned bodice was embroidered with forget-me-nots, the skirt fell in pleats from a nipped-in waist, accentuating her slim figure. Jessie came up to help with her hair, pinning blue silk roses into her dark as night curls, highlighting her delicate features and the soft flush on her pale as petals cheeks.

Taking a deep breath she braced herself, crossed her fingers and hoped with all her heart. "Please don't let it be a total disaster," she breathed.

Downstairs, in the hotel lobby with Lawrence, she danced from foot to foot waiting for the guests to arrive. The Huntington-Smythes arrived first, Chester Huntington-Smythe striding out of their carriage with Edward, Charlotte and Sybil Huntington-Smythe following behind.

"So good of you to come," Verity said, greeting them each in turn.

"Good of you to invite us," Chester said, as Lawrence shook his hand. "It's a pity we didn't get to know you better earlier. We're all sorry about your loss and the circumstances of it."

"Thank you," Verity said, the memory of her mother's funeral fresh in her mind.

"Perhaps we can make up for lost time now," Lawrence said, showing them into the lounge for pre-dinner drinks.

"Such a pleasure to be here," Sybil said, glancing around. "A pity Mrs Fitzroy couldn't make it though. We got on so well."

Verity didn't think it a pity but Lawrence said, "She'll be sorry to have missed you too."

Charlotte was more brazen, wafting in, a cloud of her heady perfume filling the room. "Good to see you again," she breathed her tone husky with promise as she greeted Lawrence, kissing his cheek. "Our last meeting was sadly cut short."

I do hope she behaves, Verity thought as she saw Lawrence struggle to contain the grin spreading across his face. "Delighted you could come," he managed.

Jeremy arrived with a pretty redhead called Prudence. Verity's heart warmed when she saw him. Thank goodness, she thought. At least with Jeremy and his guest there would be lively company.

Charlotte chatted to Jeremy while Sybil and Edward discussed the unusually warm weather with Prudence.

Verity stood with Lawrence, talking to Chester, who gazed around as though assessing the value of everything he saw. "Nice place you have here," he said. "Just the one hotel, is it? Or do you envisage a chain of similar establishments across the country?"

Lawrence glanced around too, as though seeing it through Chester's eyes. "No, not really," he said. "One is quite enough. This was my father's idea. He may well have hoped for more, but it was never to be."

"No ambition in that direction? With the railways opening up the country and ever faster and more reliable methods of transport, I guess hotels would present a good business proposition." He drew on his cigar. "I'm in finance myself." He handed Lawrence his business card. "If ever you have plans to expand."

"Thank you." Lawrence took the card and tucked it into his pocket just as Brandon Summerville and his sister Lydia arrived.

Verity's heart beat a tattoo in her chest. It was difficult to resist the man's charm, but she was acutely aware of Charlotte's feeling for him. If the evening turned into a disaster it would be Charlotte's fault, she thought. I should never have let her influence me. She put on her best smile. "Thank you for the flowers," she said kissing Lydia on the cheek. "It was kind of you."

"I'm so sorry you got caught up like that," Lydia said. "I felt awful."

"I'm glad you survived the ordeal," Brandon said, holding her hand longer than necessary, sending a blush of hot blood up her cheek. "You look none the worse for it."

"An ordeal greatly lessened by your generosity, I believe. I assume it was you who facilitated my release."

A pink tinge coloured Brandon's cheek. "It was the least I could do. I'm only sorry Lydia led you into such trouble."

"It seems I owe you a debt of gratitude," Lawrence said. "You must allow me to compensate you."

Brandon smiled "Dinner is recompense enough," he said.

Dinner, consisting of wild mushroom soup, salmon mousse, venison in red wine with seasonal vegetables followed by lemon Charlotte and profiteroles, was served in the private dining room. Verity soon found there was no need to worry about any lack of conversation. Prudence, speaking in clear, dulcet tones, filled in all the empty spaces, jumping from one topic to another with grasshopper ease, skittering over them like flies hovering over water. In her company everyone relaxed, or, Verity thought, were stunned by her effervescence.

She silently thanked Jeremy for his foresight in bringing her. Even Charlotte behaved herself. Any fears she'd had that she would spend the evening monopolising Brandon were unfounded. She appeared to be pointedly ignoring him and paid more attention to Jeremy.

Verity guessed she was doing it deliberately so that Brandon would feel slighted, but, from what she'd heard of the man she'd have more luck finding sunshine in a cave than making any impression on him.

Among the various topics discussed were social events, Ascot and racing. Jeremy mentioned Verity's love of horses. Charlotte wittered on and said something about her uncle's riding accident and the subject turned to his health, managing his property, and the estates. "Daddy may have to go up there after all," she said. "Uncle Jasper isn't getting any better."

The mention of Yorkshire reminded Verity of her father and the mystery about his death. "We're planning a visit to Leeds quite soon, aren't we, Lawrence?" Verity said.

Brandon looked up sharply. "Do you have business there, Lawrence?"

"A few loose ends tying up my aunt's estate," Lawrence said. "Nothing of any significance."

Charlotte brightened. "Oh you must try to ride out, Verity. You'd love it, riding like the wind across the moors. There's nothing like it."

"I thought Bertie was the horse-racer," Jeremy said. "Given his performance at the hunt."

Edward glared at him. "Bertie's an excellent horseman," he said, "although not everyone appreciates his prowess."

Jeremy's eyebrows went up but he bent his head to continue his meal. The tension round the table tightened.

Verity noticed a strained atmosphere between Edward and Brandon too: nothing in particular, just a few cutting remarks that got her wondering.

Lydia must have seen it as well. "I must congratulate you on the depth of your knowledge and understanding of such a wide range of topics," she said to Prudence. "It's a pleasure to meet someone so well versed."

"Oh, one has to be able to chat, doesn't one," Prudence said. "What else is there for us ladies to do?"

Brandon chuckled. "I'm sure my sister can tell you," he said. "She takes an avid interest in the plight of women."

Chester huffed. "Not one of those suffragette women are you? Stuff and nonsense. Not sure what they want to achieve. Politics is best left to men who understand it. Don't you agree, Sybil?"

Sybil, who'd hardly spoken throughout the meal smiled. "Whatever you say, Chester. I'm sure you're right." She took a delicate bite of potato.

Lydia shook her head. "It's not just politics, Chester," she said. "It's about women having control over their own lives. Not all women are treated as well as you treat your wife."

Verity heard the admonishment in her tone, but before Chester could respond Prudence cut in with a question about the latest musical. "Have any of you seen it yet?" she asked. "I was thinking of going." Thankfully the topic turned and the conversation moved on.

Lawrence mentioned an opera he was keen to see and wondered if Charlotte would like to accompany him. "Sounds wonderful," she said, clapping her hands. "Perhaps we could make up a party and all go. I'm sure Lydia and Verity would love it too."

He smiled. "Why not," he said, "I'm sure it would be delightful."

Verity felt for him. She wondered if she'd done the right thing giving him any hope that Charlotte might be interested in him. Charlotte was clearly only interested in herself.

After dinner the men passed around the port and cigars while the ladies withdrew to the lounge for coffee. Lawrence glanced around the table. He'd noticed that Jeremy had been unusually quiet through the meal and recalled his reluctance to come when he heard who the other guests were. It was only Verity's invitation that had persuaded him. Brandon's comments about the Huntington-Smythes came to mind. Why had he agreed to come? Probably at his sister's request, he guessed.

She'd seemed fond of Verity despite the brevity of their acquaintance. Edward had been fairly defensive of his brother Bertie when Jeremy mentioned his riding. Was that the only reason for the tension between them?

"That was a fine spread, an excellent dinner if I may say so," Chester said, leaning back in his chair. "You have an excellent cook. Quite an essential in your business I suppose."

"Thank you," Lawrence said. "I'll pass your comments on to Mrs T."

"Lively company too," Brandon said, glancing at Jeremy.

Jeremy smiled. "Yes, but I fear the ladies will be having a more companionable time than we can hope for," he said.

"Surely not?" Chester said. "I mean, bless their little hearts, but gossip and tittle-tattle will never replace good conversation."

"You mean serious conversation?" Jeremy asked.

Chester drew a breath. "I mean things that are important to men of the world. Things that make a difference."

Lawrence could see this straying into troubled waters. "Perhaps Edward could give us some stock broking tips to cheer us all up," he said. "That is your business isn't it?"

Edward's face turned stony. "A very small part of it," he said, "and I doubt you would be in a position to take advantage of anything I have to offer."

"Why is that?" Brandon asked.

His words hung in the air for several seconds. Lawrence had only said it as a light-hearted suggestion, to lift the atmosphere but now he felt the animosity between them building.

Eventually Edward shrugged. "It's very specialised, that's all. No offence meant."

The moment passed, but Lawrence couldn't help wondering if Brandon was right about the Huntington-Smythes. Perhaps they weren't quite what they seemed. "I hear Lord Rosebury won his third Derby at Epsom this year," he said, hoping to change the subject.

Chester brightened. "Indeed he did. Horse called Cicerio." He rubbed his hands together and grinned. "Favourite of course but still worth a punt."

Lawrence breathed a sigh of relief as the conversation turned to possible favourites at Ascot.

Later, when they joined the ladies he was pleased to see Verity smiling and seeming to enjoy herself. "I've persuaded Charlotte to accompany me to the Exhibition at the Royal Academy tomorrow," she said. "Perhaps we can have tea here afterwards."

"Of course," he said, delighted at the opportunity to see Charlotte again. "I'll ask Mrs T to make something special."

While they all had coffee Verity played the piano and Prudence sang songs from the musicals, her repertoire most impressive.

At the end of the evening, while they awaited their carriages, Chester took Lawrence on one side.

"I don't suppose you've invited us here because you like the cut of our jib," he said. "It'll be Charlotte you're interested in. Am I right?"

"Well, er. She's certainly a credit to you, sir."

"My little girl has expensive tastes and she's become accustomed to a certain standard of living," he said. "If you're interested in her you may wish to think about that chain of hotels. Goodnight." He shook Lawrence's hand.

Lawrence felt as though he'd been given a lecture by the headmaster, but he got the message – Charlotte came with a very high price tag.

Chapter Twenty Five

The next morning Daisy left Mr Lawrence's office with mixed feelings; glad he'd thought to ask for her help, but aware that, if it hadn't been for her stupidity in employing Molly Brown in the first place, he wouldn't have had need of it. She couldn't decide whether the favour asked was punishment, but it was at least an opportunity to go some way to redress the problem she'd caused.

Knowing of her continued acquaintance with Matilda who, prior to her marriage, had worked in the hotel kitchen as a pastry cook, he'd asked her to enquire whether her husband, Constable Perkins, knew anything about the circumstances of Molly Brown's death. Daisy felt sure that if Matilda was privy to any such information she wouldn't be slow in sharing it. All the same, her heart fluttered as she knocked on Matilda's door a few days later.

"Daisy, how lovely," Matilda said. "Do come in. I've just got some scones out of the oven, so you're very welcome."

Daisy went into the small, neat kitchen where a toddler sat in a high chair, pushing crumbs of scone and jam into his mouth. She smiled and her heart lifted. "He's getting big now, isn't he?" she said. "I hardly recognise him." She tousled his mop of brown curls.

Matilda glowed, her face a picture of the greatest pride and happiness. "Yes. Can't stop 'em." She laughed, rubbing her back.

"When's the next one due?" Daisy asked. "Not long now is it?"

"A few weeks." Matilda moved the kettle to the stove. "George swears it'll be a girl," she said. "I don't mind either way."

Daisy helped get the tea and they chatted about friends they both knew. Matilda asked after Mrs T and the rest of the staff and Daisy had great pleasure in updating her on all the latest gossip.

"Has George ever mentioned Molly Brown?" Daisy asked as she sipped her second cup of tea. "She used to work at the hotel, but left after a rather unsavoury incident. Now she's been murdered and I wondered if George knew anything about it."

"Someone from the hotel's been murdered? Goodness, how intriguing. I must tell George." She pondered for a moment. "What did you say her name was?"

"Molly Brown. I understand she was working as… um… well, let's just say it wasn't hotel work. Not as we know it."

"Oh." Matilda's eyes shone with curiosity. "I don't recognise the name. George hasn't said anything, but I can ask, if you like?"

Daisy felt awful but she needed to know. "Anything you can find out. It's just that it might reflect badly on the hotel, if you know what I mean."

"Oh I know," Matilda said, looking as though she was enjoying Daisy's predicament a little too much. "Mr Lawrence and his famous reputation. Still, I can't complain." She smiled broadly. "Working there did me a right favour. Just think, if I hadn't met George…"

Yes, Daisy thought. If she hadn't met George her life would have been very different.

The morning after the dinner Verity got up early, dressed and went down to breakfast. Lawrence was planning his trip to Leeds and she wanted to go with him. When she arrived downstairs she found a letter from her Aunt Elvira waiting for her. She immediately felt guilty for not having written since she returned to London. Of course her aunt would want to know how she was getting on.

Her heart sank when she read the letter. Aunt Elvira's oldest friends were travelling to France and Elvira had invited them to stop overnight at Maldon Hall. She needed Verity to be there and expected her to travel down in time for the weekend.

"I take it these friends have a son whom Mama thinks eligible?" Lawrence said when Verity showed him the letter.

"Two," Verity said. "And for good measure she's invited the Villiers. They too have a son."

"You mean Percy Villiers? The Master of the Hunt?"

"Yes. I fear we will be quite over-run with eligible young men."

Lawrence laughed. "When will you leave?"

Verity sighed. There was no question she'd have to go. "The day after tomorrow. I'm going to the Summer Exhibition with Charlotte this afternoon."

"Ah, yes. The afternoon tea. It's all arranged."

"When are you going to Leeds?"

"I'll travel up over the weekend. I have several appointments for next week. It shouldn't take too long, no more than a day or two. I doubt I'll find anything further than what we already know."

"I wish I could come."

Lawrence patted her hand. "Your time would be better spent thinking about your future rather than your parents' past."

"You sound like Aunt Elvira."

Lawrence shied. "Mama has many faults but she does have your best interest at heart. You can't blame her for that."

Verity nodded. "I know," she said, but it didn't make the weekend any more appealing.

Her worries were all forgotten later that afternoon when she visited the Royal Society Summer Exhibition with Charlotte, who was more interested in who might be there than any of the paintings. Verity, on the other hand, was enthralled. This is why I've come to London, she thought; to see the work of upcoming artists and old masters and wonder at their skill and flair. As they walked around the gallery she heard people's whispered discussions about technique and effect and felt immediately at home. She revelled in the calm atmosphere of deep respect and quiet appreciation. It felt almost sacred.

Charlotte's appreciation was easier to see. She wrinkled her nose in distaste at anything she didn't like or understand, preferring the traditional oils on canvas. They'd been perusing the gallery for over an hour when they ran into Lydia Summerville, catalogue in hand, inspecting a painting of Queen Alexandra.

"I didn't know you were a devotee of art," Charlotte said.

"Oh I like to see what's new," Lydia said. "But Brandon's the collector."

"Brandon? Is he here?" Charlotte brightened.

"He was but I think he's gone. He was very taken with John Singer Sargent's latest paintings. The portrait of *The Marlborough Family* in particular. Have you seen it?"

Verity looked down at her catalogue. "Not yet."

"It's in the upstairs gallery," Lydia said. "I'll show you."

They followed her to where the portrait hung. Verity stood in front of it taking in all the detail, mesmerised. It was worth the visit just to see this one painting. She sighed with satisfaction as warmth flowed through her. This really was an incredible place. One day I'll have a gallery of my own, she thought, although she knew she might as well ask for the moon.

"Will you join us for tea?" she asked Lydia as they were leaving, it was the least she should do after Lydia had shown them where the most prepossessing and provocative painting were housed.

"Oh yes, do," Charlotte said. "You can tell us all about your visit to Paris. I'd love to go to Paris, wouldn't you, Verity?"

Verity laughed. "Well it certainly sounds more appealing than a wet weekend in Kent with my aunt."

After lunch with Matilda, Daisy returned to the hotel. She wasn't sure she had anything worth telling Mr Lawrence but as least she'd set the ball rolling. If there was any gossip Matilda would be sure to know it.

"Is Jessie in the tea room?" she asked, not seeing her in the kitchen with the others.

"She's gone out," Peggy said. "I was going into town later myself and asked if we could go together, but she said she had plans."

"Plans," Mrs T said, banging a roll of pastry dough on the table "Since when has a chambermaid been able to have 'plans'?"

"I'll have a word with her," Daisy said. "It's probably something and nothing." Inside her stomach churned. Jessie would be meeting Charlie for sure and the whole stupid business would start over again. Surely she wasn't daft enough to be taken in for a second time, but then who knows? They say love is blind.

She had some paperwork and sewing to get on with so retired to her sitting room, but she kept an ear out for Jessie's return. When she did return her face was flushed and her eyes shone. Daisy's heart sank. She called her into the sitting room. "You didn't tell me you were going out," she said. "I trust it was something urgent for you to go without permission."

Jessie glared at her. "I'd finished the rooms. I didn't think I needed permission to go out for an hour or two when I wasn't needed here. Didn't know I was in prison and had to have a chit before I could leave."

Daisy sighed. "I was just worried when you weren't here."

"Well I'm back now ain't I? So you've no need to worry."

Daisy turned away. She hated having to ask. "Have you seen Charlie again?"

"What if I have?"

"I just worry about you, Jessie. You're not…" She was going to say not well, but that would bring up a whole host of resentment and guilt.

"Not what? Not myself? Not right in the head? Well, you've no need to worry. I can take care of myself thank you and I don't need you interfering in my marriage and my life." With that she stormed out, slamming the door behind her.

Oh dear, Daisy thought. Here we go again.

Back at the hotel, Lawrence joined Verity, Charlotte and Lydia for tea and they spent a pleasant half-hour discussing the merits of the various artists on display at the Exhibition. Lawrence found Verity's enthusiasm infectious and was impressed with Lydia's knowledge of the subject. "I'm quite minded to go myself," he said. "What did you think, Charlotte?"

Charlotte pouted. "It was all right, but I prefer something a little more lively."

"Such as?"

Charlotte beamed at him. "Well, music, dancing. Things like that." Her eyes sparkled with mischief. "There's a club I'd love to go to. They play ragtime music. It's all very avant-garde." She blinked at him as though waiting for his response.

"It sounds like fun," Lawrence said, although he didn't know why he said it. It didn't sound like fun at all but her eyes held the challenge and he'd never been known to turn down a challenge. Still, something held him back. "Perhaps some other time. I'm afraid I have several commitments in the next few days."

"Lawrence is off to Yorkshire on Saturday," Verity said. "Maybe when he returns."

"Lovely," Charlotte said. "We can make a party of it."

"Why not?" Lawrence said, but he wondered if her suggestion might have been meant to include Brandon. If so it was even less appealing and he was beginning to wish he'd never asked.

As they were leaving he heard Lydia ask Verity to tea the next day. "I'd love to hear of your experience after you were arrested," she said. "Those poor women, there must be something we can do for them." She handed Verity her card.

"Thank you," Verity said. "It will be a relief to talk about it."

"I hope you're not leading Verity into more trouble," Lawrence said. "Not going to join a march or go to any more of those meetings. I couldn't allow her to do anything like that. She was lucky to escape with her reputation intact last time."

"No, nothing like that," Lydia said, smiling. "Just letter writing and moral support for the cause."

"Well, be careful," Lawrence said and wondered if he sounded as much of a killjoy as he felt.

The next afternoon, with Lawrence's permission, Verity went to tea with Lydia. She took a cab to the house, a substantial Victorian red brick house in Bayswater. It had a pleasant outlook over the square. Verity had wondered what sort of house Brandon Summerville would live in and felt quite disappointed to find it fairly ordinary. Brass railings surrounded the small front garden, filled with summer flowers and roses in bloom. Even inside there was no ostentation, the decor being elegant, fresh and more light and airy than it appeared from outside. Several pictures graced the pastel painted walls and she wondered whether Brandon had chosen them. If so he had excellent taste, she thought.

The butler showed her into the drawing room where Lydia sat reading a magazine. She rose from one of the two large sofas that stood in front of an ornate fireplace. "I'm so glad you could come," she said. "I was hoping you would."

She rang for tea. "Now you must tell me what happened in that awful place. Was it really bad?"

Verity told her about the women she'd seen in prison, their frequent incarcerations and determination to carry on whatever the personal cost. "Honestly I was humbled by their fortitude, the unspeakable things they've had to endure. What we read in the papers is only the half of it."

The maid came in with the tea and Lydia poured Verity a cup.

Verity sipped her tea, her mind back in the cell with the other women. She wondered what had happened to them since, where they were, if they were even still alive, such was their degradation.

"I've never said anything to Lawrence, of course. He'd be as appalled as I am. They have such tremendous spirit." The memory spiralled through her mind. "I must admit to being beyond gratitude when I was released and taken home," she said, "although I felt I'd betrayed them somehow by not being committed to the cause. I'm afraid all my thoughts and fears were for my own future and wellbeing. I feared that if Aunt Elvira heard of my predicament she'd cut me off entirely and I owe her so much." She glanced at Lydia. "I felt I'd let her down, let my whole family down. I have a lot to thank your brother for."

"Oh, please think nothing of it. It's just as well that he knows the Police Commissioner and several officers at that station. They're in the same Lodge."

Verity frowned. "The same Lodge?"

Lydia put her hand to her mouth. "Oh perhaps I shouldn't have mentioned it." She put a finger on her lip then tapped the side of her nose in the same gesture as the police constable who'd taken Verity home.

"What is it? Some sort of secret society?"

Lydia laughed. "No. Not a secret society, but a society with secrets, that's for sure."

"Well, whatever it is, I'm grateful," Verity said.

Lydia had a list of prominent politicians who might be persuaded to support the Women's Suffrage Movement. Between them they drafted a letter stressing their commitment to non-violent protest and pleading for fair representation from the government. After going over both the list and the letter, Verity agreed to take half the addresses. "It'll help me feel I've gone some way to redeemed myself after my undeserved good fortune," she said.

Chapter Twenty Six

That weekend, with Miss Templeton gone home to her aunt's and Mr Lawrence away in Leeds, Daisy arranged to go back and see Matilda again. She had great satisfaction telling Mr Svenson that she was on an errand for Mr Lawrence when he asked where she was going as she put on her coat and hat.

"I just thought you might be going into town and could drop a note off to the wine merchant," he said. "It doesn't matter. I can send someone else."

She smiled, but the fact that he had the authority to ask her still rankled. When she got to Matilda's she was welcomed with tea and cake that Matilda had made. "I enjoy baking," Matilda said. "I love being here with George and little Ralfie, but I do miss the company."

"It's a pity you can't do more cooking," Daisy said. "You're very good at it. Shame it's only George that gets the benefit."

"I know, but George wouldn't have me doing owt else," she said. "He reckons looking after him and Ralfie's a full-time job."

"Well, you'll have your hands full when the next one arrives."

"Aye I will that."

They drank tea and chatted some more then Daisy asked if she'd spoken to George about Molly Brown. Matilda's eyes lit up. And Daisy remembered what a gossip she was and how she loved to relate everything George said in the greatest of detail.

"George says they've arrested Mr Jevons. Our Mr Jevons. Can you believe that?"

Daisy swallowed. "I know, but I'm sure he didn't do it. I mean. He wouldn't."

"Apparently he attacked her in the hotel and when she reported him he lost his job. George says that's motive enough."

"So they're not looking for anyone else? Given her occupation?"

"Poor girl. George says she lost her job an' all. Had to find another way to make a living." She stared at Daisy. "I couldn't do that, could you?"

Daisy's heart hardened. "I believe it was her choice," she said. "We all have choices. She could have stayed a chambermaid, but she wanted something better and thought a man could provide it."

Matilda shook her head, looking as though the weight of the world was on her shoulders.

Daisy felt she was getting nowhere. The police weren't even looking for anyone else. "I just wondered whether they might look at her brother," she said. "He came to the hotel. A nasty piece of work. It's not beyond the realms of possibility is it? I mean. We both know Mr Jevons wouldn't have done it."

Matilda sighed. "George says he feels sorry for Mr Jevons. He says there isn't any solid evidence he did it, only the brother saying he saw him. George says it's something to do with circumstances or something." She frowned.

Daisy's heart lightened. "Perhaps you could suggest George look into where she worked. It would be a feather in his cap if he found something the rest of them didn't know. She was always chatting up the men who came to the restaurant alone. Maybe someone didn't get what they expected, or did and then didn't want to pay for it." Daisy sipped her tea, the idea planted. "George is very good at that sort of thing isn't he?" she said.

Matilda brightened. "Yes. George is clever. I don't think people appreciate that." She tapped the side of her nose. "Like a bloodhound he is. Once he gets the scent of something."

"So, perhaps you could point him in that direction, do you think?"

Matilda beamed. "Yes. It's more likely that it was a disgruntled client isn't it? Mr Jevons is a gentleman. He wouldn't have done it."

Daisy left slightly reassured. At least George Perkins agreed there was room for doubt about Mr Jevons being the culprit. She trusted George to do the right thing. She wished she could speak to him herself. Maybe, when she called again, she'd make sure it was a time when he'd be in.

On the way back to the hotel she ran into Peggy who said she'd been to visit her sister. "I managed to pick up some shopping too," she said, indicating the basket of goods she carried. "Honestly the pennies don't go far these days do they? The prices always going up never down."

Daisy commiserated and they chatted as they walked. "Oh. I saw that friend of Jessie's. You know the chap she met, what was his name, Charlie."

"Oh yes?"

"Yes. He was with a lady, well she looked like a lady. Quite well dressed. They went into a boarding house. Probably his wife I suppose, although, to be fair, she looked a sight too good for him. Oh. Sorry." She put her hand to her mouth. "I shouldn't say that should I? Who am I to judge? No one, that's who. My ma always said every time I open my mouth I put my foot in it."

Daisy's heart started to beat faster. "No. You're all right. Are you sure it was the same chap?"

"Yes. I've got a good memory for faces. He didn't see me. Too engrossed in his lady friend."

"Well, as you say, probably his wife." A swell of satisfaction grew inside Daisy. Charlie was with another woman. What would Jessie say about that? Of course there could be an innocent explanation, but as it was Charlie Benton, Daisy guessed not.

Chapter Twenty Seven

Situated above a grocery store, the solicitor's premises, listed as 237a The High Street, Chapelside, Leeds were unprepossessing to say the least. Lawrence gazed up at the windows overlooking the road. He sighed and pushed the heavy wooden door open. Narrow stairs led up to a landing where, a little way along, a door on the right proclaimed it to be Smithson, Hughes and Smithson, Solicitors.

With a heavy heart Lawrence rang the bell. The door opened and an elderly lady peered out.

"Lawrence Fitzroy to see Mr Smithson," he said, handing her his card. "I have an appointment."

The lady nodded and opened the door further to allow him to enter. Closing the door behind him she shuffled ahead into the small waiting area where two chairs stood against the wall on the left. The desk ahead of him held an ancient Remington typewriter next to a pile of brown cardboard files. Gold lettering on the half-glassed door on the right showed it to be Mr Smithson's office. There didn't appear to be any other offices, only what looked like a kitchen at the end of the corridor. Lawrence wondered what had happened to the other Smithson and Hughes. The woman knocked briefly, opened the door and announced Lawrence's arrival.

"Show him in, show him in," said a voice inside the room.

Lawrence entered a room crowded with clutter. Piles of boxes, books and files leaned precariously on filing cabinets, chairs and tables. Stacks of books sat on the floor and lined the window sill. The morning light streaming in through grimy glass did nothing to diminish the impression he got of dusty antiquity. Gazing around, he wondered what he'd walked into.

A wizened old man, Lawrence guessed to be well into his eighties, sat on a padded swivel chair behind a large mahogany desk, his spidery fingers reached out to shake Lawrence's hand. "Good morning, Mr Fitzroy. Mr Henry Smithson at your service. What can I do for you today?"

Lawrence took the only empty chair in the room. Sat opposite the old man, he saw yellowed skin, and sparse grey hair clinging to a skeletal frame. His clothes, which probably fitted at one time, appeared too big for the slightness of his body, but his clear blue eyes sparkled with unexpected energy.

"I'm looking into my late uncle's affairs," Lawrence said. "Mr Douglas Templeton. I believe you dealt with his estate."

The man sat back in thought. He swivelled his chair from side to side stroking his chin. "Coffee," he said suddenly lurching forward. He rang a bell hidden from Lawrence's view by one of the towers of files either side of the extensive blotter that took up most of the rest of the desk.

The door opened and the old woman shuffled in.

"Coffee," Henry Smithson said. "And biscuits. The good ones for our guest."

The old woman tutted and left.

Mr Smithson smiled. "She can be a bit mean with the biscuits," he said. "Unless we have guests. Now, down to business." He stood and went to a pile of files balanced on a stack of books on top of a cabinet and pulled one out. Lawrence expected the rest to come tumbling down, but they didn't. Mr Smithson brushed the dust from the cover and took the file back to his chair. "If I remember right," he said, glancing up at Lawrence, "and I'm seldom wrong, this is him."

He opened the file and started to look through it as the door opened and the old woman came in carrying a tray with two cups of coffee and a plate of bourbon biscuits. She put the tray on the desk in front of Lawrence.

"Thank you," he said smiling up at her.

She shuffled out. Lawrence waited while the old man looked through the file in front of him, sucking his teeth and shaking his head as he muttered to himself. Then he stood and went to another pile of files, pulling one out. He glanced through it. "No, no, that's not it," he said greatly irritated. He slammed the file on the top of another pile of files on a chair and returned to his seat. "How's the coffee?"

Lawrence took a sip of the coffee which was surprisingly good. "It's fine, thank you."

"Good. Have a biscuit."

Lawrence took a biscuit.

Henry Smithson picked up the other cup and sipped the coffee. "Hmm," he said, as though satisfied. "Now, Douglas Templeton. Sad affair. A while ago though. Shame." He shook his head and looked thoughtful. "Not really his fault, you know. Terrible business."

Lawrence's patience was running out. "I know he committed suicide," he said. "I just want to know why. If it's a matter of money…"

The old man sat back shocked. "Money? No, no, nothing like that, it's just… I understand from your letter that you are working for the family?"

"Yes. On his daughter's behalf. I'm administering Mrs Templeton's estate."

"Ah Mrs Templeton. So very upsetting." He sniffed as though he himself had suffered a great loss.

Lawrence took out the letters he'd found among Aunt Doris's papers. "I found this letter about the disposal of the property. I also found mention of a portfolio of shares."

Mr Smithson took the offered papers. "They went bust," he said. "The brokerage. Shabby affair it was." He handed the papers back as though that were the end of the matter.

Lawrence heaved a sigh, curling his fists in exasperation. "I just want to know what happened and why," he said.

The old man sat back in his chair gazing at Lawrence. He shrugged. "Why does anyone do anything?" he said. "There are some things we never get to understand."

"Miss Templeton cared very much for her father. You can understand a daughter's concern when she finds out that he…"

The solicitor's face clouded over. "Of course," he said. "Cared for her father. Of course." He nodded and glanced up. "Never had children myself. Great pity." He glanced again at the file in front of him, sighed and turned over the pages one at a time, breathing heavily as he did so. "You've heard of The South Sea Island Bubble?" he said at last.

Lawrence frowned. He couldn't see what a seventeenth century scandal had to do with anything. "Yes, but…"

"And the fiasco about Dutch tulips?" Mr Smithson continued gazing up at him. "Speculation mania, people call it. Delusion and the madness of crowds. People invest for profit and as long as they're getting profit they don't consider where it's coming from." He got up and went looking at the piles of files on the cabinets. "It wasn't Mr Templeton's fault of course. He got caught up. Now, where is it?" He stroked his chin as he gazed at the piles of files. "He got in with a group of men all in business. He said they'd prosper through mutual support. I thought they were a bit dodgy, but Douglas was taken with them."

"But I don't see…"

"Ah, here it is." He pulled out another file and returned to his seat. "Douglas Templeton went into partnership with another chap… what was his name? Can't recall. Anyway, this chap, set up an investment company and Douglas was made a director. Name on the letterhead and all that. He bought shares. They paid him well, so he bought more, told his friends, told everyone. Everyone bought shares. The more shares people bought the greater the return, for a while."

He looked at the file. "Parsimon Investments. That what it was called. They invested primarily in mining companies." He paused. "It was all very hush, hush of course which made it more attractive. Only selected clients allowed to invest making them feel special. Of course they were special because they were well off and not inclined to dig deep to see the truth. In the beginning it paid out a good profit, up to forty per cent so naturally people bought more shares and the price went up. Nobody actually looked at the business. Too busy counting the profit." His eyebrows rose. "But, like the tulip bulbs, the shares had no intrinsic value. It was all fake. There was no company. Every time it came to paying out dividends, the partner." He paused and looked at the file. "What was his name, Monty somebody I think…" He glanced up again. "He floated more shares to get money in to pay the investors, hence more investors to pay out. It couldn't last. Eventually the bubble burst. It was doomed from the very beginning." He shook his head. "Instead of blaming their own greed everyone blamed Douglas." He closed the file. "His wasn't the only suicide."

"So, he lost everything? Even the house?"

"He bought shares on credit expecting to sell them at a profit as the price was going up." He leaned forward in a conspiratorial manner. "You have to understand how these things work. At first you make money, then you have to put more money in to protect the investment you've already made. You're always waiting for a big pay out, like a dodgy game of poker, but of course it never comes. By the time Douglas suspected there was something wrong it was too late. He was in too deep and there was no way out. Boom to bust in five years. Terrible thing." He leaned back in the chair, swivelling it from side to side. "Douglas Templeton's name was on the letterhead, you see. Everyone blamed him. He was a proud man. Yorkshire, you see. Couldn't live with what he'd done."

Lawrence sat back wondering what he could tell Verity. Her father had been swindled out of everything he owned by a crook purporting to be a friend. "This chap, the partner, Monty who? Any idea? It might help."

Mr Smithson sniffed. "Quite a character, I believe. Douglas met him in London. Larger than life, easily believable. Moved in the right circles, you see. Anyone would have been fooled. I don't blame Mr Templeton."

"But you don't recall his name or what happened to him?"

"Erm. Monty something. Montgomery, erm…
Montgomery…" He stroked his chin. "Left the
country, you know. Disappeared." He paused. "Went
to South America, or was it Africa? No. South
America, Argentina I think. Sorry. Can't tell you more
than that. I only dealt with Templeton's estate, what
was left of it."

Lawrence showed him the photograph Verity had
given him of the shooting party. "Do you recognise any
of these men? Perhaps this Monty character was one of
them?"

Smithson looked at the picture and shook his head.
"No. Sorry. I knew Douglas of course, but none of the
others." He gave a wry smile. "I am but a humble
solicitor. I didn't move in those circles."

"Thank you anyway." He put the photograph
away. "There was a trust fund, I believe," he said. "Set
up for the children. Who manages that?"

The solicitor again shook his head. "There was
nothing left. No inheritance. I understood Mrs
Templeton moved in with her brother's family. A
dreadful shame. A shame Mr Templeton couldn't live
with."

"No inheritance at all? Miss Templeton mentioned
a small allowance?"

"Not from her father's estate. Possibly from her
mother's family?"

Lawrence smiled. If Verity's allowance had come
from the Fitzroy estate he'd know about it and he
didn't. "Well, thank you for your assistance, Mr
Smithson. I won't take up any more of your time." He
rose to leave.

Mr Smithson stood up. "I'm sorry I couldn't be of
more help," he said. "Terrible business." He shook

Lawrence's hand as he showed him out. "At least we had some decent biscuits," he said loudly enough for the elderly woman sitting at the desk to hear.

Verity was glad to be travelling to Maldon Hall alone. It gave her time to think. Talking to Lydia had opened her eyes to the injustices shown to women who had no say in their lives, or the lives of their children. It's enough to put you off marriage, she thought which brought her back to Aunt Elvira's mission to get her married off. She sighed and wondered if the young men she would meet over the weekend would be as reluctant to walk down the aisle as she was.

Having caught an early train she arrived while Elvira was having coffee with the wives of farmers from the estate.

"I don't want to disturb her," she said to Meadows. "Please have my things taken to my room. I'd like to visit the Dower House while it's still empty if I may."

"Of course, Miss Verity. I'll get you the keys."

The Dower House was where she always saw her mother whenever she thought of her. Seeing it again would bring her closer. She missed her mother. She missed her smile and motherly advice and still felt the tinge of regret for not being there when she needed help. Her death had left a huge hole in her heart.

The enormity of her loss enveloped her and a flood of memories filled her mind as she pushed the door open. How empty if looks, she thought, with all her mother's things removed. Not that she had a great deal.

She walked from room to room, each one bringing a different memory. She heard her mother's voice in her head. 'Life is full of disappointment and surprises,' she often said. 'Never be afraid to follow your heart.' Well, where was her heart? She wasn't sure. She'd given it to Ned, but he'd broken it for the chance of a larger farm, or maybe bent it a little. She'd been shocked at the engagement, but she wasn't prostrate with grief, so perhaps it was just a childhood fantasy born of ignorance of any alternative opportunity.

Brandon Summerville's face popped into her head. She laughed at her own stupidity. As if she'd ever have a chance with him, when even Charlotte had failed to entrance him. Not that she wanted a chance with him. No. He was the last person on earth she'd want to spend the rest of her life with. So why did the prospect of never seeing him again make her feel so bad? She pushed the thought to one side, admonishing herself for even having it. You read too many Jane Austen books, she said to herself and laughed again.

Later she sat with Elvira going over the dinner arrangements. "There'll be ten of us," Elvira said. "Joyce and Hamish Cameron and their sons, Phillip and Sam, plus the Villiers, their daughter Belinda and their son Percy. You know him. Master of the Hunt."

"Yes, of course." Verity forced a smile. Percy Villiers was in his thirties and still unmarried. Verity understood why. She'd always found him a supercilious prig with no sense of humour or self-awareness. His sister was all right, although she had a tendency to bray like a horse.

"It'll be lovely to catch up with Joyce again," Elvira said, a rare sparkle in her eyes. "We grew up together. She was such fun." As she spoke her face relaxed and Verity thought she looked younger than she'd ever seen her. "He's Scottish of course, so be prepared for a thick burr and an excess of tartan." She smiled. "I haven't seen them since... since..." a frown creased her brow, "since Herbert passed." She paused for a moment in silence then took a breath. "You'll like them. Joyce was a great fan of Charles Dickens. She wanted to call their eldest son Pip, but Hamish insisted on Phillip. Sam was for Sam Weller in *The Pickwick Papers*. They'd be in their twenties now."

Once the seating plan was settled, Verity making sure she was nowhere near Percy Villiers, they turned to the menu. It being summer the food would be seasonal and provided by the local farms. They would start with consommé, followed by river caught trout, then roast beef and chicken with seasonal vegetables. Dessert would be a choice of strawberry tart, or mixed summer fruit pudding with ice cream or cream. Tea and coffee would be served in the drawing room.

"I've agreed it all with the cook a week ago," Elvira said, "but I wasn't sure about dessert. What do you think?"

"I think it will be splendid," Verity said, happy to help.

The Cameron family arrived in time for afternoon tea. Verity found she enjoyed talking to them. They spoke mainly about their plans to visit Europe and the Far East and the places they would be visiting.

"It all sound very exciting," Verity said, although she did get the impression that the boys would have preferred to travel alone. After tea they all went up to change.

The Villiers arrived first for dinner and Verity was left to entertain them. When Elvira showed the Camerons in, the men resplendent in full Highland dress complete with silver buckles and badges, Verity gasped with delight. They really were an awe-inspiring sight. She could hardly take her eyes off them. Maybe the dinner would be fun after all.

Over dinner they asked Verity about her time in London and she told them about the visit to the Summer Exhibition.

"Verity paints," Elvira said. "In fact she's sold some watercolours, haven't you, Verity."

Verity blushed. "Just a couple I put on show at the bookshop."

"How lovely," Phillip said. "You must show us your pictures. Do you have a studio?"

"Not really, I use the summerhouse, but I just dabble, nothing exceptional."

"Nonsense," Elvira said. "She's very talented. She also plays the piano. I'd say she's the most talented of the family."

"Rides like a Valkyrie too," Percy chipped in. "In fact there's no end to her talents."

Verity cringed. Why did he have to be so supercilious?

"Quite right too," Hamish Cameron said. "I never did see the point in false modesty." He turned to Verity. "Never hide your light under a bushel, my dear." He rolled his rrrs and 'under a bushel' sounded quite exotic, but it didn't stop her feeling worse than ever.

Phillip came to her rescue. "Perhaps we can ride out together in the morning. We'd like that, wouldn't we, Sam?"

"Aye. Champion," Sam said his face lighting up.

By the end of the dinner Verity found she'd warmed to the two Cameron boys. They seemed intent on mischief and not taking anything seriously and, as they'd be off on their travels after tomorrow, there was no threat of any expected involvement.

The next morning the three of them rode out before breakfast. They galloped their horses across fields and over hedges. With the wind in her face Verity felt alive again. She'd forgotten the thrill of thundering hooves, riding at speed and the sheer joy of the early morning as the sun rose in an orange sky. It was magical. They stopped in a copse to rest the horses.

"So, what's life really like in London?" Phillip asked. "What do you do there?"

Verity thought for a moment. "I go out to dinner, dancing, go to the theatre, meet people." It all sounded extremely futile and boring compared to the adventure ahead of the boys.

Phillip smiled. "And is love on the horizon? Any marriage plans?" His soft Scottish burr brought a jolt to her heart.

"Good heavens, no," she said a little too quickly. "I have no plans in that direction." Then she thought and said, "Don't tell Aunt Elvira but I was actually arrested once."

"Arrested! Do tell." The boys both stared wide-eyed at her. She'd obviously gone up in their estimation. She told them about the suffrage meeting and being arrested and taken to the cells. The way she told it sounded daring and heroic, but it hadn't felt like that at the time. It was the stuff of nightmares. "It was an eye opener," she said. "Some things you wouldn't believe." She saw a look of deep admiration in the boys' faces. Then she told them about the women suffragettes and what they'd had to endure and the mood changed.

"I believe you," Phillip said. "The older generation have a lot to answer for. Hopefully our generation will do better."

They sat quietly for a while until Sam said, "Well, I'm starving. Race you back to the house." They all mounted up and raced back for breakfast.

Later, as they were leaving, Verity felt a touch of sorrow at their going. They'd brought light and laughter back into her life. "I envy you your great adventure," she said as they left.

They each kissed her cheek. "We'll write," they said, but Verity doubted they'd find the time with all they planned to do. She waved as the carriage taking them to Dover pulled away and realised that, for all the time they'd been there she hadn't once thought of Brandon Summerville.

Chapter Twenty Eight

Daisy decided not to say anything to Jessie about the woman Peggy had seen Charlie with. If there was anything to it she'd find out soon enough. It was even possible that Peggy might mention it. Better coming from her, Daisy thought. If she said it Jessie would go on the defensive and once she'd made up her mind to anything it was the devil's own job to get her to change it. Anyway Jessie was working in the tea room that afternoon, so she'd be kept busy and out of trouble. Or so Daisy thought.

"There's a man in the tea room asking a lot of questions," Jessie said when she came into the kitchen to collect an order. "Asked how long I'd been here and did I know the girl who worked here before. I think he's a reporter or something. Trying to dig up some dirt, that's what they're usually at."

"What did you tell him?" Daisy asked, suddenly wary.

"Nothing. Told 'im I was new, hadn't been 'ere long. 'E said I must hear all the gossip though, but I said I never listen to gossip."

Daisy smiled. "You did right. It's against hotel policy to talk to the newspapers and you shouldn't be chatting with the clientele either. It's not your place."

Jessie huffed. "Don't worry about me. I know me place." She glared at Daisy.

"I didn't mean…"

"Yes you did. Always trying to put me down you are. I don't know why I bother." She turned and stormed out.

"Got right snap on 'er that one," Mrs T said. "I'm surprised she don't blow a gasket."

"It's my fault," Daisy said. "I rub her up the wrong way. Can't seem to do anything right."

"Well, if you asks me she'd heading for a tumble. Folks don't take well to being chewed out when they've done nowt."

No and it's a sure way to lose her job and possibly lose me my job as well, Daisy thought. She went up to the tea room to check out the customer who may have come to find out what he could about the hotel to put it in some filthy rag.

"It's all right," Bridget said. "I've sent him on his way with a flea in his ear."

A little later Daisy went back to the tea room to see what they had for the laundry the next day and noticed Jessie was missing.

"Oh she caught a snag in her stocking," Bridget said. "She's just nipped out for some wool to repair it."

"Oh right," Daisy said, but a swell of unease swirled in her stomach all the same.

*

Lawrence felt he'd got no further in his quest to find out about his uncle's death. One thing was certain; he'd killed himself after losing all his money through a fraudulent investment scheme run by a man he trusted. Why had he trusted him? He'd been in business long enough to know there were unscrupulous men who preyed on the weaknesses of others. Men who exploit their vulnerability for their own ends. Why had Douglas Templeton been fooled? Had he been so blinded by the early returns that he failed to follow his instincts? Lawrence found that hard to believe. There must have been some other reason, but Lawrence couldn't think what it could be.

The next morning he visited the offices of the local newspaper, the paper that carried the cuttings his Aunt Doris had secreted away. He couldn't help feeling that he'd come on a wild goose chase but then he remembered Verity's face when she'd asked him for help and he recalled why he was doing it.

"I'm looking into the circumstances of my uncle's death," he said to the editor who greeted him on his arrival. "I'd like to see the papers that these come from, or anything relevant." He showed him the cuttings Verity had given him.

The editor glanced through them. "It's certainly our paper," he said, "but a bit before my time. Our Miss Wetherall's the archivist. She'll help you find what you're looking for. She's been here over forty years and no one knows the archives like Miss Wetherall."

Lawrence followed him down to the basement. There a diminutive woman in an old fashioned brown corduroy suit sat at one of the three reading desks set out in front of rows of floor to ceiling shelves stretching as far as the eye could see. The shelves held row upon row of large leather bound binders.

"Miss Wetherall," the editor said. "Mr Fitzroy is interested in searching the archives for details of his uncle's death. Perhaps you can help him."

Miss Wetherall glanced up, removed her glasses and rose, patting her steel grey hair into place. "I'm happy to help," she said making her way towards them. "What exactly is it you're after?"

"I'll leave you to it," the editor said. He left looking relieved.

"I'd like to read the rest of the papers that these come from," Lawrence said, handing Miss Wetherall the cuttings.

She took them, replaced her reading glasses and read slowly through them shaking her head as she did so. "This was a terrible tragedy," she said, taking off her glasses to gaze at Lawrence. "I remember it well. Awful thing for his family."

"You remember it?" Surprise lifted Lawrence's voice and his heart. "It was a long time ago."

Miss Wetherall nodded. "I didn't know him, but I knew his wife, Doris. Lovely woman. She used to help out at the church and she visited my mother while I was at work. My mother was quite elderly and she enjoyed the company. So sad what happened." She handed the cutting back. "I remember thinking at the time, 'it's a good job Doris isn't here to read this. It'd break her heart'."

"So, she wasn't here when these articles were written?"

"No. She'd gone by then. Gone to family I believe."

"But she had these cuttings. They were found among her things."

Miss Wetherall shrugged. "Someone must have sent them to her. Why would they do that? Wasn't it enough that she'd lost her husband? Honestly, I don't know what the world's coming to. Some people have no Christian charity." Miss Wetherall looked quite cross on Doris's behalf.

"Do you know anything about the other person involved? Mr Templeton's partner. Montgomery something?"

"No. I didn't know him or his business associates. 'His friends from the Lodge', Doris used to call them. I have no idea where they lived though. I wasn't really interested."

Lawrence smiled. So that was it. The fraternity of businessmen who prospered through mutual support, the solicitor had referred to. Fine friends indeed. He took out the photograph of the shooting party. "Do you recognise any of these men?"

Miss Wetherall put on her glasses and looked at the photograph. "No. Sorry. Like I said, I only knew Doris."

"Perhaps I could read the papers from that time. There may be other articles of interest that weren't sent to my aunt."

"Of course. Please take a seat." The archivist indicated a seat at one of the desks and Lawrence sat while she disappeared amid the rows of shelving. She returned about twenty minutes later wheeling a trolley on which lay a pile of large binders filled with papers. Several strands of hair had fallen from the pins that held them in place and she looked flustered. "I think you'll find these are what you're looking for."

Over the next three hours Lawrence went through the papers, turning the pages and reading the headlines. He found the columns the cuttings had been taken from. He scanned the rest of the pages and found nothing. He tried the next issue and the next. He scanned articles of local interest looking for a name that might stand out and still found nothing.

He was about to give up when he turned to the Court Notices and saw *Bankruptcy Hearing in the name of Parsimon Investments.*

He read on: *Parsimon Investments, founded by Mr Douglas Templeton and Mr Montgomery Summerville...*

Summerville! Douglas Templeton's partner was Montgomery Summerville! Of course it could be a coincidence. Possibly not even related. Maybe another branch of the family. Summerville was a not uncommon name, but all the same a frisson of excitement stirred within him. Maybe the answer he was looking for was closer than he thought.

He called Miss Wetherall over. "I wonder if you could tell me anything about this man, Montgomery Summerville," he said. "Anything at all."

Miss Wetherall put on her glasses and gazed at the item Lawrence had open on the desk. "Summerville... Summerville. I'm not sure. The name rings a bell. Was he a local businessman? We often print articles about functions they attend, social events, that sort of thing. He may appear in some of them."

"Possibly. It says here that he was a partner in Mr Templeton's business."

Her eyebrows rose. "Was he? Well then we should have something... although... hmm..."

"What?"

"Well if it was a bad business, and it sounds as though it was, anything controversial may not have been reported." She smiled at Lawrence. "This is a local newspaper. We depend on the goodwill of local businessmen and rely on the income from their advertising. We couldn't exist without them. The editor wouldn't print anything that showed a contributor in a bad light or impacted badly on their business. A man like that, we'd only put in what he wanted put in."

"So you've no idea what happened to him after the company was wound up? I heard that he'd gone abroad. Argentina."

She shook her head. "As I said, this is a local paper. Births, Deaths and Marriages. We tend to stick to those. You can't go much wrong with Births, Deaths and Marriages."

"So you don't know if he's still alive? If he had any family?"

"Sadly no... although..." She frowned. "We do keep a register of obituaries." She disappeared back into the shelves returning with another large folder. "People often come here looking for relatives who once lived in the area. It's easier to keep them all together." She opened the folder. The contents were listed by year. She turned to those after 1892 and ran her finger down the lists as she turned the pages, year after year. "Yes. Here we are," she cried in triumph. "Montgomery Summerville, died in August 1902 aged 75. He leaves a wife, two daughters and four grandchildren."

A swell of relief flowed over Lawrence. At least it was something. A start. "Thank you, Miss Wetherall. You've been most helpful."

"Thank you, Mr Fitzroy. I've enjoyed our little foray into the past. You've no idea how dull the archives can be most of the time." She smiled.

Lawrence left his card. "If you remember anything else."

"It'll be a pleasure," Miss Wetherall said with a wide grin on her face.

On the journey home Lawrence went over what he'd learned during the last few days. None of it changed anything. It merely confirmed what the papers said. Douglas Templeton had taken his own life after losing all his money through some disastrous, fraudulent investments. Is it any better to know your father was a gullible fool and not a swindler by intent? He supposed it may be a little more palatable but it didn't change the facts. He sighed, trying to find some bright spot in the whole debacle. Douglas Templeton had sent his family away to protect them. By his actions, he had avoided a court hearing and possible prison sentence, which would have sullied the family name. Had he done it by way of a sacrifice, to save the family the shame that would accompany being dragged through the courts, his failings daily reportage for the slavering herds who relished anyone's downfall? That was one way of looking at it. Then there was Montgomery Summerville's part in it. What would he gain by telling Verity of his involvement? The man was dead. There was no evidence of any connection to the Summervilles he knew, not yet anyway. That was definitely something he'd talk to Brandon about, but he didn't want to pre-judge the outcome of any future conversations.

Then there was the question of Verity's allowance. Where was that coming from? Not from the Templeton Estate that was for sure. Something else he'd need to look into. He sighed.

By the time his train reached King's Cross he'd decided to tell Verity that her father was unintentionally dragged into a swindle by an expert and killed himself to save the family any embarrassment. He thought her best interest would be served by dropping the matter and revering the memory of the man she knew and who so loved his family he gave his life to save them from his foolishness. If only she'd take his advice, he thought, she could put it behind her and get on with the rest of her life.

Chapter Twenty Nine

The next morning Daisy went into Mr Svenson's office to collect the list of departures and arrivals. He wasn't there but she saw the daily newspaper open on his desk. She glanced at the headline and her heart hammered. She picked up the paper to read it just as the door opened and Mr Svenson came in. Hastily she put the paper down and picked up the list of arrivals and departures. "Good morning," she said. "I was just collecting…"

"Fine." Clouds of disapproval filled Mr Svenson's face. "Don't let me keep you."

Daisy hurried out. She ran to reception where the papers had been delivered and not yet distributed to those who'd ordered them. She picked one off the top of the pile and went to her sitting room to read it. The headline read: *The Maître d' and the Chambermaid.* The article went on to relate details of Molly Brown's murder linked to the fact that she'd left the employ of The Fitzroy Hotel following an altercation involving the man who was then maître d'. *Mr Arthur Jevons is now in custody awaiting trial for murder,* it said. It then went on to give details of the hotel and some of its more disreputable history. The only good thing was the disclaimer at the end that said that the hotel bore no responsibility for the events following the maître d's dismissal.

Anger swirled inside Daisy. Her fists curled. The article echoed the same gossip and speculation she'd heard voiced in the kitchen among the staff. Jessie must have spoken to that reporter after all, she thought. She jumped up and, paper in hand, went to find where Jessie was working in one of the upstairs rooms. She found her working with Annie. "Can I have a word? Jessie," she said.

Annie knew to leave them. "I'll take the dirty laundry down," she said hurrying out.

"Well, what now?" Jessie's tone was one of defiance.

Daisy waved the paper at her. "That reporter, he got his story then."

"I don't know what you mean." Jessie took the paper and read it. "You think that I did this? Well, you're wrong. I never spoke to anyone." She threw the paper at Daisy. "Typical. Anything goes wrong in your little world and it must be me." Her voice rose with righteous indignation. "You just want to get rid of me. You didn't want me here in the first place, spoiling your little kingdom. Well, hard luck, 'cos I'm staying and I've done nothing wrong so you can stick it."

Daisy's resolve and irritation melted away as she realised Jessie was telling the truth. She was many things, but she wasn't a liar. If she'd done it she'd be crowing about it in a 'so what, what are you going to do about it' way. No. She'd got it wrong and she owed Jessie an apology. "I'm sorry," she said. "When you left the tea room I thought…"

"You thought I'd popped out to make trouble for you. Well, I didn't. I had a tear in me stocking and needed wool to mend it. You can ask Bridget." She turned to return to her work, shaking out the bedspread. "I wasn't the only one knew about Mr Jevons and Molly."

"No. Of course you weren't. I'm sorry, Jessie." She took a breath. She felt bad now. After all Jessie had gone through she should be supporting her, not blaming her for everything that goes amiss. "And you're wrong. I'm not trying to get rid of you. I'm pleased that you're here. You work hard and get on with the other staff. I just wish we could be friends again."

Jessie sniffed. Clearly she wasn't going to let Daisy off so easily. "Well," she said. "Apology accepted. As for being friends, we'll see."

Daisy left a little happier than when she'd arrived.

On Monday Verity decided to visit Ira Soloman at the bookshop. She felt guilty for neglecting him for so long. The last time she saw him was at her mother's funeral and it felt like forever ago. She hadn't written either. Now she could tell him about her visit to the Summer Exhibition and ask him about her father's death. He'd been a family friend. He may know something the Fitzroys didn't.

It was mid-morning by the time she arrived at the shop. As soon as Ira saw her he rose from behind the desk to greet her. "Verity, how lovely," he said. "What a welcome sight on a dull morning. How are you?" He kissed her cheek and held her at arm's length his glance running over her. "You look very well. London obviously suits you. You must tell me all about it."

"I am well," Verity said her heart suddenly lighter. "I've missed you and the bookshop." She glanced around. "It's good to be home, even if it is only for a few hours."

"I'll put some coffee on and you must tell me all the latest London gossip."

Verity laughed. "I don't know about that. I think my foray into high society has been a little underwhelming." She followed him through to the back kitchen and they sat and talked. She told him about the balls she'd attended and the Summer Exhibition. He told her about the latest art books she might like and the peculiarities of some of his customers. They passed a pleasant couple of hours like the old friends they were.

"There is one thing that's been troubling me," she said eventually. It had been on her mind throughout but she'd hesitated to bring it up, not wanting to spoil the morning.

"What is it, little one?" He'd called her 'little one' for as long as she could remember.

She took a breath. "I found some newspaper cuttings among my mother's things. Newspaper reports about my father's death. You knew him. Is it true he committed suicide?"

Ira Soloman put his hands to his head, his chin dropped to his chest. "Oy-vey," he said. "Such a terrible thing you should know. It's all in the past. A long time ago."

"I want to know," Verity said. "I want to know the truth. The newspapers said he was a cheat and a fraudster. Is it true?"

Ira shook his head. He gazed at Verity and took her hand. "Your father was a good man. A good friend. He loved you very much. Don't think badly of him. He did everything he could for you."

Tears filled Verity's eyes. "But he hanged himself. How could he? Why would he?" The tears ran freely down her cheeks as the swell of emotion she'd been holding back rose to the surface. Misery crashed over her like a summer storm.

Ira took out his handkerchief and handed it to her. He rose and put the kettle on to re-heat the coffee.

"Here drink this," he said, tipping a slug of brandy into the coffee.

Verity shook her head. "I just want to know the truth," she said. "Tell me please."

Ira sat. He sighed. "I don't know what the papers said or how much you've read about your father's business. I doubt much of it was true."

"So what did happen?"

Ira took her hand. "Don't judge him too harshly. He was an honest man and he expected others to be honest too, but he got involved with men who were dangerous and deceitful. Men who come out of every enterprise with their fortunes intact leaving a string of less fortunate people behind. If he was guilty of anything it was being too trusting."

"You mean he was swindled. Someone else was to blame?"

"Not entirely. The man he went into business with was no fool. He preyed on other's weaknesses, their greed, their feeling of entitlement to be rewarded for no effort. Douglas got sucked in. He put all his money into the company and persuaded his friends to do likewise. He invested more than he could afford to lose. But you can't build a company on fresh air. When the company folded, as it was bound to do, he lost everything so did his friends."

"Did you lose money too?"

Ira shrugged. "A little."

"I'm sorry." Verity put her hand on Ira's arm. She took a breath as thoughts whirred in her head. "So it was a fraud? My father was a swindler?"

"No. Not Douglas. His partner. He disappeared, leaving Douglas to take the blame."

"Who was he? This partner? Did they ever find him?"

Ira shrugged. "I don't know. I never met him." He stood and poured himself another cup of coffee. "I only know what I know from attending the inquest."

Verity took out a couple of the old photographs she'd kept from her mother's album. "Do you know any of these men. Would he be one of them?"

Ira glanced at the pictures. "I'm sorry. I wasn't included in your father's circle of friends. We played chess together. That was all. I didn't know him so well."

"But you were his best friend."

Ira smiled. "I like to think I was a good friend, but I was an outsider. Douglas was good to me. He accepted me for what I am." He smiled and sipped his coffee as though remembering something in the distant past. "A few days before he died Douglas sent you, your mother and sister away. He did it to protect you. He asked me to keep an eye on you. That's why I came here and bought the bookshop. To be near you, in case you needed me. It was the least I could do."

"So you've been here all these years like a guardian angel?"

Ira laughed. "Hardly an angel," he said.

When Verity returned to London she was pleased to see that Lawrence had also come home. Anxious to learn what he'd found out in Leeds and to tell him about her conversation with Ira Soloman she cornered him in his office. "I hope I'm not disturbing you," she said. "I've just got back myself and wanted to hear how you'd got on."

Lawrence smiled. "Please, sit. Always happy to be disturbed by you," he said. "First, tell me about your visit home. How was Mama?"

"In her element." Verity laughed. "The Camerons were lovely. I'm glad I went home. It's put things into perspective."

Lawrence's face brightened. "I hope that means you've made peace with what you discovered about your father," he said. "I'm afraid nothing I found out in Leeds does anything to change the facts. I'm only sorry I can't give you better news."

A stab of disappointment brought a bitter smile to Verity's face. "I think I was expecting too much," she said. She sighed. "I spoke to Ira Soloman. He was my father's friend. He told me that Papa was swindled out of all he owned. He said he was a good man and I shouldn't judge him too harshly."

"He sounds like a very wise man."

"You know, I think he is." Her lips twitched into a smile. "I've accepted that I can't change the past. I suppose that's something." Her shoulders dropped as the tension she'd been holding in them fell away.

"Good. So, tell me all about this Ira Soloman. What else did he say?"

Verity shrugged. "Only that he knew my father and used to play chess with him. When Papa died Mr Soloman came to live in Nettlesham. Apparently my father asked him to keep an eye on us. If I think about it he's always been there, in the background, when I was growing up. He often used to visit Mama. I think she found comfort in his visits."

"He owns the bookshop doesn't he?"

"Yes. That's right. I work in the shop, but, to be honest, I think it's more for company than anything.

I'm not the world's greatest sales person. He lets me display my watercolours."

Lawrence nodded. "So, what are your plans now?"

"Well, there are a few more exhibitions I'd like to see and Charlotte's invited me to accompany her to the theatre next week. Then there's the opera you mentioned." She smiled.

"Ah. Yes, the opera. All in hand." He didn't look convinced.

Once Verity had gone Lawrence sat back and pondered what to do next. He was glad that Verity had come to terms with her loss, but still had a few loose ends to tie up. He wanted to speak to Brandon Summerville to see if he knew anything about a possible link to Douglas's partner, but first he planned to visit the bank and find out about Verity's allowance. Being the Executor of her mother's estate would be all the authorisation he needed. This Ira Soloman was something else. A friend of Douglas who knew him personally and was fond enough to keep in touch with the family after his death. Up until now he'd only spoken to people who knew of him, none who were close enough to be called a friend. Perhaps the bookshop in Nettlesham would be worth a visit. He didn't anticipate finding out anything of any great consequence, but he hated to leave a job half-done.

Chapter Thirty

The next evening Daisy was surprised to see Jessie in the kitchen when she'd had the afternoon off. She didn't look too happy either. "Is everything all right?" she asked. "I didn't expect you back so early."

Jessie shrugged. "I had some sewing to do. I thought I'd finish that blouse I started."

Daisy frowned. That didn't sound like Jessie. Something must be up. "I have some lace you could add," she said. "It would look lovely on the collar."

"If you say so." Jessie's mood didn't improve.

"It's in my sitting room."

Jessie followed her into the room.

"How's Charlie?" Daisy said once they were alone. She guessed that was the reason Jessie was so out of sorts.

Jessie bit her lip as though hesitant to speak. "I'm not sure," she said at last. "He was a bit off today. That's why I came home early. He kept asking me questions about the hotel and the staff. I said 'I thought it was me you were interested in, not the hotel' and he went all quiet. I think he's up to something."

Daisy didn't know whether to be relieved that she'd seen though him at last or worried she might be right. "What sort of up to something? What did he want to know?"

"Well, when people went bed, when we got up, that sort of thing. Do you think I should mention it to Mr Svenson? Just in case?"

"Mr Svenson? No I don't think we should bother him."

"But suppose something happens and we thought it might and never said anything? At least if we report it we'll be in the clear if he does do anything."

"Yes, but Mr Svenson…"

"He's in charge isn't he? And he's got a soft spot for you."

Daisy was shocked. "A soft spot for me? What are you talking about? Don't be ridiculous. He's got no such thing."

Jessie giggled. "'Course 'e 'as. I've seen 'im looking at you. You should grab him while you can. You'll not get many more chances." She laughed.

Daisy shook her head. "Seriously though, what do you think Charlie's planning?"

"Well, he asked if everyone got paid in cash every week. I thought it was because he wanted me to give 'im me wages, but 'e didn't ask for them. Then there was the thing about the night porter…"

"You mean a robbery?"

"Why not? There's cash kept in the safe as well as the guests' valuables. I reckon Charlie's got enough out of me to know the ins and out of the place. I'd feel awful bad if he's bin using me to further 'is evil intentions."

"Well, I must admit, it sounds like something Charlie Benton would do. I think you're right. We should tell…" she wanted to say Mr Lawrence, but she couldn't bring herself to bother him with pure speculation. Jessie was right; Mr Svenson was the right person to tell. Then, if there was nothing in it she'd only look a fool in his eyes. "…Mr Svenson. Come with me."

Jessie followed her up to Mr Svenson's office. "Have you got a moment?" Daisy said.

"Come in." He beamed at them and moved a second chair to the front of the desk so they both could sit. "What can I do for you?"

Hesitatingly and stumbling over her words Daisy told him about their suspicions. She was careful not to mention Jessie's relationship to Charlie Benton, merely saying she'd run into a chap who used to be a friend but had got into bad company. She stressed that they had no evidence, but he'd been a little too inquisitive about the routine of the hotel and, knowing his character, she thought she should bring it to his attention.

He sat back in his chair, stroking his chin. "You think this is a serious threat?"

"I'd say so," Jessie said.

"Anything of value is kept in the safe," Mr Svenson said. "I'm not sure anyone would…"

"That won't make any difference," Jessie said. "'Is old man robbed a bank. They kept everything in the safe there an' all."

Mr Svenson's eyebrows rose. "Hmm. Well, I suppose we should prepare just in case. Do you have any idea when this raid might take place?"

Jessie shook her head. "It'll be soon. He'll not hang around once 'e's made up 'is mind."

Mr Svenson drew the large diary on his desk towards him. He flicked through some of the pages. "If he knows the hotel routine the most likely day would be the day I collect the wages from the bank. That's the day after tomorrow."

Daisy and Jessie exchanged glances.

Mr Svenson closed the diary and smiled. "Thank you for telling me. I don't think I need to detain you ladies any longer. Please ask Mr Barker to come up."

"What will you do?" Daisy was anxious to know if she could help or if either her or Jessie would be involved.

Mr Svenson's lips pressed together in an impatient smile. "I shall be making arrangements to keep the hotel property safe. Thank you."

Daisy felt the dismissal. She hurried Jessie out, feeling as though the world was about to collapse around her.

Lawrence's next call was to the bank. Verity had no hesitation telling him which branch dealt with her allowance. "Papa arranged everything," she said, although Lawrence knew that not to be the case.

"I just want to check that it's all in order," he said. "Your mother didn't seem to have any allowance at all."

When he arrived at the bank the manager, a man only a few years older than Lawrence but infinitely more sombre, showed him into his office. "Miss Templeton?" he said, stroking a turning grey moustache. "I'll need to see some sort of authority or identification."

"Of course." Lawrence showed him the papers Verity has signed giving him permission to access any records the bank held. "I'm dealing with her mother's estate," he said. "She doesn't appear to receive any allowance."

The bank manager opened a large ledger on the desk in front of him. He sniffed as he perused the pages. "No," he said. "The only account I have pertains to an allowance on behalf of Miss Verity Templeton. I understand she is a minor and therefore the account is held in the name of the trustee with arrangements for her to access it."

He turned the ledger around to face Lawrence, open at a page showing regular cash withdrawals.

"Well, that seems to be in order," Lawrence said. "Do you have the Deed of Trust? Perhaps I can see that."

"Of course. I thought you might ask." He opened a folder on the desk and picked up a thick document tied with a pink ribbon. He tipped his head back to read the document. "According to the trust set up by Mr Ira Soloman the beneficiaries are Henrietta and Verity Templeton (the named persons) until they reach maturity or marry, whichever is the sooner."

"Mr Ira Soloman?" Lawrence's brows drew together in puzzlement.

"Precisely. According to the Deed of Trust the payments continue until such time as stated. Any residue remaining when the youngest named person reaches maturity, or marries, may be kept for the benefit of any children of the aforementioned named persons." He put the document down. "That's the gist of it."

"And the current balance of the trust?"

The bank manager sniffed again and wrinkled his nose so his glasses rose up slightly before dropping back down again. The capital sum invested was…" He wrote a note on a piece of paper. "And the current investment…" He wrote another figure on the paper and passed it to Lawrence. It was a healthy amount.

Lawrence nodded. "Thank you," he said. "You've put my mind at rest. I feel sure I have no need to worry further about my cousin's affairs."

The bank manager closed the ledger. With the business at hand satisfactorily completed he smiled at Lawrence and rose to show him out. "Always happy to help a client," he said.

Outside Lawrence paused, his mind in a whirl. He didn't quite know what to make of the information the bank manager had given him. Ira Soloman had set up a trust for Douglas's children. Why would he do that? What did he hope to gain from it? Where did he get the money? There must be more to it than meets the eye. Nobody puts money into trust for someone else's children without a very good reason.

He walked on deep in contemplation. Perhaps it's time for me to visit the bookshop and meet this Ira Soloman, he thought.

The next morning at breakfast he told Verity he would be spending the day at Maldon Hall on business. She said she had some letters to write and intended to spend the afternoon visiting the National Gallery with Lydia. "It's been a while since I've been," she said, "and I want to make the most of my time in town."

"I hope she's not going to lead you into more trouble," he said. "We don't want you ending up in prison again."

Verity laughed. "No fear of that. We're only going to look at the pictures. She's very knowledgeable. I value her expertise."

"Good. Give her my regards. She did appear to be quite sensible."

He arrived in Nettlesham around mid-morning and, instead of taking a cab to Maldon Hall, walked along the High Street until he found the bookshop. A glance in the window told him it was a respectable sized business with a wide selection of stock. Inside a girl behind the desk rose to greet him.

She smiled. "Can I help you?"

"I'd like to see the proprietor, erm... Mr Ira Soloman. Is he available?"

She smiled again. "Of course, sir. Whom shall I say wishes to see him?"

"Mr Lawrence Fitzroy." He handed her his card and she scurried away. A few seconds later she returned followed by an elderly, grey whiskered man Lawrence took to be Ira Soloman.

Ira Soloman held out his hand as he stepped forward. "Mr Fitzroy, a pleasure to meet you. Please come through."

Lawrence nodded to the girl and followed his host through to the back of the shop where they passed a small room, the door open to reveal a desk cluttered with papers and books. Mr Soloman showed Lawrence into what was obviously a small staff sitting room. A girl, just finishing coffee, rose as they entered. "I think we'll be more comfortable in here," Ira Soloman said. He smiled at the girl who looked a little flustered.

"I was just going," she said, putting her coffee cup on the side. "Excuse me."

Once they were alone Lawrence sat in one of the well-padded armchairs either side of a modest fireplace. The room had a cosy feel about it, neat but homely, he thought.

"The coffee's freshly made," Mr Soloman said. "May I offer you some?" He spoke with a slight accent which Lawrence found charming. He warmed to this slight, almost frail man with a friendly face and piercing blue eyes.

"Thank you," he said. "I suppose you know who I am."

Ira Soloman smiled. "Of course. You are Verity's cousin. And, if I am not mistaken, her guardian."

"As head of the family I have responsibility for her if that's what you mean."

Mr Soloman handed him a cup of coffee. "Verity talks of you often," he said. "And, since our last conversation I have been expecting you to call. I am very happy to meet you."

"Then I'll waste no time getting to the reason I've called."

"Good." Ira sat in the chair opposite Lawrence with his coffee.

Lawrence told him about his visit to Leeds, the solicitor and the newspaper office. Then he went on to his meeting with the bank manager. Ira Soloman sat, nodding throughout, occasionally sipping his coffee, his eyes bright with interest.

"You have all the facts and none of the emotion," Ira said. "It was a terrible time. Douglas knew he'd made a mistake but was in no position to correct it. He feared for his family and wanted to protect them from the furore he knew would come. I was an outsider, you understand. He felt he could turn to me and I was happy to help him."

"Tell me about the trust fund."

"Ah the trust fund." Ira chuckled. "You look at me and wonder, why did this old Jew set up a trust fund for his friend's children?" His eyes sparkled with glee. "You are right to be sceptical. I am not a man who does things without a reason." He put his coffee on a table at the side. "I know about family," he said. "My family were hounded out of Russia and came to this country with nothing. Only by working hard did we manage to survive. Even here we found prejudice and suspicion. But Douglas was different. He was a good friend. When he realised the state of the company he had become embroiled with he wanted to do something to protect his family."

"Friendship is one thing, but putting aside such a sum of money for another man's children?"

Ira smiled and bowed his head. "You may have seen from his papers that Douglas owned a house. Did you not wonder what may have happened to it?"

Lawrence nodded. "I did see there was mention of a transfer of the property, but I found no proceeds of sale."

"That is where the money for the trust came from. It was Douglas's way of making sure they were not left penniless. He knew Doris would be looked after. Her brother, your father, would take care of her. But he wanted himself to give his children some legacy, some inheritance. You understand?"

"So it was put in your name because…"

"Because, even now, if his creditors knew of any money it would be forfeited. Even now…"

Lawrence sat for a moment staring at the old man. "You took quite a risk. If anyone found out you'd be…"

"In trouble. Yes. So no one must find out. No reason they should is there? The children understand that their legacy comes from their father. It is as it should be."

"And they have no idea of your part in it?"

Ira shook his head. "What was it but a kind deed for a friend?"

Lawrence smiled. "Of course. All perfectly straight forward. You have been a good friend."

Warmth flooded the old man's face. "I have no children of my own," he said. "When I die this shop," he glanced around, "everything will go to Verity. She's been like a daughter to me."

"I know she's very fond of you," Lawrence said and she'd been even fonder if she knew the truth, he thought.

"I hope that you too will count me as a friend."

Lawrence leaned across and shook Ira's hand. "A very good friend," he said.

Chapter Thirty One

As June turned to July the summer heat mellowed. Verity looked forward to the night of the opera, even the early drizzly rain unable to dampen her spirits. It would be a special occasion and Lawrence had organised the party of six to take a box at the Royal Opera House for the first London performance of *Madame Butterfly*. Charlotte would come with her brother Edward, and Brandon would accompany Lydia, leaving Lawrence to escort her. It promised to be an enthralling night out.

When they arrived at the Opera House it was everything she'd hoped. The gilt walls, crystal chandeliers, the magnificent stage, the settings, everything was perfect. She noticed Charlotte edging herself into a seat at the front next to where Lawrence would sit. Lydia sat the other side of her next to Edward, leaving herself and Brandon who sat on the end. He smiled at her as they took their seats and the overture began. She struggled to contain the hammering of her heart.

Throughout the performance she sat entranced, hardly taking her gaze from the stage, her enjoyment heightened by Brandon whispering some of the finer points of the story to her, his voice soft and engaging. It felt magical, as though they were sharing something intimate and precious. As the story unfolded her happiness turned to tears. She gasped and squeezed her eyes shut at the end when Cio-Cio-San took out the sword her father had used to commit suicide. "Oh no," she breathed. Brandon comforted her, handing her his clean white handkerchief.

"Thank you," she said as they gathered their things to leave. "I feel such a fool."

He smiled. "It's not foolish to feel emotion," he said. "It was an incredible performance."

They went to the Carlton Rooms for supper. My word, Lawrence really has pushed the boat out, Verity thought, but she'd had such a wonderful evening nothing could spoil it. She half expected Charlotte to turn her considerable charms on Brandon for the rest of the evening, but to her surprise all her attention was taken by Lawrence. Well, he had paid for it all, Verity reasoned. Over supper they talked about the performance, which everyone had found profoundly moving.

"It's a night I'll never forget," Verity said as the memory of the music and the story on stage lingered in her mind. Even the supper was one of most convivial she could ever recall.

"It's been a wonderful evening," Charlotte said. "It's a pity it has to end. I'd love to go dancing now. What about it, Lawrence? I know the perfect place, and you did say."

"Well I…"

"You'll come, won't you, Verity?" Charlotte said. "It'll be fun."

Verity forced a smile. She'd had a lovely evening and could understand why Charlotte didn't want it to end, but she couldn't sleep in until noon like Charlotte.

"Oh come on. Don't be an old curmudgeon."

Verity saw Lawrence's reluctance, but Charlotte was bound to get her way. She always did. Edward declined to go and Lydia likewise, dropped out of the party.

"Count me in," Brandon said, much to Verity's surprise. "I'm not about to pass up a chance to dance with Miss Templeton."

"Verity, please," Verity said.

"Verity." The way he said it gave her goose bumps all over.

In the end it was just the four of them, Edward happy to see Lydia safely home. Verity couldn't work out why Brandon had decided to come to along. He hadn't seemed like a dancer to her. Could it be that he wanted to be with Charlotte after all? She could think of no other explanation.

When they arrived at the club Verity's doubts began to surface. They descended into a smoky, dimly-lit cellar where tables were set out around a small dance floor. A pianist sat on a raised dais accompanied by a saxophonist and a trumpet player all playing foot-tapping music, which, to Verity's ears, after the opera, sounded like a cacophony of noise. Charlotte was delighted. "Isn't it amazing," she said, slipping her coat off. "Come on."

They found a table and, as they took their seats around it, a waiter appeared. "Champagne," Charlotte called out. "We must have champagne."

He brought the champagne and they sat and watched couples moving around the floor. Most people sat listening to the music. A group of men crowded around a small bar in the corner.

"Come on," Charlotte said, dragging Lawrence onto the floor. At least she's enjoying herself, Verity thought.

"I'm not sure what sort of dance one does to this music," Brandon said. "But I'm willing to give it a go if you are."

Verity nodded and before she knew it she was up in his arms. They swayed gently to the music moving slowly around the floor. She breathed in the warm woody smell of him and her heart raced. Something else I'll never forget, she thought.

When the music stopped they returned to the table. Whether it was the noise, the champagne or the hot stuffy atmosphere, Verity wasn't sure, but her head began to spin and she felt hot all over. Feeling ill at ease and not wanting to spoil everyone's evening, she excused herself to go to the ladies room. I just need a bit of air, she thought. The men stood as she left.

In the ladies room she took a couple of breaths, splashed her face and hands with cold water and chided herself for being so stupid. Everyone else was enjoying themselves, why couldn't she? She'd just have to carry on and make the best of it. Having calmed the anxiety that raged inside her she went out to make her way back to the table where the others were sitting.

The band had resumed playing and, as she passed the bar, a man lurched towards her. He grabbed her and pulled her onto the floor. "Come and dance with me," he slurred, the smell of drink heavy on his breath.

"Get off me." Verity tried to push him away but he was too strong for her. The memory of Bertie at the Boat Race Ball filled her mind. She felt sick and frightened. She closed her eyes to shut the horror out. Suddenly she felt him pulled away from her. When she opened her eyes she saw Brandon, his hands gripping the man's lapels, lifting him off the ground and pushing him against the bar. "Leave the lady alone," he said. "Unless you want to breathe through a hole in your throat for the rest of your life."

The man's eyes bulged. He could hardly speak. "Sorry," he managed to squeak. "My mistake."

Brandon put him down and turned to Verity, his face dark as thunder. "Come on," he said. "Let's get out of here."

Back at the table Charlotte was still laughing and drinking champagne.

"Verity needs to go home," Brandon said.

Lawrence jumped up. "Is everything all right?"

"I can take her, if you want to stay."

Lawrence didn't look as though he wanted to stay, but he could hardly leave Charlotte who pouted, "Leaving already. It's still early."

"It's all right, Lawrence," Verity said, seeing his difficulty. "I'm happy to go with Mr Summerville."

"Brandon, please,"

Verity smiled. "Brandon."

"We won't be long," Lawrence said, casting a worried glance at Charlotte. "If you're sure?"

"I'm sure," Verity said and sighed with relief.

Outside the air felt fresh and cool. The earlier rain had stopped and street lights reflected in wet pavements. Brandon called a cab and they rattled through empty streets.

"I'm surprised you didn't stay with Charlotte," Verity said. "She'd be better company that me."

A smile lit his face. "I like Charlotte but one can have too much of a good thing. Her constant frivolity becomes tiresome after a while."

How pompous he sounds, she thought. "At least there's no danger of any frivolity with me," she said. "You have no fear of that."

He chuckled. "I'm glad to hear it." The mirth dancing in his eyes made Verity's heart leap. What an infuriating man he is, she thought.

She glanced out of the window as they passed dark buildings silhouetted against a lightening sky. Sitting together in the cab she felt the nearness of him. It was a pleasant feeling. "It must be nearly dawn," she said.

"In an hour or two, maybe."

"There's something magical about watching the sun rise isn't there? Seeing the start of a new day," she mused.

"It depends, I suppose, on what the day has in store. What lies ahead of you." His voice was soft with warmth.

"Of course," she said, smiling. "It reminds me of lambing time, or waiting up all night for a mare to foal." She took a breath, realising how provincial she sounded. "I'm sorry, it's another life."

"And a charming one from the sound of it."

She laughed. "You wouldn't say that if you lived on a farm. Mostly it's hard work with little reward, but there are moments." She lapsed into silence as though remembering those moments.

"I envy you," he said.

Her brow furrowed. "Really?"

"Really," he nodded.

Daisy Carter had decided not to go to bed when Mr Svenson, Barker and Hollis were taking turns to keep watch in the office in case Jessie had been right about Charlie Benton's plan. She decided to settle down for the night in her sitting room where she'd be able to hear any commotion upstairs or any alarm sounding. She dozed fitfully in a chair covered with a blanket.

What if nothing happened and they'd stayed up all night for nothing? She couldn't think about that. She was in Mr Svenson's bad books enough already. This would make it worse, but on the other hand she couldn't let Charlie rob the hotel without making an effort to stop him.

It must have been almost dawn before anything happened. She heard the alarm and Barker shouting. She leapt up and ran upstairs, tripping over her petticoats in her haste. Cursing under her breath she almost reached the office when a man barged past knocking her to the ground. Mr Svenson followed clutching his arm. She lay there, winded, her head spun. The man wasn't Charlie. Where was Charlie? She heard Barker cursing and tried to get up. Her shoulder hurt and she'd twisted an ankle but she struggled up. I'll be damned if he's going to get away with it, she thought. Through the open door she saw Barker pushing Charlie against the wall, his arm twisted up behind him. At nineteen, Charlie was thin and gangly and no match for Barker's bulk and experience.

"I've got 'im. I've got 'im," Barker cried out the delight clear in his voice. "The police are on the way. We've got 'im, Daisy."

She limped over to where Barker was holding Charlie. "Got you, Charlie Benton," she said, her voice laced with spite. "You'll be going to prison for a long time and I'll tell you something else. If you ever come anywhere near Jessie again I'll be after you and I'll swing for you, Charlie Benton. You can bet your life on it."

When Verity and Brandon arrived back at the hotel he helped her out of the cab. "Thank you, I'll be fine now. Please take the cab…"

"I'll just see you in." Brandon motioned for the cabbie to wait. They went into the hotel and were immediately confronted by the sight of a large man stumbling towards them waving a knife in the air. Mr Svenson, the hotel under manager, staggered along behind him while trying to stem the flow of blood from a gash in his arm. "Stop thief," Mr Svenson yelled.

Verity froze, but Brandon's reactions were quicker. He hurled himself at the man, tackling him to the ground. She watched in horror as they rolled back and forth. The man being heavier rolled on top of Brandon. He raised the knife ready to plunge it into his adversary. A large potted aspidistra sat on a plinth in the hallway. Without thinking Verity picked it up and smashed it over the man's head, sending him sprawling on top of Brandon.

"Well done, Miss Templeton," Mr Svenson said coming up beside her just as the hotel porter arrived with two police constables.

"Well done, Hollis," Mr Svenson, who looked a little pale, said.

"We'll take over now," one of the constables said. "You'd best get to the hospital with that. It'll need a stitch." He nodded at Mr Svenson's arm and Verity noticed blood seeping through his fingers. She was still shaking. Hollis helped the other constable lift the man off Brandon.

"Is he alright? I haven't killed him have I?"

"No. He's fine. Just a bit concussed. He'll have a terrible headache though," the constable said.

Brandon brushed himself down as he got up. "I do believe you've saved my life," he said to Verity.

Verity gazed into his eyes. She was still shaking, her knees turned to jelly. The blood drained from her face as, suddenly overcome by the enormity of what she'd done, she fainted. Luckily Brandon was there to catch her.

Chapter Thirty Two

Lawrence arrived back at the hotel shortly after dawn in an irritated mood. He'd seen first-hand what Chester meant about his little girl having expensive tastes. Not only had Charlotte ordered a constant supply of champagne and danced until the early hours, she then insisted he take her for a drive along by the Thames to watch the sun rise and quoted Wordsworth at him. Any other time, if he hadn't been so tired and worried about Verity, he'd have enjoyed the romance of it, but as it was, it was just another expense to add to the cost of the evening.

He'd taken her home, hoping to at least be able to grab a couple of hours sleep before his morning's work began, only to find Barker, with a torn uniform and a black eye, waiting for him in reception.

Barker greeted him. "Don't worry, Mr Lawrence. We got 'em. Got 'em bang to rights. They won't be giving us any more trouble."

"Got whom? What do you mean? What exactly happened here?" he asked, puzzled as to why things didn't look quite right.

Barker grinned. "Well, you see, we 'ad a tip-off." He tapped the side of his nose. "We was ready for 'em. Mr Svenson, Hollis and me. Don't worry they wouldn't have got owt anyway. Mr Svenson emptied the safe, all the cash and valuables are in 'is room. We fooled 'em proper. A good night's work, if you don't mind me saying, sir."

Lawrence took a moment to take it in. "You mean a robbery? Here at the hotel?"

"That's right, sir. But forewarned is forearmed as they say. So, we got 'em. Shame about Mr Svenson.

We didn't reckon on more 'an one see. But it's only a flesh wound, they say. He'll be right as rain in no time."

Confused, Lawrence felt like a ship at sea, adrift with the wind taken out of its sails, the evening's irritation replaced by overwhelming concern. "Is everyone all right?"

"Oh aye, sir. All of us, thanks in part to Miss Templeton. She played a blinder, if you don't mind me saying, sir."

"Miss Templeton was involved?" Sudden fear stirred in his stomach. "Where is she?"

"Mr Summerville took 'er to 'er room, sir. He's gone now, but Jessie's staying with her. No need to worry, sir. All taken care of."

It all felt far from taken care of. "Thank you, Barker." He smiled. "It seems I left the hotel in good hands. Mr Svenson is…?"

"At the 'ospital, sir. Miss Carter's in your office with a policeman. She'll tell you all about it."

"Thank you." He made his way to the office, unsure of what he would find there but seeing Daisy Carter talking to a police constable he was suddenly reassured.

The reassurance didn't last long. Miss Carter was visibly upset and her garbled explanation left him wondering. Her words had come out with a torrent of tears and he could hardly make sense of them. When Mr Svenson returned, his arm bandaged and in a sling, it was clear he would be unfit for work for at least a couple of days. He gave Barker, Hollis and Miss Carter the morning off, telling them only to return to work when they felt able.

"Just a quick wash and change and I'll be back, sir," Barker said, like the old soldier he was. "Don't worry about me."

"Thank you." Lawrence smiled, relieved at his reliability. "Get Mrs T to give you something for that eye."

"Yes, sir. Thank you, sir." Barker grinned.

Now, just as he'd got things settled Inspector Rolleston wanted to see him and he hadn't even had time for breakfast.

"Come in, Inspector," Lawrence said showing him to a seat. "Although I'm not sure how I can help you. Miss Carter has already made a statement to one of your constables."

"Indeed, sir, but there are one or two details I need to clarify." He sat and took out a battered notebook.

"You would be better speaking to Mr Svenson. He will be able to help you more than I can."

"Mr Svenson?" The Inspector glanced at his notebook, looking baffled. "I don't have his name down here."

"I wasn't here. Mr Svenson was. He caught them red-handed. He's in his room. I can send for him."

"Red handed? You mean a burglary?"

"Isn't that why you're here?"

"No, sir. Not at all. I'm checking facts regarding the attack on Miss Molly Brown."

"Molly Brown?"

"The chambermaid who was murdered."

"I know very well who she is – or was – but I don't see what I can add to my previous statement." The irritation he'd felt earlier returned.

"That's the thing, sir. Your statement. In it you say Miss Brown accused Mr Jevons of attacking her."

"Correct – although I knew it to be utter nonsense, which has since proved to be the case."

"Quite so, sir, but in your statement you say you sent for Mr Jevons but he couldn't be found."

"Correct."

Inspector Rolleston nodded. "So the man purporting to be Miss Brown's brother," he consulted his notebook, "Mr Jimmy Daikins, commonly known as 'Blagger', never saw Mr Jevons?"

"That's correct."

"And yet he identified him by name as being the man seen arguing with Miss Brown shortly before her death. You see my problem, sir. How could he identify him having never seen him before?"

"Well, obviously he lied, just as he lied about the original attack."

"My thoughts entirely, sir." Inspector Rolleston sighed, closed his notebook and put it back in his pocket. "In the circumstances I have no option but to release Mr Jevons."

"I'm glad to hear it." Some good news at last, Lawrence thought. "Mr Jevons isn't a killer."

"No, but someone killed her. We just have to find out who."

Soft morning light filtered through the lace curtained window as Verity awoke lying on her bed, fully clothed, with one of the maids standing over her. "You all right, miss?" the girl said. "Mr Summerville was right worried."

The memory of what had happened ran through Verity's mind in slow motion. She still couldn't believe it. She'd picked up a pot and smashed it over a man's head. How could she do that? "Mr Summerville? Is he...?"

"He's gone, miss. Just said I was to stay and watch over you."

The memory of his strong arms around her filled her mind. She pushed it away. "I'm fine," she said, mentally checking every muscle in her body. "I must have dozed off. What time is it?"

"Just gone seven, miss. You'll have time to wash and change before breakfast. If there's nothing else..."

"No. Thank you. I mustn't keep you."

"I'll let Mr Lawrence know you're all right. He's bin right worried an' all."

"Really? Yes, I expect he has. Thank you." She dismissed the girl with a nod.

The girl bobbed a curtsy before leaving. I must look a mess, Verity thought, easing herself onto her feet. She still felt a little wobbly, but took a breath. In the bathroom she splashed her face and changed into a green and white printed cotton day dress with a high lace collar and lace-trimmed cuffs. She brushed her dark hair until it shone and pinned it up with a tortoiseshell comb. She pinched her cheeks to bring a little colour before going down to breakfast.

Downstairs Lawrence rose to greet her. "Verity. How are you?" He kissed her cheek. "I was so worried. I'm sorry I shouldn't have left you last night. It was unforgivable."

"Nonsense. I was in good hands, and so it proved. You have no need to blame yourself. Anyway, I'm fine. Fully recovered." She glanced around. A huge bouquet of roses, hydrangea, lilies, carnations and summer flowers stood on the side.

"Those came for you," Lawrence said. "I had them put in here as I didn't want to disturb you."

Verity's lips spread into a smile. "How lovely. Who…"

"Who do you think?"

Verity opened the card and read *With thanks and gratitude, Always, Brandon.* "Oh," she gasped. "Brandon. How kind." Her heart beat a tattoo in her chest and hot blood rushed to her face. She hoped Lawrence hadn't noticed.

"I'll have them taken to you room." Lawrence rang for the maid. "I heard what happened. You were quite the heroine. Brandon has much to be thankful for."

Verity found herself blushing again as the memory filled her mind. "I think he was the hero," she said. "Tackling the ruffian like that. I swear my heart nearly stopped."

"You were very brave and quick thinking. I can't imagine what would have happened if you hadn't stepped in."

Verity laughed. "Brandon said I saved his life. I didn't of course. He'd have got the better of that villain eventually."

"I'm not so sure but I'll be seeing Brandon later to thank him for his part in it. Apparently you and my staff managed to avert a burglary for which I'll be eternally grateful. It's not just the money, it's the hotel's reputation."

"I trust they too have been rewarded."

Lawrence grinned. "Of course. There'll be a bit extra in their pay packets this week." He ushered her up to the table. "Now come and have some breakfast and tell me what happened at the club last night. Why you left in such a rush. I have a feeling there was something wrong. Was there?"

Verity shrugged. She helped herself to some scrambled eggs and bacon from the dishes on the side. "A drunk at the bar got a little too friendly," she said. "Brandon came to my rescue. It was nothing."

"Nothing? It didn't seem like nothing last night. I wish I'd been there. It seems I have something else to thank Brandon for."

"It's fine, Lawrence. Honestly. Now how did you get on with Charlotte?"

A fleeting look of irritation crossed his face. "I wish we'd never gone to that place. I can't imagine what Charlotte sees in it." He picked up a slice of toast and buttered it. "I'm afraid I wasn't at my best. I'm sorry."

"Charlotte likes to think of herself as a rebel," Verity said. "I'm sure she was impressed and delighted that you indulged her."

"I have a feeling that being indulged is a fair part of her *raison d'être*. I'm not sure I could keep up with her expectations."

Verity laughed. "Don't put yourself down, Lawrence. You're far too good for her."

"Hmm. I wish." He bit into his toast.

Verity got on with her breakfast but Brandon was never far from her mind.

"I've been thinking," Lawrence said, after a while. "It may be best if you go home to Maldon Hall for a while. Mama would be glad of the company and it'll give you time to get over your ordeal."

Verity jerked to attention. "Go home? Why? I'm perfectly happy here."

"I was thinking of your safety. After yesterday…"

Verity's heart sank. Go home. Just when she was beginning to enjoy herself. "No, Lawrence. I'm fine and I have plans. I don't want to let people down." It wasn't true. She didn't have any plans, but she had hopes and they counted didn't they?

"Very well, if you're sure, although I'd be happier if you were with someone, just in case."

"There's no need, Lawrence. Honestly, I'm sure."

Chapter Thirty Three

The news of Mr Jevon's release soon reached the kitchen. "I knew 'e didn't do it," Bridget said. "Poor man. Typical police though. Pick a suspect and then try to make the facts fit."

"Do you think he'll get his job back?" Peggy asked. "After all he hasn't done anything."

"No. Not even 'is job. Poor man indeed, but once they turn to drink…"

"I can't see Mr Svenson having him back," Hollis said. "He'll be in charge now won't 'e. So much for years of service."

"Well, I'm glad 'e's not coming back," Annie said. "I like the new man better. Old Mr Jevons got a bit above 'imself if you ask me."

"No one did ask you," Mrs T said.

Hearing the gossip Daisy wondered if it was time to visit Matilda again. If Mr Jevons was out, where were the police looking now? If she could find out any further information it might go some way to putting her back in Mr Lawrence's good books. Heaven knows she needed it. He'd been a bit off with her ever since the Molly incident. Now she wanted to put things right. Anyway, an afternoon with Matilda always involved a lot of gossip and anything she could pick up would make her feel better.

The afternoon sun dappled through the trees as she walked. She could have taken a bus but decided to make the most of the good weather. The streets were busy with shoppers and people about their business. She'd brought some of Peggy's jam tarts as a treat for Matilda to have with their tea. Ralfie would be down for his afternoon nap and Matilda would be glad of a chance to sit and gossip.

"Phew," Matilda said when she arrived. "I'm glad to see you. I'm fair done in today."

Daisy followed her into the small kitchen overlooking a tidy garden. The back door was open to let in some air. She took off her hat and coat. "I'll make the tea, should I?" she said. "You have a sit-down for a change."

"Thanks," Matilda said manoeuvring herself into a chair. "I'll be glad when this one comes, 'e's bin giving me gip."

Daisy made the tea and set out the jam tarts on a plate on the table. She noticed the dark shadows under Matilda's eyes and guessed she hadn't been sleeping much. "How have you been?" she asked,

"Oh, you know."

Daisy started by telling her all the news of the hotel and the other staff. Then she mentioned Mr Jevon's release.

"I know," Matilda said. "'Course we all knew 'e didn't do it. George says they've 'ad to think again." She picked up her cup and took a sip of tea. Daisy waited.

"George says they're looking at the club where she worked. You know, them toffs. He says it's a place no better than it should be. A place where men with enough money can do whatever they like and no one asks any questions. Disgusting he calls it." She took another sip of tea and rubbed her back as though in pain. "You know my George. Straight as a church pew."

"Indeed I do," Daisy said. "I know he'll want to do what's right. Any idea of what they intend?"

"Well, between you and me," Matilda leaned forward her voice dropped to a whisper, "and this mustn't go any further – he thinks they're going to raid the club one night. Shake the tree, he says and see what falls out." She sat back a satisfied grin on her face.

"Good for them," Daisy said. She took a sip of her tea. "Any idea when?"

Matilda shrugged. "George has been put on extra shifts this week, so it could be any day. Ooo..." She leaned back her face creased in pain. "Ahrrr. That hurt. I bin getting these pains all morning. Oh good gracious, I think this baby's decided to come." She stood up and braced herself against the table, leaning over taking deep breaths until the pain passed.

"Is there anything I can do?"

"Fetch Mrs Braithwaite at number twenty-seven. She'll know what to do. She delivered Ralfie for me. Ooo." Matilda bent over in obvious pain. "Here, help me upstairs."

Daisy helped Matilda up to the bedroom and settled her in bed before running down to number twenty-seven and banging on the door. Mrs Braithwaite answered. "It's Mrs Perkins at number seven," she said. "She's started..."

Mrs Braithwaite didn't need any further explanation. She went inside, grabbed her bag and followed Daisy back to Matilda's. Daisy waited while Mrs Braithwaite examined Matilda.

"It'll be a while yet," the midwife said. "But it might be an idea to tell her husband. No rush. I doubt it'll come before midnight. Oh and knock next door. Get Jenny to come in and keep an eye on Ralfie."

"I know where George works. I'll get a message to him." Daisy kissed Matilda's cheek. "I'll let George know. I expect he'll want to be here to wet the baby's head when it's born."

Matilda smiled. "Thanks, Daisy. I'm glad you were here. Oooo..." she moaned as another wave of pain washed over her.

Outside Daisy took a breath. She felt for Matilda and all she was going through but knew the baby would bring joy to both its parents. It's a pity men don't have babies, she thought as she ran next door to fetch Jenny, the neighbour's twelve-year-old daughter, there'd be far fewer of them. Once she'd been assured Jenny would see to Ralfie she hurried towards the police station.

Sergeant McBride was behind the desk at the police station. Daisy remembered him from Matilda and George's wedding. He remembered her too. "Miss Carter," he said. "What can we do for you today?"

"Good afternoon, Sergeant McBride," she said. "I'm on a mission of mercy. I need to let George Perkins know his wife has gone into labour. Do you know where he is?"

The sergeant looked up at the clock on the wall. He scratched his chin. "Three thirty, he'll be on his way back to the station. Probably around Aldwych by now." He sniffed. "I'll give him the message." His face lit with a smile. "Shame he'll miss all the excitement."

"The excitement?" Daisy thought his wife giving birth would be excitement enough for anyone.

"Oh sorry. Shouldn't have said anything." Sergeant McBride tapped the side of his nose. "Police business."

Daisy guessed what that police business was. "Thank you, Sergeant McBride. I'll leave it in your capable hands."

"Good to see you again, Miss Carter. Take care."

"Thank you, Sergeant, I will."

Daisy left with lightness in her heart. So the police raid was going to be tonight. Well that was something she could tell Mr Lawrence.

Chapter Thirty Four

After a late lunch Lawrence took a cab to Brandon Summerville's house in Bayswater. He wasn't sure why he was going. It had seemed clear when he thought about it, but following his conversation with Ira Soloman he'd been reassured. Although Verity had not come to terms with the circumstances of her father's death, she had at least gained some understanding of it. Was there any point in pursuing the matter further? Death before Dishonour sounded fine as a regimental motto, but he wasn't sure it applied in business. Douglas Templeton had taken his life to save his family from humiliation. Lawrence couldn't blame him for that. He was glad Verity had accepted it, but she didn't know about the Summerville connection. He'd kept that from her for her peace of mind, but that didn't stop him wanting to know more.

He sighed at his own self-doubt. Brandon Summerville was a wealthy man. Had he benefited from his grandfather's misdeeds? He wasn't sure he could maintain a friendship with a man whose prosperity was built on the misfortune of others. It would certainly put him in a different light and he'd be duty bound to tell Verity. Her family would have been destitute were it not for Lawrence's father and the kindness of a good friend.

He recalled his time in the Guards with Brandon as a fellow officer. Brave in battle but often reckless. Lawrence remembered his loyalty, his courage under fire. Some said he was lucky, others that he made his own luck. Either way he was a man you'd choose to fight alongside. He'd had a reputation with women too. The irrefutable attraction of women was something that had never bothered Lawrence, he'd never envied him that, but he wondered if his reputation was well deserved. Clearly Charlotte was enamoured of him, and he suspected Verity was too. That was something he did care about which was why he needed to know the truth.

When he arrived the butler was showing him in when Lydia appeared.

"Lawrence," she said. "How lovely to see you. I'm afraid Brandon is tied up at the moment. I'm about to have tea, won't you join me? He won't be long." She smiled and her face lit up. She wasn't conventionally pretty but there was a warmth about her and a level of maturity which Lawrence found intriguing.

He followed her into the drawing room where a maid had set a tray of tea on a table in front of the fireplace. Lydia asked her to bring another cup. She sat on the settee and Lawrence took a chair next to her. "I have to thank Brandon for his intervention last night," he said. "Verity said he was a hero. I hope he didn't come off too badly."

Lydia chuckled. "He didn't get away as lightly as he likes to make out," she said. "He forgets he's not twenty-one anymore. He has a nasty gash on his head and his shoulder will take a while to recover, but he's quite full of himself, so please don't worry about him. I'm sure your gift will more than make up for any discomfort."

Lawrence had sent a case of best Scotch whisky by way of thanks. "It was the least I could do."

"I hope Verity's all right," Lydia said. "Brandon was beside himself. I believe he's become quite fond of her." She smiled and Lawrence didn't know what to make of that remark. Fond? As in fond of a pet? Or something else?

"She appeared perky enough this morning," he said, "and she said to thank him for the flowers."

The maid came in with the extra cup and Lydia poured the tea, turning the talk to pleasanter things. Lawrence found her knowledge of art and politics surprising and impressive. She was also well-travelled.

"Just because I'm a woman doesn't mean I don't understand things," she said.

He felt immediately chastened.

They'd been talking for about forty-five minutes when the butler came in. "Mr Summerville will see you now," he said, so Lawrence rose to follow him out.

"I'm hosting a party for Brandon's birthday next month," Lydia said as he said goodbye. "I do hope you and Verity can come."

"Thank you," Lawrence said. "And thank you for the tea."

"A pleasure," she said, the warmth of her smile lighting up her soft brown eyes. Yes, indeed, Lawrence thought. It really had been a pleasure.

The butler showed him into the library where Brandon sat at a desk, going through some paperwork. He rose when Lawrence entered and came round the desk to shake his hand. "Good to see you," he said. "Please." He indicated a brace of easy chairs in front of a fireplace. "I'm sorry to keep you waiting I trust Lydia kept you entertained."

Lawrence smiled. "Thank you, yes."

"How is Verity? I've been quite concerned. I'm afraid the events of the evening may have been too much for her."

Lawrence, affronted on her behalf, suddenly felt the need to defend her. "She's more resilient than you might suppose," he said and immediately regretted sounding so cold and uncaring, which he wasn't at all. "I mean, she's... fine. She thanks you for the flowers." Now he felt really uncomfortable. "I'm sorry, Brandon. Sorry that you had to take her home last night. It was my responsibility and if I'd have been there..."

"You'd have done the same as me. At least they caught the blighters. But that's not what you came for is it?"

"No." He took a breath trying to get the words straight in his mind. He took out the newspaper cuttings and the notes he'd made following his visit to Leeds. "I wanted to ask you about this." He passed Brandon the papers.

Brandon read through them, his face growing darker as he did so. When he came to the notes regarding Montgomery Summerville he shook his head. "I knew nothing about this," he said. "I'm assuming the Douglas Templeton referred to is something to do with your cousin?"

"Her father."

Brandon looked devastated. "I'm sorry." He handed the papers back. "Montgomery Summerville was my grandfather. I knew there was some sort of scandal but if you recall we were overseas twelve years ago. You can't hold me responsible for something my grandfather did any more than you are to blame for the misdeeds of your grandfather."

That hit home. Lawrence's father had worked hard to recover the family fortunes after his grandfather's death. "I don't hold you responsible," he said. "I just want to know what happened. I can't help but wonder…"

"What? If my money came from his fraudulent dealings? No. It didn't." He got up, walked to a side table and poured them each a glass of whisky. He handed one to Lawrence and sank into a chair. "When I left the Guards I knew there'd been some sort of scandal. My parents fled to America to avoid the humiliation, my mother died on the ship on the way over, my father soon after. I went there for Lydia. We had nothing but my army pension. I worked hard, took risks, Lydia worked alongside me." He took a sip of whisky. "She's a remarkable woman. I couldn't have done it without her. America really is the land of opportunity if you're prepared to work for it. I made my fortune, but made it honestly. You can be assured of that."

"And your grandfather?"

"He died in Argentina. No one knows what happened to the money, but he wasn't the only one to get rich. There were others." He took another slug of whisky.

Lawrence showed him the photograph of the shooting party. "Do you know who these men are?"

Brandon took a deep breath as he looked at the picture. "That's my grandfather." He pointed to the elderly man next to Douglas Templeton. "Not sure of the others." He looked a little closer. "That one," he pointed to the man the other side of Douglas, "Looks like Jasper Huntington-Smythe. They knew Monty. Good friends in fact. You might want to look more closely at where they got their money."

He threw back the rest of his Scotch. "Want another?"

"No, thanks." Lawrence finished his drink. "I think I've taken up enough of your time."

"I'm sorry about Verity's father," Brandon said. "It must have been a shock, coming out now. I hope she's all right."

"She doesn't know about your family's connection to it, if that's what you mean."

"It wasn't but now you mention it I'll leave it your judgement whether you tell her or not, but the sins of the fathers, and all that."

Lawrence thought he looked quite uncomfortable. He nodded. "No point raking over old coals," he said. "It's in the past and that's where it'll stay."

"Thanks." Brandon shook his hand. "She's a lovely girl." His voice softened as he spoke. "If she was my cousin I wouldn't let her out of my sight." A wide grin spread across his face. "It's refreshing to find someone so unspoilt."

Yes and unspoilt is how she'll stay, Lawrence thought as he bid Brandon goodbye. The way Brandon spoke of Verity unsettled him. Perhaps I should insist she return home, he thought, a thought as fleeting as it was ridiculous.

Chapter Thirty Five

That evening, when Daisy got back to the hotel, she went to find Mr Lawrence. At least she had some news. She told him what Matilda had said about the notorious club in Whitechapel. "She thinks the police will be mounting a raid tonight," she said.

"That's good," Lawrence said. "Let's hope it will take attention from the hotel and Molly Brown's time here."

"I hope they find what they're looking for," Daisy said.

"Indeed." He smiled. "I understand that your sister, Mrs Ferguson, knew the man who attempted to burgle the hotel yesterday and she was the one who gave Mr Svenson the tip off."

Daisy's heart sank. How much did he know about Jessie's part in it? "I believe she overheard something."

"Really?" Surprise lifted his eyebrows. "Where would she hear something like that?"

Daisy shrugged. "Somewhere in town, I'm not sure."

"Hmm. I must say I'd be concerned if that was the sort of company she keeps. I can't approve of staff associating with criminals."

"Oh no. Of course not. I believe it was someone she knew in the past. There wouldn't have been any recent connection."

Lawrence stared at her. "I hope not, for both your sakes." He handed her the list of arrivals and departures.

Daisy left the office with her heart pumping like an out of kilter engine. She'd never known him be so abrupt. Got out of the wrong side of the bed, she thought, then remembered he hadn't actually been to bed. Still it rankled.

Jessie had done the right thing and she was still being blamed. It wasn't fair. After all she'd gone through. And saving the hotel from being burgled. It was alright for the likes of Mr Lawrence, she thought, brought up in a big house with close family and no need to struggle. Jessie was working hard to put her past behind her. Why couldn't they give her a chance? At least Mr Svenson appreciated what she'd done. He'd made a point of thanking them both personally as soon as he got back from the hospital.

"We owe you a debt of gratitude," he'd said to Jessie. "Well done. And you too, Miss Carter. Thank you."

She'd blushed. Maybe he wasn't so bad after all.

The next morning Daisy picked up a newspaper as soon as they were delivered. She'd have time to go through it before starting work. She glanced at the headlines as she turned the pages, looking for anything that might concern a raid on a club in Whitechapel. She found it in a small item in column three on page five. She read:

In the early hours of this morning the police investigating the murder of prostitute Molly Brown raided a gentleman's club in Whitechapel. The Hades Club, situated in a run-down area of East London, is the known haunt of prostitutes, gamblers, petty criminals and those with occupations of a nefarious nature. Several men were arrested and will appear in court this morning charged with gross indecency and violent affray. The investigation into the death of Miss Molly Brown continues. A police spokesman said 'We

*are interviewing several men and following a number
of leads. An arrest is imminent.'*

At last, Daisy thought. They're on the right track
and the glare of publicity will move away from the
hotel. She did wonder about the arrests. She wouldn't
be able to go until the afternoon, but visiting Matilda
after the birth of her baby would give her the perfect
opportunity to find out if George Perkins could tell her
anything more. She'd even take a present for the baby.

She cut the item out of the paper, wrote a short
note explaining what it was and that she hoped to find
out more and put it in an envelope addressed to Mr
Lawrence. On her way to the office to see Mr Svenson
she gave the envelope to the girl covering reception.

Lawrence picked up the note from Daisy on his way
out that morning. He wasn't particularly interested in
the murder of Molly Brown, only that it didn't reflect
badly on the hotel. She had been a chambermaid who
falsely accused one of his staff of molesting her and
then blackmailed him to keep it quiet. She didn't
deserve to die, he didn't think that, but he had no
interest in who had killed her. Mr Jevons had been set
free, that had been his only concern.

He supposed Miss Carter had given him the
cutting in an attempt to make up for her error in
employing the girl in the first place. Trying to show
that her murder had nothing to do with the hotel. He
had been a bit hard on her over the burglary business.
After all, if her sister hadn't tipped them off... He
sighed and shook his head.

In his mind's eye he saw the girl, Molly. A pretty
girl, too young to die. Then there was her so-called
brother. He wouldn't mind seeing him behind bars.

Was he one of the men arrested? They were appearing in court this morning. He had to pass the assizes building on his way to lunch at his club with Jeremy and he had time, so he decided to satisfy his own curiosity and call in to watch the proceedings.

The day began with the usual procession of women brought in for soliciting. All pleaded guilty and were duly fined. About eleven o'clock several men were brought up, most charged with violent affray, resisting arrest and various offences connected with prostitution.

They were bound over to keep the peace and fined. Lawrence was about to leave when a red-eyed, dishevelled man in his late thirties was brought up. His face was puffy and bruised, his hair awry. Lawrence hardly recognised him. The court officer read out the charge: Edward St John Huntington-Smythe was charged with gross indecency and living off immoral earnings. A police officer read out the circumstances of the arrest. Not only did he own the club, but he'd been found in *flagrante delicto* with another man.

Lawrence sat stunned while Edward Huntington-Smythe was committed for trial.

The next case brought up was Bertram Aloysius Huntington-Smythe, charged with violent affray and the murder of known prostitute, Molly Brown. He pleaded not guilty and was also committed for trial at the Central Criminal Court.

Lawrence sat staring into space, unable to absorb what he was hearing. The Huntington-Smythes were being charged with the most horrendous crimes. He couldn't believe it. Then he thought of Charlotte. Poor, dear Charlotte. What on earth would happen to her now? Once the papers got hold of the names of the transgressors they would have a field-day. The Huntington-Smythe name would be attached to the most salacious stories and vulgar gossip. How could she live with that?

He left the court, hardly able to think or see where he was going. When he arrived at his club Jeremy was already at the bar. He ordered a drink for Lawrence. "What's up with you?" he asked. "You look as though you've seen a ghost."

Lawrence showed him the newspaper cutting. "You'll never guess who they've arrested."

Jeremy studied the paper. "The Hades Club. I've heard of it. Not a place any self-respecting gentleman would wish to be seen in if the gossip is anything to go by. Go on, tell me who?"

"The Huntington-Smythes. They've arrested Edward and Bertie Huntington-Smythe."

Chapter Thirty Six

Verity spent the morning in her room writing letters. She'd received several invitations which needed replies and Aunt Elvira had sent a long missive with all the local news and snippets of gossip, interspersed with suggestions for places Verity might visit and things she might take an interest in. The letter was littered with subtle references to Verity's social life, which she read as seeking information about any possible liaisons which might lead to proposals of marriage.

As she wrote, the memory of the attempted burglary and the vision of Brandon bravely tackling the escaping villain kept running through her mind. How she'd love to tell Aunt Elvira about it, but then she'd insist she went home as staying would be too dangerous. Every time she glanced at the flowers he'd sent, her lips spread into a smile and her heart flushed with warmth. She enjoyed his company, but any hope of anything more was a distant dream. She'd have to stand in line behind Charlotte and several other women and she wasn't prepared to do that. If only her heart wouldn't flutter so much every time she recalled his strong arms around her and how kind he'd been at the nightclub. She sighed. Why did life have to be so difficult?

She was putting on her hat to go out to visit a small gallery that Lydia had recommended when a messenger arrived with a note from Charlotte.

Meet me for lunch. Please come at once. Usual place. Please hurry.

Puzzled, she tipped the messenger and set out to meet Charlotte. She couldn't think what was so urgent, but Charlotte was always full of fun and the gallery could wait until another day. She stepped out into the sunshine as warmth filled the street. A light breeze nudged fluffy clouds across a summer blue sky. She would have enjoyed the walk to the tea shop in Hyde Park, but the urgency of the note concerned her, so Barker got her a cab for the short journey.

Charlotte was already seated at a table when she arrived. She greeted Verity with an empty stare, her usually sparkling eyes red-rimmed and dull with misery. Ashen-faced, with her lips turned down she looked as though she was about to burst into tears.

"What on earth's the matter?" Verity asked, taking a seat opposite her at the table. "You look awful."

"I feel awful. It is awful, the most dreadful thing has happened. I can hardly bear to tell you about it."

A waitress appeared at the table and Verity ordered tea although she thought brandy would be more appropriate. She reached out and took Charlotte's hand. "There's nothing you can tell me would make me think any less of you," she said. "You're my friend and always will be."

Charlotte shook her head. A look of pure misery filled her face. "It's not me, not my fault, it's just so unfair." She took a handkerchief from her bag and blew her nose. Verity waited. Charlotte sniffed and wiped her nose again. She leaned forward, her voice a whisper. "Edward and Bertie have been arrested."

"Arrested!"

Charlotte glanced around her eyes wide with fear. She put her finger to her lips. "Shush. No need for the whole world to know."

"I'm sorry, but why? What have they done?" Puzzlement creased Verity's brow.

"Nothing. They're both completely innocent. Just in the wrong place at the wrong time. It's a travesty of justice, that's what it is."

The waitress arrived with the tea and Verity took her time setting it out. Her mind was racing. What on earth could they have done to be arrested? Bertie she could understand, short-tempered and prone to lash out, but Edward had seemed such a kind, caring man.

"Oh, I don't want to go into details," Charlotte said waving her handkerchief in the air as though trying to bat away the awful truth. "Suffice to say Daddy's furious and he's taking us all away. That's why I wanted to see you. We're leaving for South America tonight."

Verity sat back amazed. "South America?" Shock stole her breath. "I don't understand."

Charlotte sighed, now more in control of her senses. "It's complicated but Daddy says we have friends there and we'd be better off out of it. They're innocent of course, but mud sticks and our name will be in all the newspapers." She took a sip of tea, Verity thought to compose herself. "Daddy says there are lots of opportunities for well-bred young ladies in Argentina." A wan smile twitched her lips and Verity saw resignation in her eyes.

Of course, she thought. If they stayed here and there was a scandal Charlotte's chances of making a good marriage would be as likely as snow in August. "Ah, I see." Verity struggled to find the words she needed to comfort her friend. "I'm sure he's right," she said eventually. "If they've any sense they'll all be after you. You'll be able to take your pick."

Charlotte pulled her shoulders up and took a deep breath sitting up straight. "Let's hope so," she said, putting on a brave face.

"I'll miss you terribly," Verity said. "You must write. Promise?"

Charlotte's face crumpled, she reached out to Verity. "I'll miss you too." She sniffed and pulled herself upright again. "Now," she said, "let's look on the bright side. I'll have lots of interesting things to tell you and you must write and tell me all about what's happening in London."

Verity smiled, but Charlotte's bravado didn't fool her. This was the end of the world as she knew it, for Charlotte and Verity's heart went out to her. "I will and I wish you well."

Charlotte nodded. "And don't believe anything you read in the newspapers," she said.

As soon as Verity got back to the hotel she burst into Lawrence's office with the news. "I've just seen Charlotte," she said. "You'll never guess what's happened. They've arrested her brothers." Breathless with the horror of what she was saying she gasped as she sat down. "Charlotte's being sent away. I can't believe it. Who would do such a thing and why?"

Lawrence stared at her. "Please, Verity, calm down and take a seat. I'll get us some tea, unless you'd prefer something stronger."

"Yes please." She watched Lawrence pour them each a brandy. He didn't seem at all perturbed by her news. "Have you heard anything? What's it all about?"

He handed her the brandy and pulled up a chair next to her. "I'm afraid it's not going to go well for the Huntington-Smythes," he said. "I'm as surprised as you, but it seems that Edward and Bertie have been involved in something less than honourable. You say Charlotte's being sent away? Probably for the best." He took a drink.

"But what's it all about, Lawrence? What have they done?"

"I'm not sure. I only know what they've been accused of and it's not pleasant. There'll be a trial and it'll be in all the newspapers. Honestly, Verity, for your own good, any association you have with that family will have to end."

"Any association!" Shock and rage churned in her stomach. "The only association I have is with Charlotte and she's done nothing wrong. Anyway, she's being sent to Argentina so any further association as you put it is unlikely." Tears pricked her eyes as a well of misery crashed over her. It was so unfair.

"Argentina? Well I suppose…"

"Suppose nothing. It's so unfair." The tears threatened to fall.

"I'm sorry you've lost your friend," Lawrence said. "I do wonder if it wouldn't be best for you to return home after all. Mama will understand."

"No. I won't be chased out of town by malicious gossip and untrue accusations. Honestly, Lawrence, I thought you were better than that." Suddenly it all became too much for her and she collapsed into Lawrence's arms, sobbing.

Chapter Thirty Seven

Lawrence had just reached his office the next morning when Jeremy came bursting in. "Have you seen this?" He waved the newspaper in his hand.

Lawrence stared at him, unsettled by the interruption. "What, the paper? No, not yet. What is it?"

"Here. On page three." Jeremy shoved the paper folded to page three in front of Lawrence's face. Lawrence scanned the page. "What? I can't see anything."

Jeremy leaned over the paper and pointed to an item halfway down. The headline read *Prisoner Takes His Own Life.* As Lawrence read it his stomach churned and his breath shortened. He gasped, his hand over his mouth as he stared at Jeremy. "I don't believe it. Edward's dead?"

"Found hanged in his cell after his court appearance. I guess he couldn't face the shame and disgrace of being found out. It'll fall on the whole family. You mark my words, they'll all suffer for it."

Lawrence shook his head in bewilderment. "It's unbelievable, all of it. I didn't take to the man, but all the same…" He sank onto the chair behind his desk.

"It doesn't say anything about Bertie. He's the one charged with murder." A look of pure revulsion crossed Jeremy's face. "Never trust a man who beats a horse," he said. "I can't say I feel any sympathy for him."

Lawrence recalled Jeremy's disgust at the way Bertie treated his horse at the hunt. "It's Charlotte and the rest of the family I feel sorry for," Lawrence said. "She'll take it hard."

"Charlotte? Of course. Sorry, old man, forgot you were quite taken with her."

Lawrence took a breath. "She's on her way to Argentina with Chester and Sybil. Probably best all round." He smiled at Jeremy. "I hate to say it but, to be honest, I think we've all had a narrow escape."

Jeremy chuckled. "You're probably right. Shame about Edward though. I didn't think he was all bad."

"He's done the decent thing, I suppose." Lawrence glanced again at the paper. "Didn't want his family and his proclivities dragged through court for everyone to read about over their Sunday dinner."

Jeremy nodded. "What about Verity? Do you think she knows? Does she read the paper?"

"Oh my Lord, no. She won't know and she'll take it badly. She was distraught at Charlotte leaving. This will be even worse."

"Would you like me to tell her?"

Lawrence shook his head. "No. I'll do it. It's my responsibility. Can't say I'm looking forward to it though. I'll try to persuade her to go home. A change of scene might do her good. Get her out of London."

"She's stronger than you think. You don't give her enough credit. And as for sending her home – what do you think Mama will say about that? The season's not over yet and you'd have to give a reason. I can't see Verity agreeing to go home a failure in Mama's eyes."

"What do you mean a failure?"

"Well, I wouldn't advise telling Mama about the guests she's entertained in her home being in prison for murder and gross indecency. And leaving London before the end of the season with no beau in sight…"

Lawrence sighed. "You're right of course. No point in worrying Mama with things she doesn't need to know." All the same, he cursed the day they'd ever met the Huntington-Smythes. "I'll speak to Verity. Put it as gently as I can." He threw the paper down. "Damn them. Damn them all."

Jeremy took a seat opposite the desk. "It'll be the talk of the town. We'll all be tainted by association. That'll make it hard for Verity."

"Hmm. I'm not so sure. The way the gossip-mongers work they'll all want a piece of her. Want to know if she knew anything about Edward's preferences." He pouted with his chin in his hand. "I wish I could get her out of town."

"There is one thing in our favour," Jeremy said.

"What?"

"The Summervilles. Lydia's invitation to Brandon's birthday party next month. They're influential. Our appearance there will go a long way to distance us from the Huntington-Smythes. I'll be taking Prudence. I take it you'll be there with Verity?"

Lawrence nodded. "Yes. We've been invited. I think Verity's looking forward to it. She'll miss Charlotte of course." He sighed. "Brandon's taking quite an interest in her. I'm not sure whether or not I approve."

Jeremy chuckled. "I think you'll find Verity has a mind of her own when it comes to men and marriage. She won't have her head turned by a charmer like Brandon."

Lawrence shrugged. "I'm not so sure," he said. "Brandon has an uncanny knack when it comes to women. Never known one to refuse him."

Tears sprang to Verity's eyes when she read the piece Lawrence showed her in the paper. "Charlotte will be devastated," she said. "I can't believe he'd do such at thing, but I suppose…" She read it again and sank onto the bed. "I suppose he thought it the honourable thing to do. Like my father." She glanced at Lawrence and handed him back the paper. "Now everyone will think him guilty, whether he was or not. Where will he be buried?"

"Erm. I'm not sure." Lawrence looked as distraught as she felt. "He hasn't been found guilty of anything, so he's still innocent in the eyes of the law, although suicide is itself a criminal offence."

"A criminal offence? Surely he's beyond the reach of the law now?"

"The law, yes. I believe the Church of England allows for a private funeral in such circumstances, but possibly without a Christian service."

"So just stuck in the ground with no one praying for his salvation. It's barbaric." She paused, hardly able to say the words. A swell of grief swirled in her stomach. "Do you know, I have no idea where my father is buried. No place to go to mourn or remember." The vision of her father's face filled her mind. She closed her eyes to shut it out.

"I'm sorry." Lawrence sank onto the bed beside her. "We keep our memories in our hearts. You don't need a grave to grieve."

"So it will be the same for Charlotte and her family?"

He shrugged. "Not necessarily. He can be buried in the family grave and as for the service… I think these things can be arranged, if you know the right people."

"Of course. Anything can be arranged – if you know the right people." Suddenly a wave of sadness overtook her. "I'd like to go." A tear ran over her cheek. "For Charlotte, for the family."

Lawrence stared at her. "I'm not sure…"

"Please. I liked him. He never did me any harm. In fact he once did me a favour. I'd like to go."

She saw Lawrence's determination crumble. "If you insist. I suppose I could go with you. As a friend of the family."

She managed a wan smile. "Thank you. Then I will be able to write to Charlotte. It may be some comfort to know he wasn't alone when he was finally laid to rest." She stood up and paced the room. "What a horrible world we live in," she said. "Why must we judge one another? Why can't we be left alone to live our lives in any way we wish? It's not fair."

Lawrence shook his head, stood and put his arms around her. "Who said life was fair? We have to make the best of what chances we're given. Edward made his choice. We have to allow him that."

"I suppose so." She sighed. She felt safe in Lawrence's arms. As safe as she'd felt in Brandon's.

*

That morning Daisy also scanned the paper. Her afternoon with Matilda had proved unfruitful, other than several hours spent with the new baby and a blow by blow account of its birth.

"Thankfully an easy one," Matilda said, "compared to Ralfie. 'E took forever. Mrs Braithwaite says boys are always more difficult than girls." She smiled and Daisy saw a flash of the old Matilda. Her eyes shone with pride. "An' she's no trouble." She rocked the child gently in her arms. Daisy asked if George had said anything about the arrests following the raid, but all Matilda would say was, "You were right. They've rounded up a load of toffs. One of them must have done it."

She turned the pages of the paper checking the headlines. She'd only got as far as page three when Barker interrupted her, putting his head around the door. "Mr Svenson wants to see us."

Daisy's heart sank, even as her irritation grew. "What's he want now?" she muttered, folding the paper away to peruse later.

"Dunno. 'E wants to see Jessie an' all if she's free. I think it's about the blokes we collared." His face broke into a smile. "Might be a bonus."

"Well, she isn't free. I'll come now and tell her later or the work will never get done. I don't know what this place is coming to." She carried on muttering her displeasure as they made their way to the office. When they arrived, the look on Mr Svenson's face told her it wasn't about a bonus. They took their seats opposite the desk.

"I'll come straight to the point," he said. "It's about the attempted burglary. There's going to be a trial and we've to appear as witnesses. They have our statements but the prosecutor wants further details. I trust this won't be a problem."

"A trial? But they were caught red-handed," Barker said. "Surely there's no doubt about their guilt?"

Mr Svenson's thin-lipped smile showed his impatience. "I believe it's about their intention. In order to convict for burglary they have to prove intent. They could say they were drunk and came in by mistake. Unless they plead guilty, which they haven't so far."

"By mistake? They were at the safe trying to open it. A mistake? Load of cobblers… pardon my language with a young lady present."

Barker's face flushed with fury.

"I know, but it's the law. They want to talk to Jessie as well. She was the one who tipped us off, they'll want to know all about that."

Fear and foreboding crunched Daisy's stomach. Jessie couldn't go into the witness box. If she did all their subterfuge about who she was would be revealed. They'd both lose their jobs and the newspapers would have a field day with the fact that she was the wife of the accused. Not only that, Mr Lawrence would know she'd lied to him. Lied to him on more than one occasion. Any respect he had for her would be gone and her heart would break. She'd be dismissed without a reference.

"I'll speak to Jessie," she said, "but surely they can't force us to appear in court, or can they?"

Mr Svenson's gaze burned into her. "I would have thought that, as employees of the hotel, you would want to do everything within your power to bring these villains to book. Unless there's something you're not telling me?"

"No. No, of course not." Daisy's heart fluttered. "It's just that Jessie's not as strong as some. She's had her difficulties. Mr Lawrence is well of aware of them. I don't want her put under unnecessary pressure if she's not up to it." She smoothed her apron over her skirt wishing she was anywhere but where she was.

"I see. Well, I'll do everything I can to make things easier for her, but if they decide she's integral to the case then she'll have no option but to comply. Is that clear?"

He looked so smug she wanted to hit him. "Yes, sir. Clear as day. If that's all?"

He shuffled the papers on the desk looking as irritated as she'd ever seen him. Of course he didn't know the truth about Jessie so perhaps she was being hard on him. Still, she didn't feel like giving him the benefit of the doubt.

"Yes, that's all. Thank you."

She nodded as she got up to go. Barker followed her out. "Well, there's a turn up. Us appearing in court. Might be in the papers. Might even get a medal."

Daisy didn't think so.

Chapter Thirty Eight

Few mourners attended Edward Huntington-Smythe's funeral. The weather had turned autumnal and the morning chill added to the sombre atmosphere. Verity wore the same black dress, coat and hat she'd worn to her mother's funeral and the memory of it lingered in every stitch of fabric. Lawrence had hired a carriage for the journey to the Huntington-Smythe's country estate, where Edward would be buried in the family grave. A cool breeze whipped the churchyard trees as they made their way into the church. Pale sunlight through the windows cast shadows over the pews where estate workers sat in solemn silence. A shiver ran down Verity's spine as they took their seats.

They stood as the coffin was carried in, Bertie, in handcuffs, walked behind accompanied by two prison warders. Pale and vulnerable, he looked younger than his years. Verity's heart went out to him. He appeared shrivelled, his swagger gone, his bravado crushed. How awful, she thought, to lose a brother. She'd never liked him, but she felt sorry for him all the same.

He hung his head as he sat in silence. The service was a short one, the voices of the small congregation drowned out by the music from the organ playing 'Guide Me O Thou Great Redeemer'. The vicar, an elderly man swathed in whiskers and sadness, said a few words, focussing on God's understanding of human frailties, the Lord's compassion and the forgiveness of sins. He talked about the cleansing of the spirit and the certainty of eternal life. There were prayers and a closing hymn followed by a blessing. Then the congregation filed out. There was no eulogy, no one to speak about Edward or his life.

The vicar said a few words at the graveside and Verity watched the coffin being lowered into the grave. "Goodbye, Edward," she whispered. "May God be with you." Deep sorrow circled her heart. She wiped her eyes with the handkerchief she knew she'd need. Why Edward, she thought. He didn't deserve to die.

After the burial Bertie was led away, still handcuffed. He hadn't spoken the whole time and once again Verity felt for him. He didn't deserve what happened to him either, she thought, although if he killed that girl, perhaps he did.

After the funeral Lawrence took her out to lunch at the best restaurant they could find. They drank wine and talked about family matters, friends, plans and dreams. Anything except what was on both their minds – how far and how fast the Huntington-Smythes had fallen and what would happen to them now.

Chapter Thirty Nine

The day of Brandon Summerville's birthday party Verity wasn't sure she wanted to go. It had been several weeks since Edward's funeral, but she still felt the pain of it, for Charlotte's sake. If it hadn't been for the fact that Lydia had arranged it and invited her and that Lawrence, Jeremy and Prudence were going, she would have backed out. As it was she had little hope of finding it in any way enjoyable.

Lawrence had insisted she have a new gown. "Something to cheer you up," he said. "After the horrible time you've had."

She knew he meant well, but it would take more than a new dress to lift her spirits. She missed Charlotte and felt for her over the loss of her brother. Going dancing was the last thing she felt like doing.

She sighed as she glanced in the mirror. The dress Mrs Henderson had produced was exquisite. The lace puffed sleeves, tight bodice with an extravagant tulle collar and cerise silk, floor length skirt showed off her slim waist, while the taffeta under-skirts rustled as she moved. Jessie had pinned fresh rose buds into her hair. Around her neck she wore a pearl collar set with amethyst and diamante, borrowed from her Aunt Elvira.

"I'll be the envy of every man in the room," Lawrence said, offering his arm when he came to collect her. She smiled but wasn't reassured.

Their carriage drove through bustling streets as the sun set, leaving a smear of gold across a darkening sky, the warmth of the day still lingered. The party was held in a gallery owned by a friend of the Summervilles. As they entered Verity saw the coloured lights set up around the room which made it feel like walking into a rainbow. A small ensemble set up on a dais played softy, barely audible over the hubbub of conversation. Waiters circulated with trays of glasses of champagne. Brandon greeted them, shaking hands with Lawrence and Jeremy and saying how pleased he was to see them.

Lydia welcomed Verity with a brush of her lips to her cheek and warmth in her eyes. "I'm so glad you came," she said.

Verity recognised several couples from other balls she'd attended. It all appeared very informal and friendly.

"A small but exclusive crowd," Jeremy said, glancing around. "I can't think what we've done to be invited."

"Lydia invited us," Verity said, surprised at his remark. "She's a friend." She hadn't thought Jeremy so much of a snob.

Soon she found herself whisked onto the floor for one dance after another. The time seemed to fly. After a while the musicians stopped for a supper-break.

Supper was laid out on long white-clothed tables in an upstairs gallery. She saw oysters, lobster, several fish dishes, a variety of game pies, a spread of cold meats, flans and quiches with every type of pickles and salad. Sweetmeats, trifles of every colour and description, cakes and a plethora of cheeses rounded up the sumptuous feast, along with a magnificent punch-bowl and a selection of wines.

"A feast indeed," Jeremy said, helping himself to several slices of cold meat, potato salad and pickles. Verity chose salad with quiche and Lawrence roast beef with horseradish and a Vienna roll.

After supper Verity wandered around the gallery looking at the paintings. She couldn't help thinking how Charlotte would have loved it. The thought brought memories of Edward and a stab to her heart. All these people cared about was a constant round of parties, balls and entertainment, she thought.

"Penny for them."

She spun round, expecting to see Jeremy or Lawrence but found herself staring into Brandon's brooding brown eyes. "I beg your pardon," he said, his voice soft with unexpected concern. "You looked as though you were lost in thought. I wondered what intrigued you so."

She shrugged, trying to slow the hammering of her heart. The mere scent of him seemed to send her into a dither. "Just what a wonderful turn out," she lied. "And what a lovely place for a party."

"I'm glad you approve. Are you enjoying the paintings?"

"They're exquisite."

He smiled, his eyes lit with interest. "Which is your favourite?"

She didn't know what to say. Her brain seemed to have stopped functioning. "They're all so lovely, it's difficult to choose."

"I hear you're an artist yourself," he said. "Watercolours isn't it?"

Was it her imagination or was he laughing at her. "I dabble. Nothing like the pictures on display here." She sipped her champagne to cover her embarrassment. Still, her heart fluttered at the nearness of him.

"You're too modest." He took a sip of champagne from the glass he was holding. "What is your preference, landscapes or portraits?"

She took a breath. Talking about paintings she was on safer territory. "Landscapes can be breathtakingly beautiful," she said. "The difference of light and shade, the capturing of colour and sunlight, distance and perspective, making you feel as though you're really there," she paused. "But I think perhaps there's more skill in capturing the essence of a person in a portrait. Reproducing the thing that makes them unique and brings them to life." As she spoke her voice warmed with enthusiasm, her passion clear in her face.

He nodded but didn't speak. Her heart sank. She'd got carried away. What must he think of her, going on about the art of putting paint on canvas? He wasn't interested in her opinion. He was just making polite conversation. She hastily sipped her drink, glancing around for an escape.

"Lydia said you had an eye," he said eventually.

The band struck up for the next dance and people started moving onto the floor. A woman in a purple dress came hurrying over.

"You promised me this dance," she said, taking Brandon's arm.

"Of course." He turned to smile at Verity and her hear beat even faster. "Excuse me. Duty calls."

Then they were gone. Verity sighed with relief. She'd made a complete fool of herself, but part of her thrilled at his interest. Stupid, she thought. As if he'd be interested in me.

Jeremy appeared to save her, sweeping her onto the dance floor to rejoin the fray. She noticed Brandon had a different girl in his arms for every dance, but wasn't that the job of a host?

Later she excused herself and went to the ladies power room, where she found Prudence fixing her hair where a strand had fallen out of place.

"So, what do you think of our host," Prudence asked. "Isn't he the dashing hero?"

Verity glanced around and saw they were alone. "He's the most fascinating man I've ever met," she said. "But I'll deny it if you ever tell anyone I said so."

Prudence laughed. "Men," she said. "What can you do? I hear he's got a reputation."

"I believe so. What do you think?"

Prudence pouted. She caught Verity's gaze in the mirror. "I think you should make up your own mind," she said.

At midnight the band stopped playing and Lydia stepped onto the dais. The bandleader called the room to silence and waiters circulated with trays of champagne.

"I want to thank you all for coming," Lydia said. "Please, fill your glasses and wish my brother the best birthday ever." Once everyone had a glass in their hand she raised hers. "Happy birthday, Brandon."

Everyone in the room called, "Happy birthday, Brandon." Then they called for a speech.

Brandon, glass in hand, stepped up next to his sister. He glanced around the room. "I too want to thank you for so many things." He took a breath and recited:

When friends are far and few,
And all the world's about us,
Raise a toast to those we knew,
Would never ever doubt us.

The words were as simple as they were heartfelt. He raised his glass. "To good friends and better times."

Everyone in the room cheered and raised their glasses. "To good friends and better times," they chanted.

What a surprise, Verity thought as he stepped down, shaking hands with the men nearest to him. What an extraordinary man.

By the time they left at dawn Verity noticed Brandon had danced with every female there, except her. The fact that she longed to be in his arms did nothing to stop the evening being one of the best she could remember.

Chapter Forty

Once the rooms were finished Daisy called Jessie into her room for a chat, leaving Annie to see to the laundry. She collected a tray of tea and cakes from the kitchen and motioned for Jessie to sit.

Jessie sat gingerly on the edge of the chair. "What's up?" Anger danced in her eyes. "You ain't brought me in 'ere for nothing. Another dressing down is it? What have I done now?"

"Nothing. You've done nothing wrong. I've no complaint about you or your work. You've settled in very well. No. It's about Charlie and the attempted burglary."

She poured Jessie a cup of tea and handed it to her as nonchalantly as she could manage. The last thing she needed was Jessie flaring up. "Mr Svenson says Charlie's pleading not guilty and there's to be a trial. All the staff have to make further statements and may be called as witnesses."

"Witnesses? What's that got to do with me? I wasn't there, remember?" She took the offered cup and saucer.

"No, but you tipped us off. They'll want to know about that. I said you'd overheard a conversation. We obviously can't tell them the truth."

"The truth? I'm not telling them anything. They can't make me." She glared at Daisy. "Can they?" Her brow furrowed in alarm.

Daisy shrugged. "I don't know. I know we'd have a hard job explaining to Mr Svenson why not."

Jessie gasped. "Svenson's the least of me worries. The police will say I was part of it. I told 'em about the staff, the safe, the money. They'll put me away an' all. I won't do it. I won't."

Daisy clapped her hand over her mouth. Of course Jessie was right. The police would connect her to the robbery and she'd go to prison. She couldn't allow that.

Fear for her life filled Jessie's eyes as she stared at Daisy. "I won't do it! I won't dob Charlie in to the law. 'E's still me 'usband. He'd murder me, you know what he can do. What he did before."

Daisy felt her fear. It was true, Charlie would find some way of taking his revenge and it wouldn't be pretty. A vision of Jessie's face after the last beating filled her mind.

"I wish I'd never said owt." Jessie dropped her head in her hands. "I wish I'd let 'im rob the place. We'd all be better off."

"You did the right thing. You know he'll never go straight. It'd always be one thing or another. You're better off out of it. Honest to God, I wish you'd never got involved with him." She paced the room trying to think of a way out.

"Bit late now." Jessie's voice was sullen. "I should never have said owt. I knew I couldn't trust you." She raised her head. "My mistake." Anger curled her fists.

"Don't worry, Jess. I'll talk to Mr Svenson. We'll sort something out. I won't let anything happen to you." Even as she said it she knew she was clutching at straws. There was nothing she could do. She'd let Jessie down and it was the worst feeling in the world.

*

A few days after the party, Verity received an invitation to join Lydia for tea at the Savoy. *There's someone I'd like you to meet*, she wrote. Intrigued,

Verity accepted the invitation. When she arrived Lydia was already seated with her guest. "This is Kitty," she said, her voice burning with pride. "She's a suffragette."

Verity immediately thought of the women she'd met during her brief stay in a prison cell. She'd admired their fortitude. "Pleased to meet you," she said. "I bet you've a few tales to tell."

"Indeed I have," Kitty said. "But Lydia tells me you've been helping too. Writing letters and drumming up support."

"I'm afraid my contribution pales beside that of others," Verity said. "I wish I could do more, but I'm afraid I could never do what you do."

Kitty laughed. "Sometimes I wonder how I do it." Then, over tea and cake in the most opulent dining room in London, she told them about the degradation she suffered in prison and the horrors of being forcibly fed with a tube up her nose. "I had an irresistible urge to continue the fight," she said. "We want justice and a better life for all women. Why shouldn't we have control over our lives the way men do?"

Verity heard echoes of Charlotte saying the same thing, but, despite envying men's freedom she would never do anything to change her comfortable life.

"Tell Verity about your plans for the Lord Mayor's Show," Lydia said.

Kitty told her about the plan to throw leaflets over the parade. "We've studied the route," she said. "There are several buildings along the way where we think we can secure access to upstairs rooms overlooking the parade. It'll be miles long, so there are lots of opportunities and the streets will be crowded. We're having two thousand leaflets printed. I know it won't make a great difference, but it may bring us some publicity. It's a chance to keep the campaign in the public eye."

"Well, I suppose it's better than breaking windows," Verity said.

"Yes. But what we really want is parliamentary representation," Lydia said. "That's why the letters are so important. We need to get the politicians on our side. I know the *Deeds not Words* campaign started by Mrs Pankhurst does a lot to bring attention to our cause, but it can be counter-productive. A lot of people disagree with it."

Kitty looked defensive. "It's to show them that we're willing to die for our cause," she said. "I don't think you can argue about people's commitment when they put their lives at risk."

"No. Of course not," Lydia said. "Just a different way of going about things." Verity guessed that Lydia, while admiring the spirit of the suffragettes, didn't approve of their more violent methods.

"So, what about the Lord Mayor's Show? Are you game?" Kitty's voice burned with enthusiasm.

"As long as nobody gets hurt," Verity said. "I promised Lawrence."

"The worst that can happen is being arrested and fined," Kitty said.

Lydia smiled. "Brandon is a compassionate man and sympathises with our cause, but he could never countenance a deliberate attempt to get arrested. Still, littering doesn't seem all that bad."

"And it will further our cause." Kitty sounded hopeful.

"I'll think about it," Verity said. "Ninth of November?"

"Yes. We're meeting up in Covent Garden."

"I'll think about it too," Lydia said, looking doubtful. "But I'm really not sure."

Chapter Forty One

Several days later Verity received an invitation to attend the opening of an Exhibition of Impressionist Art at the National Gallery as a guest of Mr Brandon Summerville. As first she thrilled at the thought. It would be a wonderful event. A chance to see the masterpieces of the world's greatest artists, something she'd love in ordinary circumstance but, on second thoughts she wondered it if was wise. Why had he invited her particularly? She was especially curious when she found that neither Lawrence nor Jeremy had been invited. It would be improper for her to go with him alone, even in these enlightened days.

"It'll be quite busy I expect," she said to Lawrence when she told him over breakfast. "It's something I've always wanted to do. There'll be paintings by Monet, Renoir and Degas that I'd never see in a lifetime. It would be a wonderful opportunity to see them."

"In that case I think you should go," Lawrence said. "It's not every day you'd be invited. I'm sure Brandon has your best interest at heart." He flicked the paper he was reading, only half paying attention.

"Do you think so? I'm not so sure," she said. "I didn't exactly cover myself with glory at our last meeting."

He looked up. "No. But you saved his life, remember." He chuckled. "That means he's indebted to you. I expect this is his way of repaying you. Just the sort of thing he would do." He turned his attention back to the newspaper. Verity sighed. She'd love to go, but she'd be bound to embarrass herself in his presence again. Was it worth the humiliation?

She was able to find out more when she ran into him on her way into town.

"Good morning, Verity." He raised his hat. "I was hoping to run into you. I trust you received my invitation."

"I did indeed," she said. "It's very kind of you to invite me, but I'm not sure I can attend." Disappointment swelled inside her as she said it. It would break her heart not to go, but could she trust herself not to do something stupid?

His face creased into a frown. "That's a shame. I know Lydia would appreciate your company. She finds these things quite dull. I myself enjoy them immensely and thought you might too."

So, Lydia was going? That resolved any doubts she had about attending. "I most certainly would. In that case, I'll be happy to accompany you and Lydia." She emphasised the last word.

He smiled and her heart swelled. "Good. I'll send my carriage."

The day of the gallery opening Verity dressed with care. She wore a new straw hat festooned with jade green ribbons and full blown roses. She knew the forest green jacket and skirt suited her, bringing out the gold flecks in her emerald eyes. She brushed her dark hair until it shone. The cream of London society would be there and, for some reason she didn't understand, she didn't want to let Brandon down.

Champagne was served as they arrived and she soon found herself entranced by the paintings which took her breath away.

"A feast for the eyes," she said to Lydia, "and so awe-inspiring. How wonderful to be able to paint like that."

Clearly Lydia didn't find it dull, but spoke knowledgeably about each one, telling her little known details of the artist. Brandon, however, appeared distracted, hardly paying any attention to the pictures on display.

They'd been there an hour or so and the crowd was thinning out when she found herself alone in an upstairs gallery. Thinking Lydia must have wandered off she glanced around to see Brandon approaching. Her pulse raced and warmth spread up her neck to her face. Why did he always have this effect on me she thought, irritated that it should be so.

He smiled, although he looked as discomforted as she felt. "I'm glad to have found you alone," he said. "I wanted to speak to you, privately." She glanced around. She was sure Lydia had come upstairs with her, in fact led her upstairs, but now she was nowhere to be seen. Neither was anyone else.

"There's something I have to tell you." He indicated a bench where they could sit. Her stomach knotted as she sat. What on earth could he be about to tell her?

He looked as though he was struggling to find the words. She waited.

"I was sorry to hear about the circumstances of your father's death," he said at last. "I didn't know."

She felt a thud in her heart. The enormity of the shame it brought to her family washed over her. She bowed her head, unable to look at him. "As far as I know, no one knew. It's not something one shouts to the world about." The tone of her voice was calm but cold. She took a breath to steady her nerves. If this was about her father it would be painful to hear. She felt shame enough without him rubbing it in.

"Lawrence came to me because my grandfather was your father's partner. He wanted to know how much I knew, which was nothing at all."

Her head shot up and she stared at him. "Lawrence told you? Why would he do that?"

He took her hand. "Because my grandfather, Monty Summerville, was the man who swindled your father out of everything he owned."

Her heart contracted, she felt sick inside as a wave of horror washed over her. She couldn't breathe. She pulled her hand away and jumped up, staring down at him. He was telling her that his family were to blame for her father's death. Why would he tell her that? And why now? After all the years? "Your grandfather was the swindler? Not my father?" She couldn't take it in. She sank down onto the bench again, her mind in a whirl as the memory of the pain she'd felt when she found the newspaper cutting filled her mind. "Why are you telling me this?"

He took a breath, his face granite. "Because I thought you should know the truth, the whole truth. I swear I knew nothing about it until Lawrence came to me."

Her chin set as fury rose up inside her. "Lawrence knew and didn't tell me. He told me my father was gulled out of his money by a fraudster. He didn't tell me who he was. He told me to forget the past, and he knew all the time?" She could make no sense of it. If Lawrence knew…

"Lawrence isn't the villain here," Brandon said softly. "He kept quiet because he thought it best. There was no point raking over old coals. No good could come of it, only harm to you and your family. Why

281

bring it up again when it's in the past.? It won't change anything."

"And yet, here we are." Sudden realisation hit her like an out of control coach and four. He was gloating. She felt sicker and angrier than she'd ever been. Her fists curled as she tried to contain her absolute fury. "If you're telling me this to further humiliate me and send me scurrying back, head hung in shame, to where I came from, then you've very much mistaken in your judgment of me. My father may have been a gullible fool, but his only fault was trusting people who couldn't be trusted." Her voice grew louder, even as tears of rage rose to her eyes.

He jumped up. "No. Good God! Is that what you think of me?" He sat down next to her again, grabbed her shoulders and turned her to look at him. "If there's anyone here should be humiliated it's me. My grandfather was an out and out scoundrel, a good for nothing wretch who left his family to fend for themselves when he skipped the country with his ill-gotten gains. Your father was blameless. One of his many victims." Contrition shone in his eyes. "If there was anything I could do to change it I would, but there isn't." He let her go and dropped his hands to his sides, his head bowed.

"So, why tell me now? Why bring it all up again?"

He glanced up at her, his face a picture of remorse. "Because I didn't want any secrets between us. I didn't want us to start off on the wrong foot."

Now she was more confused than ever. "Lawrence never told me."

"No. He said he wouldn't, but I wanted you to know. To start with a clean sheet."

To start what, she wondered. "Does Lydia know?"

"No. And I trust you won't tell her." She saw the worry in his face. "She knows he left the country under a cloud but not the full extent of his wrong-doings. The scandal killed our parents. We've worked hard to put it behind us. If she knew about your father…" He gave a helpless shrug. "She'd take it to heart. It would destroy her. She'd feel guilty and try to make amends. She does enough to right the wrongs of today, never mind those of the past."

"So, you're telling me on Lydia's behalf? Not your own?"

"Not at all. It's your opinion of me I value. I hoped you would judge me for my actions, not those of my predecessor or the opinions of others." He spoke softly and hung his head. "Although, I understand if you cannot… perhaps it's too much to ask."

The shock she'd felt earlier turned again to anger. "I assure you I am quite capable of making up my own mind about things. I don't need others to tell me what to think."

He smiled and raised his head to look at her. "That's all I ask. And Lydia?"

"She'll hear nothing from me."

"Thank you." He sighed.

She felt a sudden a bond between them. The confession had brought them closer. Was that the intention behind it? She couldn't decide. All she knew was that she trusted him more now than she had before. Perhaps he wasn't the villain they all said he was.

Lawrence finished the paperwork on his desk and sat back. Several things played on his mind. He mulled over his conversation with Verity. He wasn't going to stop her going to the exhibition opening at the National

Gallery, a once in a lifetime opportunity. She'd never forgive him. No, it was Brandon's part in it and his interest in her. Of course there was the thing with the attempted robbery at the hotel, and Brandon's heroic effort to stop the burglar. That must have given him pause for thought, then more worrying, was the conversation he'd had with him about his grandfather.

Was that behind his interest? Some sort of misguided attempt at atonement? Was it possible that he felt badly enough about his grandfather's action to try to make amends? If so it was a terrible mistake that would do more harm than good. Verity could easily misread his intentions which would result in humiliation for all of them. No point in getting the girl's hopes up, he thought. Perhaps he should have a word with Brandon, man to man. Fellow officers so to speak. He shook his head. Brandon would laugh in his face and Lawrence wouldn't blame him. Lydia had probably told him of Verity's interest in art and it was the action of one art-lover to another. Nothing more than that. Still, it worried him.

She'd become very friendly with Lydia too. Was that because she was missing Charlotte? He liked Lydia and could see no harm in the friendship, although he wasn't sure he could support her stand on the women's suffrage issue. Fair treatment was one thing, criminal damage was quite another. Verity had had one close shave with the law. Her reputation wouldn't survive another.

Then there was the disquiet among the staff over the police requesting further statements. Something that seemed to be causing more upset than expected. What was behind that? Again, he felt as though he'd missed something. Something he didn't know about. It was an uncomfortable feeling. He'd been distracted. He was losing his grip on things.

The other thing on his mind was Mr Jevons. Having been released from prison and cleared of all blame, both for the alleged assault on the chambermaid, and her murder, was he hoping to get his job back? There was the drinking, of course, but Jevons had written to tell him that he had sworn off drink and would never let another drop pass his lips. Did he owe him another chance, given his long years of service?

He sighed and picked up his papers. He'd pass them to Svenson and visit Jeremy. He'd have a better idea of Verity's thoughts, being more experienced with the female of the species and he'd value his opinion about Jevons. He knew him better than anyone too.

*

Things didn't improve for Daisy either. She had finished dressing the next morning when Annie came pounding on her door. "What it is it?"

"It's Jessie. She's gone."

Daisy's heart somersaulted in her chest. "Gone? What do you mean gone?"

"She was gone when I woke up. Her stuff's gone an' all. I think she's done a runner."

Daisy closed her eyes, her stomach churned. Of course, she thought. Just like Jessie to run. "All right. I think I know where she may have gone. You start the rooms. And, Annie…" Annie gazed at her. "Not a word to anyone."

Annie shrugged. "Whatever you say, Miss Carter."

Daisy rushed downstairs. There'd be no problem with the kitchen staff, although they may wonder why Jessie wasn't at breakfast, but she didn't want Mr

Svenson to know. Not yet anyway. She had a few things to do before she could leave the hotel without causing suspicion. She guessed Jessie wouldn't go anywhere without going home first to see Ma. If Daisy could get there by mid-morning she might be able to bring her back, or at least make some excuse for her absence.

Anxiety swirled inside her all the way to Silvertown. When she reached home she found Ma in the kitchen preparing the mid-day meal. She wasn't surprised to see her. "I suppose you've come about Jessie?" she said, turning to fill the kettle for tea.

"That's right. Is she here? I need to speak to her."

"Been and gone. She told me what you wanted her to do. Not very wise, dobbing blokes like Charlie in to the law."

Daisy sank onto a chair. Ma was right. Charlie and his ilk would seek revenge and Jessie would suffer.

Ma put the kettle on the stove and rattled the cups and saucers as she set them out her face hard as granite rock. "Jessie did you a favour. She don't deserve to be punished for it."

"No. Of course she doesn't. I'm sorry. I should have thought."

"Bit late now."

"Where is she? I'd like to talk to her."

"She's somewhere you won't find 'er. Nor will that scrote Charlie Benton."

"Good," Daisy said. "I'm glad."

Among the thoughts whirring through her brain, what she was going to say to Mr Svenson, her obligation to the hotel, the lies she'd told to Mr Lawrence and the worry about losing another chambermaid, the overriding pain came from the knowledge that, once again, she'd done something to drive a wedge between her and her younger sister. A sister she loved with all her heart, despite their spats and difficulties. She'd let Jessie down, the one person in the world she should have protected. "I'm sorry, Ma," she said. "I should have thought."

"Aye. Well, she's safe enough now." She made the tea and put the teapot on the table. "What will you tell 'em at the hotel?"

"I'll say she's been taken ill. I'll speak to Mr Svenson. I doubt I can keep her job open though."

"But you'll give her a good reference?"

Daisy smiled. "I'll write it myself."

Chapter Forty Two

When she got back to the hotel Daisy went to the office to find Mr Svenson. She paused outside the door, taking a deep breath before she knocked and went in. The under-manager sat at his desk writing in a ledger. He looked up as she entered.

"I won't be a moment," he said. "Please take a seat."

Daisy sat on the edge of the chair. He held her future in his hands. She'd been under a cloud ever since the Molly business. Losing another chambermaid would not be viewed well. Trepidation churned inside her.

He finished writing, closed the book and smiled at Daisy. "What can I do for you?" he said.

"It's about Jessie. She's been taken ill. I've had to send her home." The lie tripped off her tongue.

"Oh dear. I hope it's not serious." Concern creased his face. "Is there anything I can do? Send for a doctor, perhaps?" He picked up the telephone on his desk.

"No. No. Really, it's fine." She hadn't expected kindness.

"Is the work too much for her? Perhaps reduce her hours?"

His solicitude undid her. Her resolve crumbled. The more lies she told the worse things got. She wanted to fight for Jessie, but lying wasn't the way. She'd told enough lies. "I'm sorry. I…" Nausea rose up to her throat. "The fact is, she's not ill. She's disappeared. I'm afraid this business about the police has been too much for her. I said she was fragile."

He sat back and stared at her. "Oh. I see." He gazed at her for a moment. She wished she could disappear into the wall. The silence stretched between them. Then he leaned forward and said, "This leaves us in a pretty pickle doesn't it? I'm guessing that your sister knew more about the burglars than she's telling. She was, perhaps, in some way connected to them? Am I right?"

Daisy couldn't speak. She nodded.

He stood and paced for a while, then resumed his seat. "I can say I can't recall who warned us about the possibility of intruders. That there have been a number of burglaries in the area and I was being over-cautious. No one but you and I know of your sister's involvement. For the sake of the hotel it may be best to keep it that way."

Relief and gratitude flooded over her. "You'd do that? For Jessie?"

"For the hotel, Miss Carter. A member of staff, no matter how lowly, being involved with a criminal wouldn't look good on our résumé."

"No. Of course not. I can't thank you enough. I will of course employ another chambermaid."

"Hmm yes. I trust the next one will be more reliable than the last two." He smiled and his eyes twinkled. He was mocking her. She guessed she deserved it.

"Give your sister my best regards when you see her. She was a good worker and I'm sure undeserving of what has happened to her."

Daisy almost bobbed a curtsy as she got up to leave. Who knew, the man had a heart after all.

*

Lawrence found Jeremy at his club, sitting in one of the red leather upholstered armchairs, reading the newspaper.

"Good morning," he said. "An unexpected pleasure. Can I get you some coffee?"

"Please."

Jeremy ordered coffee. "What bring you into town today? Not trouble at the hotel I hope."

"No. Well, not really. Just a few things on my mind I'd like to talk over with you." He smiled. "Nothing too serious."

"Good. I'm not in the mood for serious. What is it?"

Lawrence told him about Verity's father's suicide and how she'd asked him to look into it. "The devil of it was that I found it intriguing and I think I pursued it as much for my own curiosity as Verity's."

The coffee arrived and they each took a cup. Lawrence went on to tell Jeremy about his visit to Leeds and what he'd found out. Jeremy listened in astonishment.

"So, you see," Lawrence said. "When I found out that Brandon's grandfather was involved I had a word with him."

Jeremy's brow furrowed "You did what?"

"I spoke to him. Of course he knew nothing. He was in India with me when it happened. Then he went to America. I'm not sure what I expected." He sipped his coffee. "The thing is, since then Brandon is paying Verity a lot of attention and I suspect his motives. I don't want her to get hurt."

Jeremy shook his head. "Damn fool," he said, "ever to get involved in the first place. I'm sure Uncle Douglas knew what he was doing when he sent his family to stay with us. He did it for their peace of mind. So they wouldn't suffer for his actions. Raking it all up will do no good at all." There was no disguising the disgust in his voice.

"Well, I know that now. But I wasn't sure what to do about it."

"If in doubt, do nowt," Jeremy said. "It's best to let these things work themselves out. Verity's not stupid and she's more resilient than you think. She has a mind of her own."

"That's the other thing. She's spending a lot of time with Lydia, Brandon's sister. I'm concerned she's getting involved with her women's suffrage pals. That can only lead to trouble. I'm at a loss what to do, other than send her home."

Jeremy laughed. "I'd like to see you try. She won't go. I'll have a word with her if you like. She might listen to me."

Lawrence nodded. "She misses Charlotte Huntington-Smythe. I don't want to alienate her entirely."

"Taking of the Huntington-Smythes," Jeremy said. "Bertie's trial starts next week. Are you going?"

Lawrence sighed. "That's another thing. I'm afraid Verity will want to go. She's in touch with Charlotte and will think it her duty to be able to give her the news first hand. I'm not sure it'll be good for her. It'll only upset her all over again."

"You worry too much," Jeremy said. "Me? I wouldn't miss it for the world." His eyes shone with glee.

They finished their coffee and Jeremy order two brandies. Then Lawrence asked him what he thought he should do about Mr Jevons. "Do nothing," Jeremy said. "One thing you can't get in trouble for is doing nothing."

Chapter Forty Three

Daisy left Mr Svenson a little happier than when she'd arrived, but she still wasn't satisfied. The news of a burglary and trial in the paper would drag the hotel and all their names through the mud. Why couldn't Charlie admit what he'd done? It would save them all a lot of trouble. The more she thought about it the more determined she became to see him and try to persuade him to plead guilty. Perhaps being in prison had given him time to think things through.

She knew prisoners could receive letters and were allowed visitors, so she wrote to him, asking if she could see him. *It's about Jessie*, she put, hoping he still cared for her. They'd been in love once, surely there was some feeling for her left in him?

The day of the visit she put on her best navy blue suit and hat. She wanted to look business-like but not intimidating. She knew Charlie and his family well enough, they went back a long way. The youngest of five boys with a father in prison and a drunk for a mother, he hadn't had much of a start in life. When he married Jessie she thought him different from the others. It didn't take long for her to change her mind. Still, perhaps there was hope. He'd married Jessie. She was counting on that meaning something.

The place where he was being held was dark and intimidating outside and cold inside. She told the warders that she'd come on behalf of the prisoner's wife, showed them the letter he'd written agreeing to see her. A warder led her to a small room, attended by a sentry standing guard. The last time she'd seen Charlie she'd screamed at him. This time she had to convince him that she was speaking for Jessie, who loved and trusted him.

She hardly recognised Charlie when he was brought in. The striding braggart he used to be was gone, in its place she saw a hurt, confused young lad, out of his depth and unwilling to acknowledge it. Too thin, his cheeks sunken and his eyes dull he had the look of a frightened animal hunted to ground. Strands of greasy, unkempt hair fell across his forehead. A bruise darkened under one eye. His sullen look made her heart tremble.

"Hello, Charlie," she said.

He grunted.

"I know we haven't always been friends," she said, "but I'm sorry to see you in such a state. I've brought you these." She took a packet of biscuits out of her bag. The warder jumped forward but, after inspection, nodded and allowed Charlie to take them.

"Thanks," he mumbled.

"I've come about Jessie," she said. "She's frightened, Charlie. Frightened for you and frightened for herself." She glanced at the guard and lowered her voice. "She's afraid they're going to charge her with being an accomplice."

He sat up. "Charge Jessie? Why?"

"Because that's what they do. You know that. If the matter goes to trial, your relationship will be revealed. She's your wife. She works at the hotel. They'll think she was in on it and whether she was or not, they'll charge her."

"She weren't nothing to do with it."

"I know that. You loved her once, Charlie. You know what she's been through, losing the baby and that. Prison will kill her, Charlie. You have to save her."

"Save her? How can I do that? In 'ere?" He looked pensive. "An' I did... do love 'er. She's the best thing that ever 'appened to me. It was me mucked it all up. I know that."

Daisy felt heartened. "Yes. And it won't go well for you at trial either, if it comes out how you beat her up and pushed her down the stairs, killing the baby." It was stark, meant to shock and it had the desired effect.

"I didn't mean owt. It were an accident. She fell."

Daisy shrugged. "So you say. Still it won't go in your favour."

"What do you s'pect me to do? I can't do nothing, in 'ere."

"Plead guilty. Then there won't be a trial. You're going to prison, Charlie, one way or another. Don't take Jessie down with you. She doesn't deserve that."

He sighed and sat looking morose. "I s'pose it don't make much difference, one way or t'other," he said eventually. "Jessie was always my girl, you know that don't you, Dais?"

"I do, Charlie, and she only had eyes for you. It was a shame what happened."

He sat with his head bowed, all fight gone out of him. Still young and vulnerable he'd been born into a world too harsh for him.

Daisy reached out to touch his hand. The warder jumped forward. "No touching."

She withdrew her hand. "I'm sorry, Charlie. Sorry for everything."

He nodded. "I didn't want to do it, you know. It was Barney's idea, robbing the hotel. 'E talked me into it."

"It'll go easier on you if you tell the truth, Charlie. Plead guilty, do the time, then you can come out with a clean slate. Maybe start again."

"Nah. Thieving's in me bones. I was born into it and I'll probably die doing it. But I won't take Jessie down. I'll plead guilty and Barney'll do the same. 'Es brawn, not brains. I can talk 'im into it. Tell Jessie she'll get no grief from me. I owe 'er that."

Daisy's heart was lighter when she left the prison, stepping out to the chill autumn afternoon. Now at least she could write to Jessie, sending it to Ma, so she'd have no need to worry about Charlie. What a strange man he was, she thought. Deprived of love all his life, she supposed Jessie's love was all he had to cling on to.

Chapter Forty Four

Verity grew more and more concerned about Charlotte when she hadn't heard from her, despite Lawrence's assurance that it took weeks for letters to arrive from South America. "Do you think she knows about Edward and Bertie?" she asked one morning at breakfast.

"I've no doubt the family solicitor will have been in touch with Chester," Lawrence said. "They're quite civilised in Argentina. He'll have telegraphed."

"How awful for her. I wasn't sure what to say in my letters. I didn't want to mention it if she didn't know." She buttered a piece of toast. "I feel awful going out and enjoying myself while she's having to bear such sorrow. It doesn't feel right somehow."

Lawrence frowned. "It's not your fault. You shouldn't feel badly about it. Bertie's predicament is the consequence of his own actions and as for Edward…" He sighed. "He knew what he was doing. It's young Molly Brown deserves your sympathy. She didn't deserve what happened to her."

"Will you be going to the trial?"

He folded the paper he was reading and laid it down. "I feel I should go, even if to ensure that none of it reflects badly on the hotel. She did work here. I know that's not relevant, but that doesn't mean it won't be mentioned. I do hope not."

"I'd like to come. I feel in some way responsible, not for Bertie of course, but for Charlotte. Being her friend and bringing her here with her family."

"That's nonsense. What happened was nothing to do with your friendship."

"But it's the reason I care so much and why you're so interested in the outcome. Be honest, if you'd never met the Huntington-Smythes you wouldn't give a jot about the case."

"I'd care a jot, perhaps, but you're right, having met the family it does bring it closer to home. Still, I don't think a murder trial is an appropriate place for a young lady. It will be most unpleasant."

"No worse than reading about it and hearing exaggerated second and third hand details. Please, Lawrence, let me go with you. I want to be able to tell Charlotte the truth, without the journalistic embellishments. I promise I'll leave if it gets too awful."

"I suppose you're going to insist. There's no talking you out of it?"

"No."

"Well, all right. Better you go with me than on your own, I suppose."

"Thank you, Lawrence." She jumped up and kissed his cheek.

Every day she scanned the newspapers, cutting out everything she found and adding it to the cuttings she'd already saved from the raid, the arrest and Edward's death. As she did it she thought of the cuttings she'd found in her mother's cupboard, hidden away. Who had sent them? She'd always thought it a malicious act, but now she wasn't so sure. Was it a friend, letting Mama know what had happen to her husband? An act of kindness?

Verity wasn't sure whether what she was doing was the right thing or not. Perhaps it was better for Charlotte not to know. But then, isn't it always better to know the truth, however bad? Especially if it's knowledge that can protect you from future discoveries?

If Verity had known about her father from childhood, would she have loved him less? Her perception of him would certainly have been different. Perhaps in Charlotte's case ignorance would be bliss too.

As the date of Charlie's trial loomed nearer, Daisy worried he may go back on his word. Just like Charlie, she thought. Say one thing and do another. She'd written to Jessie, telling her of the visit. It would be awful if he didn't go through with it. Jessie would think even worse of her than she did now.

That's what was on her mind when Hollis told her Mr Svenson was looking for her. With a heavy heart she went to his office.

"Ah. Miss Carter, good news," he said. "The police have been in touch regarding the attempted burglary. It seems that the accused, in the face of overwhelming evidence, have admitted their guilt. There will be no actual trial, just a sentencing hearing assessing any mitigating circumstances. I'll be going, but there's no need for anyone else to attend."

Daisy took that as an instruction to stay away. Just as well, she thought. She hadn't relished facing Charlie again. Not after all that had happened. "I'm pleased to hear it," she said. "I expect the rest of the staff will be too."

"Yes. Indeed. I'll let them know. Now, is there any news about a replacement chambermaid?"

Daisy forced a smile. "It's early days. I've approached the agency and put an advertisement in *The Lady*, but had no response as yet."

"I see. That's just as I thought. In that case you'll be pleased to hear that I've had a letter from a chap I used to work with on the ships. He was a steward and a jolly good fellow, a hard worker. He has a daughter who's looking for a position. She's worked on the ships as a cabin-maid but suffers from seasickness. It will be your decision of course, but I've asked her to call this afternoon at two o'clock. I hope that's convenient. Here are her details." He handed her a slip of paper. "She'll have excellent references."

Daisy didn't know what to say. It was a bit high-handed of him, taking on her role, but she could hardly protest. Her last two attempts at choosing staff had hardly been a roaring success. Annie had already started complaining about her increased workload and she'd received no other applications. She clenched her jaw. "That will be fine," she said, her irritation rising. "I'll see her and make my decision then. Thank you."

"Good. She'll have time to settle in before the Christmas rush. We don't want to be short-staffed at the busiest time of year."

At least the other staff welcomed the news when she told them she was seeing a possible replacement for Jessie. She even thought she heard a muttered, "Hope she lasts longer than the last two," but decided to ignore it.

The girl, Miss Elise Harris, arrived promptly at two o'clock at the kitchen door which was a good sign. Smartly dressed, wearing sensible shoes and her chestnut brown hair neatly styled under a dark green felt hat, Daisy was at first reassured. She offered her tea and took her into her sitting room.

"I see your name's Elise. Pretty name," and a bit too fancy for everyday use, Daisy thought. "We use first names for below-stairs staff here, so I shall call you Elsie. You will call me Miss Carter. I hope that's acceptable."

Elise smiled, a dazzling smile that did nothing to allay Daisy's doubts about her. "Perfectly fine." She spoke with a slight accent.

Over tea and cake Daisy found out that she was seventeen, nearly eighteen, her father was English, her mother French. She spoke both languages as well as a little German. She'd worked on the ships for almost a year.

"I expect you've seen the world then," Daisy said. "You may find it a bit dull here."

"We spent all our time below decks," Elise said. "We were only allowed topside when the ship docked and the visitors went ashore on tours. I missed fresh air and the freedom to walk around without being hemmed in by walls. It made me ill. Mr Svenson said you may have a place for me. I would be most grateful." Her eyes lit up when she said his name.

"You've met Mr Svenson?"

"Yes. When he worked with my father. He's a very nice man and kind to recommend me. I don't mind hard work, but I want to get on. I hope I can do a good job here."

Daisy looked through her references. They were, as Mr Svenson had said, excellent. She could see no reason not to give her the job, especially as no one else had applied. "Very well, you may start tomorrow."

"Oh, thank you, Miss Carter, but I can start today. I have very little belongings. There is no problem."

Daisy's eyebrows rose. "Well, then if there's nothing else. You'll be sharing with Annie. She's the first chambermaid. She'll show you around and tell you what to do. You'll work in the bedrooms, then in the tea room in the afternoon and the restaurant in the evenings if required. There'll be no fraternising with the male staff and we insist on discretion and decorum at all times. Is that clear?"

"Oh yes, Miss Carter. Decorum is my middle name."

Daisy took her up to meet Annie and left her with her. She didn't know why she'd said that bit about discretion and decorum and the girl's reaction to Mr Svenson bothered her. Still, she thought, if this one goes wrong it won't be entirely my fault. I can blame 'nice Mr Svenson'.

Chapter Forty Five

Bertie Huntington-Smythe's trial was set for a day in mid October. Golden light filled the sky as leaves on the trees turned rust and gold and summer roses lost their bloom. An autumnal breeze blew clouds across the sky.

Verity got up early and dressed in her sombre brown suit and matching felt hat with a velvet band. It was several years old but she didn't want to stand out. She had an early breakfast with Lawrence who'd arranged a cab to take them to the Central Criminal Court.

When they arrived butterflies fluttered inside her as she made her way up the winding steps to the public gallery. She'd expected there to be a lot of interest in the case and she wasn't wrong. The gallery had begun to fill from early on.

They found seats in the middle rows which gave a sufficiently broad view of the courtroom below. Glancing around Verity saw people from all walks of life and levels of society. She'd expected that. Many of them would be here to see Molly Brown got justice.

The well of the court gradually filled with barristers, clerks, journalists, solicitors and ushers, a quiet murmur rising up as they took their places. Then the jury were led in. Twelve men of good standing. The court rose as Judge Bowden-Brown took his place beneath the Royal Coat of Arms symbolising the authority of the Crown over the proceedings.

The members of the jury were sworn in and the clerk of court asked Bertie to confirm his name. Then the charge of murder in the first degree was put to him. "How do you plead?"

"Not guilty," Bertie, standing in the dock between two prison guards, said, belligerence bridled his voice and demeanour.

The barristers introduced themselves as Robert Childerhouse for the prosecution and Sir Oswald Rockingham for the defence.

"He's got the best," Lawrence whispered when Sir Oswald introduced himself. "I guess his father made sure of that."

The case began with details of finding the body of Molly Brown, the nature of her injuries and the police investigation. Several police officers were called to give evidence. The pathologist gave graphic details of the victim's injuries. So graphic Verity felt sick. As he spoke about the strangulation, the memory of Bertie pushing her against the wall, his hand around her neck, ran through her mind. A shiver ran down her spine. He did it, she thought. I'm sure he did it.

There followed an account from Inspector Rolleston of the investigation. He gave details of her place of work, how she made her living and the sort of customers who used the services she offered.

"And the defendant was one of them?" Mr Childerhouse asked.

"He was indeed. His family owned the club where she worked. His brother managed it."

"And he was arrested during a raid there. Can you tell us please, what led to the raid and the subsequent arrest?"

"Yes, sir. We received information that the defendant had motive, means and opportunity. Following further investigation he was duly arrested."

"Thank you. No further questions."

Sir Oswald stood. "Inspector Rolleston, my client was arrested at Miss Brown's place of work during a raid on the premises, is that correct?"

"Yes, sir."

"Was my client Molly Brown's only customer?"

"No, sir. I believe she had a large clientele. I understand he preferred her to the other girls though and would choose her most often."

"Hmm seems rather short-sighted to kill one's preferred choice."

Mr Childerhouse rose. Judge Bowden-Brown spoke before he could say anything. "Sir Oswald, you know better than to express your own opinion. Please contain your views and constrain yourself to asking questions."

"I apologise, My Lord. Inspector Rolleston, my client was not the first man arrested for the murder of Molly Brown was he?"

The inspector looked uncomfortable. "No, sir. He was not."

"Please tell the court why the first suspect was arrested and then released. I'm sure we'd all like to know."

"A witness gave us a statement that we later found to be untrue."

"A witness? Are you telling us that this witness gave false evidence?"

Mr Childerhouse again stood up. "My Lord, that witness is not on trial. What happened prior to the defendant's arrest is irrelevant."

"That may be so," the judge said, "but I'm sure we're all interested to hear the answer."

The inspector scowled. "Yes. We later found his evidence to be unfounded. The suspect had an alibi and no connection to the crime."

"So you are satisfied that he was innocent and went looking elsewhere? Is that correct?"

"Yes, sir."

"Any port in a storm eh? Sorry. I withdraw the question. Nothing further." He resumed his seat with a satisfied look on his face.

"Good," the judge said. "I see the clock has moved on. We'll adjourn for lunch." He banged his gavel and the court adjourned.

Verity and Lawrence stepped out into the busy London street. People milled around on the pavement and the road heaved with cabs, carts, drays and carriages. They managed to cross to a tavern where Lawrence ordered beer for him, sherry for Verity and two rounds of beef sandwiches.

"How do you think it's going?" Verity asked, halfway through her first sandwich and grateful for it. She hadn't realised how hungry she was.

Lawrence shrugged. "The men on the jury will have more in common with the Huntington-Smythes than with Molly Brown. Several of them will probably have used the services of prostitutes and their experience, good or bad, may colour their judgement. They may look at Bertie and see their own sons. Anything is possible."

"You mean they'll find him innocent, because they went to the same school or move in the same social circles?"

"Possibly."

"But that's terrible. I mean I hope for Charlotte's sake that he's innocent, but if he did it she should be punished."

"Guilty or not the mud will stick. People have long memories."

She finished her sandwich, but the thought kept circling her mind. "What do you think? Did he do it? Did he kill Molly Brown?"

Lawrence tutted. "I'm undecided but, seeing him, I wouldn't be surprised."

The afternoon session brought a parade of girls and young women who worked at the club. They all knew Bertie and spoke in lurid detail of their time in his company. They were all aware of his temper and most could attest to some sort of violent behaviour. They all appeared to relish the opportunity to tell their stories before an audience, gasping at their revelations and hanging on to their every word. Verity soon noticed that the crowd around her fully supported the notion that 'the toff should get his comeuppance'.

Sir Oswald soon demolished their credibility, calling it the malicious outpourings of immoral women extracting revenge for their impoverished lives. Their words were twisted, their motives questioned. He subjected them to a piercing examination of their morals and purpose, accusing each of them of deriving benefit or satisfaction from the predicament of a man who'd done nothing more than use the services they offered and paid well for the privilege. He called it a character assassination by doxies and harlots, most of it opinion, gossip and hearsay. None of them could provide any actual evidence.

By the end of the day Verity felt deflated and terribly disheartened. "I'm surprised anyone gets convicted of anything," she said in the cab on the way home. "It's an awful performance to achieve so little."

Chapter Forty Six

The next morning a subdued Verity breakfasted with Lawrence. After yesterday's performance she wasn't sure she wanted to go to the court after all. If it hadn't been for her friendship with Charlotte and her desire to be able to tell her everything that went on, she would have backed-out.

"I didn't realise it would be so long-winded," she said. "So stuffy and formal. So much standing up and sitting down, stopping and starting. It's a wonder they get anything done."

"Ah the wheels of justice grind slow, but they grind exceeding small," Lawrence said. "Justice has, not only to be done, but has to be seen to be done. Everyone has to have their chance to say their piece, whether it's relevant or not. It should go better today. I've a feeling Mr Childerhouse has something up his sleeve to get the ball rolling. He'll want to get his teeth into the matter."

They settled in their seats in the gallery and Verity sat back to watch. The session opened with the same performance as the previous day, jurors were reminded they were still on oath and the session began.

Mr Childerhouse called Terrance Dolan, the fourteen-year-old boy who'd been arrested with Edward Huntington-Smythe. In the public gallery the watchers perked up. A ripple went through the court when he was brought in: a skinny, pale-faced boy with slicked down dark hair, black doleful eyes and a suit two sizes too big for him. A suspenseful silence hung over the court while they waited for him to be sworn in.

Mr Childerhouse opened by apologising for bringing him in, acknowledging how difficult it would be for him to speak, but how necessary if a guilty man was to be convicted. He asked him to confirm his name and tell the court how he came to be working at The Hades Club.

A hush fell over the court when the boy spoke, his voice barely a whisper. He told the court how he'd been picked up off the street with the promise of work, imprisoned, beaten, starved and forced to work as a rent boy performing whatever perverted acts the customer demanded.

"And you agreed to this?"

"Didn't 'ave much choice. I did run away once, but they caught me." He undid his jacket and shirt, turned and dropped them to show his back, a mess of scarring and welts where he'd been beaten.

The court gasped.

"Who did that to you?"

The boy turned and pointed to Bertie. "'E did, an' 'e enjoyed doing it. 'E weren't the only one. They took photographs an' all," he said, pulling his shirt and jacket back on.

Bertie jumped up and shouted, "You bloody deserved it, traitor!"

The prison guards grabbed Bertie and forced him down. The court erupted with people shouting abuse. The judge banged his gavel. "Silence in court. I won't have this disruption. Sir Oswald, please control your client or I will have him removed."

The noise died down to a murmur. The judge turned to the witness. "Are you prepared to continue?"

"Yes, sir. Just want this over and done with."

"Mr Childerhouse, you may continue and I'll have quiet in the court or people will be removed."

"Thank you, My Lord." Mr Childerhouse turned to the boy, speaking softly. "How long was your association with Edward Huntington-Smythe?"

"He called 'imself Edward Smith," the boy said. He glanced down and mumbled.

"I'm sorry the court needs to hear your answer. "How long did you know Mr Edward Smith?"

"Nearly a year."

"And you performed acts of a sexual nature with the man calling himself Mr Smith?"

"I did 'im and 'e did me if that's what you mean. Yes, sir."

The court gasped.

"Were you Mr Smith's only lover?"

"No, sir. 'E 'ad many lovers." Tears filled the boy's soulful eyes. One ran down his cheek. He wiped it away with the back of his hand.

The judge asked if he'd like a moment to compose himself.

He shook his head.

"You may continue, Mr Childerhouse."

"Thank you, My Lord." He smiled at the witness. "Did you know Molly Brown?"

"Yes, sir. She was kind to me. We were friends."

"And she knew about your association with Mr Smith?"

"Yes, sir. We talked about it. She said it weren't right and she was going to speak to the police."

A ripple went through the court. Verity felt the sympathy of the people around her for this small, mistreated boy. Her heart went out to him.

Mr Childerhouse continued. "She told you that?"

"Yes, sir. And she told Edward."

"What did Edward say?"

"'E said she'd better keep 'er mouth shut, or 'e'd shut it for her." The court took a breath.

"Thank you."

People around Verity nodded and whispered. It was clear whose side they were on.

Sir Oswald rose and began by thanking the witness for his appearance and acknowledging how difficult it must have been for him. He tried to question him in the same way as he had the women the previous day, but it was clear the boy had the sympathy of the court and any further pressure he brought to be bear would only alienate the jury. There was nothing he could do or say would make the lad's life any less awful than it was, so, in the end, he thanked him and sat down.

It being lunch time, the court adjourned.

"What do you think of that?" Verity asked Lawrence as they sat down to lunch in the tavern across the road from the court.

"What? Bertie's outburst? Didn't do him any favours did it?"

"No. Did you see Sir Oswald's face? I've never seen a man so stricken."

Lawrence chuckled. "Nor me. Although, it probably won't count for much, if Sir Oswald manages to turn it round. There are probably men on the jury who beat their wives and servants, who will think it a justifiable treatment for someone who needs to learn a lesson."

Verity shuddered. "That's awful. I felt sorry for the poor boy."

"I think that was the idea. Childerhouse will have to come up with something more substantial than the testimony of a boy who's been ill-used and may want revenge."

"You think that's how he'll play it?"

"Certainly. If it comes down to the word of a rent boy against the word of a man, supposedly a scholar and a gentleman, despite his faults, then I'm afraid they'll go for the one most like themselves."

"So his outburst won't have done him any harm?"

"Well, Sir Oswald will describe it as youthful impetuosity. A rightful response to a slur against his brother. Family honour being threatened, who wouldn't do the same?"

Verity found she'd lost her appetite. Bertie would get away with murder, because of who he was, not what he'd done.

The afternoon started with Mr Childerhouse calling Mr James Daikins. He quickly established that he was known to Molly Brown, although did not give the precise nature of that knowledge.

"Oh dear," Lawrence whispered.

Surprised, Verity frowned. "Do you know him?"

"I've had dealings with him, yes. A man not to be trusted. This will not go well."

Verity sat back and listened as Mr Childerhouse began his questioning.

"Did Molly Brown mention anything about The Hades Club and her work there?" Childerhouse asked.

"'Course she did. There weren't no secrets between me an' Molly."

"So she told you what she knew about Mr Edward Huntington-Smythe?"

"Said his name was Edward Smith, but yeah, I knew."

"And what was Miss Brown going to do about it."

"Said she'd go to the police."

"And did she tell Mr Edward Smith, as he was known to her, what she was going to do."

"She told me she was going to speak to 'im." He pointed at Bertie.

"The defendant?"

"That's him. Poncy boy. Smith's brother."

"Thank you. That will be all." Mr Childerhouse sat and Sir Oswald rose. He paced the floor, as though deciding what he was going to say next.

"Did Molly Brown tell you that she had spoken to my client?" he asked eventually.

"Nah. Only that she was going to. I 'spect she did. That's why he strangled her."

A gasp ran though the gallery.

"Hmm that's pure supposition, but let's leave it for now. Did Miss Brown mention anything about money? The possibility that someone would pay to keep her quiet?"

Daikins grimaced. "She might have said somat."

"Did she in fact ask my client for one thousand pounds?"

Ooos and arhhs rang around the court.

"I wouldn't know. I wasn't there. If I 'ad 'ave been 'e wouldn't have killed her, would 'e?"

"Thank you." Sir Oswald perused some papers on the desk. "You have a criminal record…"

Mr Childerhouse jumped up.

"Yes, thank you." Judge Bowden-Brown glared at him. "Sir Oswald. The witness is not on trial. His criminal record is of no consequence."

"I apologise, My Lord. I was just trying to ascertain the probability of truth from this witness."

"So now we all know about it," Lawrence whispered to Verity.

Sir Oswald smiled as he continued. "You made a statement to the police about this case on a previous occasion, did you not?"

Daikins glanced around. "Yes, but…"

"But you lied?"

Mr Childerhouse jumped up again. "My Lord, the defence is impugning the witness. He's referring to a previous suspect who was cleared and is irrelevant today."

"I was merely trying to verify the veracity of this witness's testimony, My Lord. It seems he changes his mind with the weather."

"I was mistaken," Daikins said. "But I'm not wrong about that murdering b—" He pointed to Bertie.

Bertie, who'd been sitting glowering at the witness, jumped up. "Cow deserved it. My brother's dead because of her."

The court burst into uproar. Sir Oswald sank onto his chair, head in his hands. The prison officers wrestled Bertie back into his seat. Judge Bowden-Brown banged his gavel. It took several minutes for the noise to quieten.

A disgruntled Judge Bowden-Brown banged his gavel and court was adjourned.

"Phew," Verity said in the cab on the way home. "Bertie's done it this time, hasn't he? More or less admitted it. Surely even someone as brilliant as Sir Oswald Rockingham can't get him out of that?"

Lawrence chuckled. "No. I must admit, he should have controlled his temper. But all is not lost. Sir

Oswald will argue justification. Bertie is only nineteen. He is of previous good character. The men on the jury will have sons who may step out of line and sow wild oats. They will not expect them to be punished for it. Then there's the matter of family honour. If he can persuade the jury that Bertie did it to protect his family, it'll go a long way to make it seem acceptable. Who was Molly Brown anyway? A prostitute, selling her body for money, a blackmailer, one of life's undeserving unfortunates, that's how he will paint her. He may admit the crime, but plead mitigation. The boy lost his brother. His whole family have deserted him. A good education, a promising career gone go waste for one foolish, impetuous action. I believe that's how he will play it. He'll say he didn't mean to kill her. It was an accident. I believe that will be the thrust of his argument."

And so it proved the next day in court. Sir Oswald, summing up, made the same points as Lawrence had surmised. He said his client had been provoked, threatened. He was protecting his brother, who had since himself made the final sacrifice to save any disgrace that may befall his family for his unconscionable actions.

"Can we allow that to count for nothing?" he said. "Surely our sympathies must be with this young boy, who has lost so much only trying to save his family's honour? Who among us would not do the same?"

Mr Childerhouse's call for justice for the victim and a plea for equal treatment regardless of status or position was readily accepted by the onlookers in the public gallery, but Verity felt sure the jurors were more inclined to listen to the man representing one of their peers.

The judge in his summing up referred to English Law. "In order to find the defendant guilty of murder you must be convinced that he did, with malice aforethought, kill Miss Molly Brown in contravention of the law. If you find that the defendant did kill Miss Molly Brown other than with malice aforethought, but rather in a spontaneous act in response to some provocation, you may find him guilty of the lesser charge of manslaughter."

The jury retired to consider their verdict.

Two days later the verdict was announced. Lawrence scanned the papers but found very little about the trial concerning the murder of a London prostitute. When it did appear it was on page five. Bertie had been found guilty of manslaughter and sentenced to twenty years in prison.

"Doesn't sound much for taking a life," Verity said. "If it had been the other way round she'd have hanged."

Lawrence agreed. "The jury were naturally prejudiced," he said. "They are men of the world, Bertie's one of their own. They're bound to find in his favour. I'm surprised they found him guilty at all."

"You mean he could have got off? No punishment at all?"

"It happens," Lawrence said. "That's how prejudice works. We all have prejudice, the preference of one thing over another. The trick is to be aware of it and not let it affect our judgement. I think the jury did a good job. It was a fair trial. There was provocation."

"You mean she asked for it?"

"No. That's not what I mean, but he who rides with the devil... She was a blackmailer who tried it on the wrong person."

"And paid heavily for her mistake."

"Would you rather he hanged?"

"No. Of course not," she said, horrified. "I'm glad he got off so lightly, if only for Charlotte's sake. She's lost one brother, to lose another would be unbearable."

Chapter Forty Seven

Mr Svenson called Daisy into the office to tell her the result of the attempted burglars' sentence hearing. "The old chap, the one who knifed me and tried to kill Mr Summerville, was charged with assault and actual bodily harm as well as attempted burglary. He got two years imprisonment. The younger lad got off lightly, thanks to his guilty plea. He got six months, but that's very little for what he planned to do. It's a shame your sister disappeared. I expect she would have liked to know the outcome. If it hadn't been for her we would have been in a far worse situation. It's a pity I can't thank her in person."

Daisy felt a flood of relief. At least Charlie Benton would be off the streets if Jessie did decide to come home. "Thank you for letting me know, sir," she said. "If I hear from Jessie I'll pass it on."

"Good. How's the new girl settling in? She's bright and very willing, from what I've seen of her."

Daisy was aware that he saw quite a bit of her as she always volunteered to clean his room and take his morning coffee and afternoon tea up. Very willing, indeed she thought. Still, she had to admit she could find no fault with her work. "She seems to be doing well, thank you, sir. I've had no complaints from the other staff."

"Excellent. We'll need to be at full strength for Christmas." He smiled and Daisy felt his dismissal.

Over the following weeks as Elise settled in, Daisy came to accept that she obviously had experience and was eager to please. She was perfect for the job and, with Christmas just over a month away, it was essential that everything ran smoothly. Added to that, Daisy couldn't afford to lose another chambermaid.

Always pleasant, Elise became popular with the other staff. Annie liked her because she was a hard worker, quick to see what needed doing and not slow to pitch in and do it.

She complimented Mrs T on her cooking, which went down well, although Mrs T would never admit to being dazzled by flattery.

Even Barker, usually conservative in his comments, warmed to her, especially when she told him she thought soldiers must be very brave. Daisy watched him puff up with pride.

"I knew an 'Arris in the Brigade, in Africa," he said. "Good bloke. I wonder if 'e's any relation."

"Papa was a baker before he joined the White Star Line," she said. "I don't think he ever served, but I admire any man who did."

Bridget too had many a good word for her. She was always polite to customers, but never over-familiar. She didn't mind the extra hours when they were busy and never complained about being on her feet all day.

At least Mr Svenson's happy, Daisy thought. Why wouldn't he be? The girl dances attendance on him, often putting a scone or biscuits on the tray when she took his tea or coffee up, even if he hadn't asked for them.

"She's got her eye on 'im," Mrs T said to Daisy. "Clear as day. She'll be after your job next."

Daisy laughed, but wondered whether Mrs T may have a point. "I don't know about that," she said, peeved at the thought. "The girl's popular but then so was Molly and look what happened to her."

Lawrence too contemplated his future. He'd had a letter from his mother asking when he'd be coming home. He read the impatience in her words. *There are thing needing to be done that cannot wait. You work too hard. Decisions need to be made that require your presence.* He sighed.

He glanced around at the photos on the wall, his father, the family, the hotel his father had built up from nothing. The summer had passed and winter would soon be upon them. They'd have to be thinking about Christmas, always a busy time. The town would be heaving with people coming to town to shop or visit the theatre and other attractions. They'd be Christmas parties to plan, extra supplies to order, special menus to prepare. They'd have to offer entertainment and something to attract Christmas shoppers in for hot drinks with seasonal fare. Could he go home and leave all that to Svenson? No doubt, with Jeremy's help they could manage perfectly well. Maldon Hall needed a family within its wall. It was time he settled down and provided one.

He was thinking about Christmas at Maldon Hall when Verity came into the office.

"I hope I'm not disturbing you," she said.

"Not at all. I was just thinking of Christmas at Maldon Hall. You'll be home by then, won't you?"

She smiled. "Yes. I've had a letter from Aunt Elvira asking when I'm coming home. I'm not sure if she misses me or she'd got something else planned."

Lawrence laughed. "You too? I had one asking the same thing. I see her point though. Perhaps it's time." He paused. "Unless there's something to keep you here?"

"A proposal of marriage you mean? No nothing like that."

Was that regret he heard in her voice he wondered. "I expect your friend in the bookshop will want you back before Christmas. It must be a busy time for him too."

"Ira? Yes. I expect he misses me but I'm not vain enough to think he can't do without me for a little longer."

"So you do have a reason to stay?"

"Only until the beginning of November. I said I'd help Lydia out with something."

Lawrence frowned. "You've been seeing a lot of Lydia lately. Is there something I should know? Something about her brother, perhaps?"

"Brandon? Good heavens, no." To Lawrence's mind the denial came a little too quickly. Rushed without thought, like a child denying stealing a biscuit when sugar crystals hung on his lip.

Verity went on, "I like Lydia. She's good company and cares about more than the latest fashion or who danced with whom at the latest charity ball. She's intelligent, charming and knowledgeable. She takes an interest in things."

Lawrence wasn't appeased. "Like Votes for Women? I do hope she's not leading you into more trouble."

"Of course not." She smiled but Lawrence still wasn't convinced.

"Very well then. I'll tell Mama we'll be home at the end of November. She'll want to arrange parties and invite the whole neighbourhood. I expect she'll relish the opportunity of more matchmaking on both our behalves."

"Well, she needn't bother on my account. I'm happy to stay single."

"I'm sure you don't mean that."

Verity laughed. "Oh but I do."

Chapter Forty Eight

The day of the Lord Mayor's Show dawned cold and crisp. Pale sunlight glistened on roof tops in the frost sharpened air, the November sky clear and blue. Luckily there was no sign of the rain that would put a damper on the whole event. Verity rose early and dressed in her warmest clothes. After breakfast she walked towards Covent Garden, passing shops already decorated for Christmas. Early shoppers crowded the pavements. She wasn't sure where she'd find Kitty but luckily ran into her before she got there.

"I hope I'm not late," she said.

"No, the others have gone ahead. I just stayed to collect some more leaflets. Here, take some." She halved the bundle of pamphlets she carried and gave them to Verity. "Just throw them out of the window. The wind'll do the rest."

"Are you sure it's all right? I mean, we won't be prosecuted or anything?"

"Of course not. It's no different from handing them out in the street, only quicker."

Reassured, Verity walked on with her to the building in Ludgate Hill selected for the scattering. They went down an alley and Kitty opened the building's back door. "The caretaker's gone to watch the parade," she said. "He's been well paid to make sure he does. You go in. I have to take these to our other post in Cheapside." She smiled. "And don't worry, it'll be fun and you get to see the parade too, which is always worthwhile."

Verity went in and up the narrow stairs. Kitty had told her to go to the top floor, so she went on up. The stairs led to a storeroom half full of old furniture, boxes and crates stacked almost ceiling high. She saw two men and a woman filling rubber balloons with coloured liquid.

"What are you doing?" she asked.

"Oh, hello. You must be one of the volunteers Kitty mentioned," the woman said. "We're filling these to throw out." She must have seen the leaflets Verity still carried. "Good. You've brought the pamphlets. Here let me have some." She took a bundle from Verity's hand.

"Kitty never said anything about balloons," Verity said, perturbed. "I thought we were just dropping papers."

"Don't worry, it's just dye. It'll wash out, but it'll make more of a splash than these." She waved the papers. "We have to make our mark."

Verity had a bad feeling in her stomach. She glanced around. "Have you seen Lydia Summerville? I thought she was coming."

The woman shrugged. "No idea," she said. The music of the bands in the parade coming along the road drifted up to Verity's ears. The men moved to the window. "Come on open it," one yelled.

The other man tried for several minutes. "I can't. It's stuck," he said.

"Give it a push."

"It's stuck fast."

Verity glanced out of a window to see the parade passing below while the men struggled to open the window next to her.

"Here let me try." The burlier one elbowed the other one out of the way while the parade below went marching on. He started swearing and cursing, as he huffed and puffed at the window, the sort of language

Verity hadn't heard since one of the cows almost drowned in a ditch and had to be pulled out by a team of horses. In the street below the bands marched on.

"Stand out of the way," the first man yelled, wielding an iron chair he'd picked up.

Before Verity knew what was happening he swung the chair at the window which shattered with a loud crash sending splinters and slivers of glass to the pavement below. The next thing she heard was the gasp as they all drew breath, then all hell broke loose. The sound of police whistles coming towards them added to the music of the marching bands.

One of the men shouted, "Bloody hell, run," and they all dashed towards the stairs. Verity, standing at the top of the staircase, turned to run down just as the first man barged past her, knocking her forward. As he pushed past she lost her footing and tumbled down the stairs, banging her head as she reached the bottom. She heard pounding feet on the treads and police whistles getting nearer before a great cloud of darkness enveloped her.

The next thing she became aware of was strong arms lifting her off the floor and a muffled voice that seems to come from a great distance calling, "In here," followed by the slamming of a door. She lay still for a while as her senses slowly returned. Pain pulsated in her shoulder and something like a knife stabbed at her ankle. She drew a breath and forced her eyes open. The room swam. Gradually, as her eyes focussed she saw she was staring into the anxious brown eyes and alarmed face of Brandon Summerville.

"Thank God, you're all right," he said, his voice soft, insistent, caressing. "I was worried sick."

"What happened?" she whispered, unable to find her voice.

He brushed a tress of her hair off her face, his hand gentle as a summer breeze. "I came as soon as Lydia told me what they intended to do. I knew they wouldn't be satisfied with merely chucking out leaflets."

She saw Lydia hovering in the background. "What exactly happened up there," she said.

Verity tried to order the thoughts that raced through her brain. "The window. They couldn't open the window."

"So they smashed it? That's what brought the police running. Idiots."

Fresh footsteps stomped on the stairs outside and she heard a loud furious banging on the door. Lydia rushed to it.

"This one's locked," Verity heard a voice say.

"Well they couldn't have got in there then could they?" another voice said. "I think we got 'em all." There was a scuffle then the footsteps receded.

"Do you think they've gone?" Brandon asked.

"I think we should wait a while to be sure," Lydia said, "if you can bear it, Verity. Where does it hurt?"

Verity ached all over. She tried to move, sending a shooting pain across her shoulder and another one up from her ankle. She groaned in pain.

"She needs a doctor," Brandon said, his earlier concern turning to fierce fury. "Bloody fools. They should be made to pay for what they've done. They could have killed her." Anger burned like coals in his eyes.

"I'm sure I'll be fine," Verity said in an attempt to calm him. "It's just a few bruises."

Lydia examined her ankle and shoulder. "We need to get you home and to a doctor," she said. "Can you stand?"

With Brandon's help she tried to stand but her ankle gave way sending another knife of pain up her leg. Brandon swiftly swept her off her feet. "Let's get out of here," he said, tension clear in his voice.

Lydia opened the door and peered out. "All right," she said. "I'll go first if you think you can manage."

"Go."

They followed Lydia down the stairs into the narrow road outside. Lydia managed to stop a cart, the carrier on his way back to the depot. Brandon paid handsomely for a lift to their home in Bayswater. All the while Verity saw anger boiling up inside him.

"I'm sorry," she said. "I thought they were only going to throw leaflets. I didn't think it would do any harm."

"Of course you didn't," he said. "It's not you I'm blaming." He touched her face, his eyes filled with tenderness. "I was worried you might get hurt."

Verity smiled. His concern warmed her heart. It was worth any amount of pain to have him care about her. If only it were real, she thought, for she was sure she must be dreaming.

When they arrived at the house he carried her into the drawing room, laying her down on the settee. Lydia checked her injuries again. "I don't think anything's broken," she said. "Just badly bruised. I'll get some bandages and arnica and I'm going to call the doctor."

Brandon poured them each a brandy and sat beside her. "You look very pale," he said. "I expect it's the shock. Drink this. It'll make you feel better." He handed her a glass and she sipped the warming liquid.

"I'm sorry to have caused you such bother," she said. "I hope you'll forgive me."

He smiled. "I'd forgive you anything. Surely you know by now how I feel about you?" He sipped his drink as though to give him courage. "You must have noticed that I keep turning up wherever you are, like a love-sick puppy."

"I… I thought you were after Charlotte."

"Charlotte?" He frowned then chuckled. "I like Charlotte, she's fun, but you're the one I really care about." He bowed his head. "It's funny, but I can't stop thinking about you. Ever since the first time I saw you at dinner with Jeremy Fitzroy. I was so taken with you and as time's gone on my feelings have deepened. I can't seem to stay away. I hoped that one day you might feel the same about me."

Verity's heart swelled so it almost burst. "Is that why you keep rescuing me?"

He smiled and his face lit with the deepest pleasure. "You saved my life once. I'll happily keep rescuing you for the rest of your life if you'll let me. Perhaps we can rescue each another?"

He leaned towards her and, as his lips brushed hers and she responded, the whole of her body tingled, the pain melting away like snow in early sunshine. She wished his kiss would go on forever. But it didn't. He drew back and said, "I suppose I'll have to marry you now?" There was no disguising the chuckle in his voice and the deep love in his eyes.

She laughed. "Yes please."

So he kissed her again.

Chapter Forty Nine

A notice of the engagement appeared in *The Times* once Brandon had spoken to Lawrence and asked his permission to marry his cousin. Verity cut it out and put it in her scrap-book with the cards and notes of congratulation she received. She wrote to Charlotte, hoping Charlotte would forgive her and understand. After all it was Charlotte who'd brought them together.

When she returned home Brandon went with her for the weekend to meet the rest of the family.

Aunt Elvira wanted to organise a huge engagement party, but had to settle for a family dinner as, although the bruises on her shoulder were fading, Verity walked on crutches as the doctor had decreed at least a month's rest for her ankle. "No dancing," he said. "You'll only make it worse."

"As soon as you're better we'll have to celebrate in style," Aunt Elvira said and Verity couldn't help but smile at her glee. She wondered if she'd have been so thrilled if she'd bagged someone other than one of the wealthiest men in London.

Ira Soloman called with his best wishes as soon as he heard the news. "You'd better take care of her," he said to Brandon. "Or you'll have me to answer to." He turned to Verity. "Your father would be proud of you," he said and Verity kissed him. He'd been like a father to her and she hoped he'd still be part of her family.

By Christmas Eve her ankle had healed and she was able to walk again. She went to her mother's grave to lay a wreath of winter flowers. She stood a while in the cold, fresh breeze that rustled the trees. "I know about Papa" she said. "I found the newspaper cuttings. It wasn't his fault, I know that now and I can forgive him, just as you did all those years ago." She stopped to brush a wisp of hair away from her cheek where it had blown. "Do I forgive his partner?" She sighed "It's not for me to judge. He'll be judged by a higher authority. I'm just sorry you couldn't tell me and Hettie. It might have helped."

She glanced around the churchyard. Leaves swirled in the wind before settling on the ground. She took a breath. "I'm getting married, Ma. You'd like him. He's brave and reckless, but I love him for it. Life will never be dull. He makes me laugh too, we're happy together. I hope you're happy for me."

As she said it a robin came and perched on the headstone. He chirped a few merry chirps before flying away. She watched his flight up into the clear blue winter sky.

"Goodbye, Ma," she said. "I love you." She blew a kiss into the air and walked away.

That evening Lawrence and Jeremy arrived with Brandon and Lydia in time for cocktails before dinner. Christmas Day followed the usual family traditions, but with Brandon by her side everything felt fresh and new. Even Aunt Elvira was happy.

"Two birds with one stone," she said after Christmas dinner, when Lawrence had taken Brandon and Lydia on a tour of the garden.

"What do you mean?" Verity asked.

Elvira chuckled. "Lawrence and Lydia. Don't they make a lovely couple?"

"Aunt Elvira, you're incorrigible," Verity said, her voice high with indignation. But she had to admit, she was right. They were perfect for each other.

Daisy managed to visit her mother on Christmas Eve. She took some of Mrs T's mince pies and sausage rolls. She'd bought her mother a new blouse and some presents to go under the tree for the rest of the family.

"There's a letter for you," her Ma said. "It's from Jessie."

Daisy tore the envelope open. Jessie had written. She must have forgiven her. Her heart lifted. She hated to be at odds with her sister. Jessie's letter said that she'd got a job in a shop. She was taking a secretarial course in the evenings and hoped to find work in an office when she finished the course. She'd written to Charlie and told him she'd only stay with him if he went straight. No more thieving. She had a nice room in a house in the town and was very happy there. She wished Daisy a Happy Christmas and would write again soon.

"Well, that's the best Christmas present ever," Daisy said. "Knowing that she's safe and well. I'm glad for her."

Christmas dinner for the staff at the hotel was a sumptuous meal, as usual. This year Daisy was surprised when Mr Svenson joined them. Elise beamed all over her face and offered to sit next to him, but he chose to sit next to Daisy. The atmosphere was one of fun and laughter. They all chatted over the meal and afterwards, over coffee and mints provided by Mrs T, Barker regaled them with jokes and tales of his time in the army. Mr Svenson told them about some of the places he'd visited on the ship, which made Elise's day as she said she'd been there too, albeit below decks and never off the ship.

In the evening Mr Svenson suggested that, as the hotel was quiet and the family away, they all go upstairs to the bar where he had a phonograph with some records they could dance to.

He asked Daisy for the first dance and, in his arms, she decided, perhaps he wasn't so bad after all.

Chapter Fifty

June, 1906

The night before the wedding Lawrence joined Brandon and his friends for a drink. Many of them had been in the Guards with him so he knew them. The talk was of times past, battles and victories won.

"She's stolen your heart," Rupert, his best man said. "That's the biggest victory of all."

Brandon laughed. "I gave it freely. There's no one I'd rather spend my life with. She's beautiful and her capacity for kindness took my breath away. I'm the luckiest man in the world."

They all drank to that.

Later in the evening Brandon took Lawrence to one side. "I know you gave your permission for me to marry Verity," he said. "But I wasn't sure I had your approval."

Lawrence sighed. "I like you, Brandon, always have, but you do have something of a reputation. I was afraid she might get hurt."

"I'd never hurt her and I'd kill any man who did," he said, "and as for my reputation, hard won in business but a flight of fancy and wild imaginings as far at the fairer sex are concerned. Verity's the only one I've ever really cared about."

Lawrence took a swig of his drink. "Having seen you in battle I don't doubt the first part," he said. "As long as you make her happy you have my approval."

"Good. I plan to make her the happiest girl in the world."

The next morning Verity stood in her room in Maldon Hall gazing at a photograph of her mother and father on their wedding day. It was one she'd found in one of her mother's albums and put in a silver frame. The look of love in their eyes was unmistakable. That'll be me and Brandon in half-an-hour, she thought.

Hettie, her matron of honour, burst into the room. "Come on, hurry up. Lawrence is waiting downstairs."

Verity took one last look in the mirror to check that everything looked just right.

"You look incredible," Hettie assured her. "Brandon's heart will melt." She adjusted the folds in Verity's oyster white, silk dress. "You know you're breaking the heart of every eligible young lady in London, marrying him, don't you? He's quite a catch."

Verity laughed. "I know. That's what Charlotte said when we saw him at the Boat Race Ball." She paused and tugged at a ringlet that hung over her shoulder. "I wrote to Charlotte but she never replied. I hope she's all right. I hope she doesn't hate me."

"I'm sure she's fine and she may be a little envious, but she could never hate you. Now come along. You don't want to be late."

Verity followed her downstairs to where Lydia, her chief bridesmaid, waited with two of the village children, also bridesmaids. Lydia beamed at her. "You look wonderful. Brandon's a lucky man."

Verity's heart swelled. "I'm the lucky one," she said.

Lydia ushered the other bridesmaids out to the waiting carriage. Verity went into the drawing room where Lawrence waited, a glass of whisky in his hand.

"Wow," he said, his eyes wide with appreciation. "You'll take his breath away. Elegant and charming at the same time." He kissed her cheek. "I hope Brandon knows how lucky he is." He raised his glass. "Want one?"

Verity nodded and he poured her a whisky.

"To the future," he said.

"To the future." She took a sip and her nerves melted away.

"Nervous?" he asked.

She shook her head. "No. Excited. It's what I want."

"You're sure?"

"I'm sure."

He finished his drink and held out his arm. "Come on then."

Verity tipped back the rest of her drink and took his arm. He led her out to the waiting carriage where Hettie and Lydia were trying to keep the other excited the bridesmaids in order. They went in the first carriage and she went with Lawrence in the second for the short journey to the church.

As she stepped out into the June sunshine she breathed in the air filled with the scent of summer roses. A group of villagers had gathered on the worn cobbles in front of the church door. They gasped with delight as she alighted, all craning for a better view. One woman stepped forward and offered her a bunch of lucky white heather. "Good luck, lass," she said. "You've done us proud."

Hettie adjusted her dress and, on Lawrence's arm, she walked down the aisle. The first person she saw was Charlotte, who smiled and waved. Warmth flowed through Verity when she saw her.

"She came home specially," Lawrence whispered. "Probably hoped you'd change your mind and she could take your place."

Verity struggled to stifle her giggles, but as she walked towards the man she'd loved since she first saw him, she calmed. This was what she wanted, to be with him in sickness and in health, for better for worse, forever.

The organ music swelled as she took her place beside him. He turned and smiled and the world stood still. Her heart almost burst with happiness.

The reception at Maldon Hall was the highlight of the year. A golden day of revelry and laughter, hope and optimism for what lay ahead of them. Cousin Clara congratulated her and wished her every happiness for the future. Lawrence danced with Lydia and Jeremy danced with Charlotte, while Elvira looked gleefully on. She's a scheming old devil, Verity thought, but perhaps she was right all along. Making a good marriage was the best thing that could happen to a girl.

Later that night, as Brandon took her in his arms all her worries faded away. She knew they were right for each other. She'd reached a safe harbour and she'd never, ever need to be rescued again.

About the Author

Kay Seeley is a talented storyteller and bestselling author. Her short stories have been published in women's magazines and short-listed in competitions. Her novels had been finalists in The Wishing Shelf Book Awards. She lives in London and loves its history. Her stories are well researched, beautifully written with compelling characters where love triumphs over adversity. Kay writes stories that will capture your heart and leave you wanting more. Often heart-wrenching but always satisfyingly uplifting, her books are perfect for fans of Anna Jacobs, Emma Hornby and Josephine Cox. All her novels are available for Kindle, in paperback, audio and in Large Print.

A Troubled Heart is her eighth historical novel set in London.

Kay is a member of The Alliance of Indie Authors and The Society of Women Writers and Journalists.

If you've read and enjoyed this book would you be kind enough to leave a review so other readers can enjoy it too?

Why not sign up to my newsletter for news about my latest books, free short stories and historical trivia? I'd love to hear from you. http://bit.ly/kayauthor

Facebook page:
https://www.facebook.com/kayseeley.writer

Twitter: https://twitter.com/KaySeeley1

Acknowledgements

I couldn't have written this book without the support and encouragement of my family and writing friends. I particularly want to thank my daughters Lorraine and Liz for reading it and their helpful suggestions. Thanks also go to Helen Baggott for her valuable assistance and Jane Dixon Smith for the wonderful cover. Mostly I'd like to thank my readers for their continued support and encouragement. Hearing from people who've read and enjoyed my books makes it all worthwhile.

Thank you.

If you enjoyed this book you may also enjoy Kay's other books:

One Beat of a Heart (A Fitzroy Hotel Story)

One Beat of a Heart, is all it takes to change a life forever.

Edwardian London 1902
.

Clara Fitzroy, spoiled and entitled, refuses to conform to convention. Her reckless behaviour has devastating consequences and an ill-judged liaison threatens to destroy everything she's hoped for.
Daisy Carter, the hotel housekeeper, has problems of her own. A family relationship brings grief and heartache and a well meaning action ends in disaster.
When tragedy strikes at The Fitzroy Hotel on Coronation Day, their lives are thrown into turmoil.
Can Clara find the courage to follow her heart?
Can Daisy keep her family together when fate is pulling them apart?
Clara and Daisy are bonded by the secrets they keep.
Can they rely on each other when their futures depend on it?

Follow the fortunes of Clara and Daisy in the first of The Fitzroy Hotel Stories

The Hope Series

A Girl Called Hope

In Victorian London's East End, life for Hope Daniels in the public house run by her parents is not as it seems. Pa drinks and gambles, brother John longs for a place of his own, sister Violet dreams of a life on stage and little Alfie is being bullied at school.

Silas Quirk, the charismatic owner of a local gentlemen's club and disreputable gambling den her father frequents, has his own plans for Hope.

A Girl Called Violet

Violet Daniels isn't perfect. She's made mistakes in her life, but the deep love she has for her five-year-old twins is beyond dispute.

When their feckless and often violent father turns up out of the blue, demanding to see them, she's terrified he might snatch them from her.

She flees with them to a place of safety where she meets the handsome and charming Gabriel Stone. He shows her a better way of life, but is he everything he appears to be?

A Girl Called Rose

The close, loving family life Rose has known is shattered when the country goes to war. Rose resolves to do her bit so, aged sixteen, she leaves home to train as a nurse in London. There she finds freedom, excitement and a different way of life.

The Water Gypsy

Struggling to survive on Britain's waterways Tilly Thompson, a girl from the canal, is caught stealing a pie from the terrace of The Imperial Hotel, Athelstone. Only the intervention of Captain Charles Thackery saves her from prison. Tilly soon finds out the reason for the rescue.
With the Captain Tilly sees life away from the poverty and hardship of the waterways, but

The Watercress Girls

Annie knows the secrets men whisper in her ears to impress her. When she disappears who will care? Who will look for her?
Two girls sell cress on the streets of Victorian London. When they grow up they each take a different path. Annie's reckless ambition takes her to Paris to dance at the Folies Bergère. When she comes home she takes up a far more dangerous occupation.

The Guardian Angel

When Nell Draper leaves the workhouse to care for Robert, the five-year-old son and heir of Lord Eversham, a wealthy landowner, she has no idea of the heartache that lies ahead of her. She soon discovers that Robert can't speak or communicate with her, his family or the staff that work for his father. Can Nell save him from a desolate future, secure his inheritance and ensure he takes his rightful place in society?

You may also enjoy Kay's short story collections:

The Cappuccino Collection
20 stories to warm the heart

All the stories in *The Cappuccino Collection*, except one, have been previously published in magazines, anthologies or on the internet. They are romantic, humorous and thought provoking stories that reflect real life, love in all its guises and the ties that bind. Enjoy them in small bites.

The Summer Stories
12 Romantic tales to make you smile

From first to last a joy to read. Romance blossoms like summer flowers in these delightfully different stories filled with humour, love, life and surprises. Perfect for holiday reading or sitting in the sun in the garden with a glass of wine.

The Christmas Stories
6 magical Christmas Stories

When it's snowing outside and frost sparkles on the window pane, there's nothing better than roasting chestnuts by the fire with a glass of mulled wine and a book of six magical stories to bring a smile to your face and joy to your heart. Here are the stories. You'll have to provide the chestnuts, fire and wine yourself.

Please feel free to contact Kay through her website www.kayseeleyauthor.com She'd love to hear from you.

Or follow Kay on her Facebook Page
https://www.facebook.com/kayseeley.writer/

Printed in Great Britain
by Amazon